Jeannette Walls was born in Phoenix, Arizona, and grew up in the southwest and in Welch, West Virginia. She graduated from Barnard College and was a journalist in New York City for twenty years. She is married to John Taylor and lives in northern Virginia.

HALF BROKE HORSES

Lily Casey Smith is a sassy, straight-talking heroine for whom saving lives, taming wild horses and beating ranch hands at poker are all in a day's work. Born in 1901, in a dirt house in the rolling gritty grassland of Texas, at age six she is helping her father break horses. At fifteen she leaves home to teach in a town five hundred miles away, riding there on her pony, all alone. Lily handles everything that life throws at her — flash floods and tornadoes, the Great Depression; the most heartbreaking personal tragedy — with immense courage and determination and a wide smile. Lily's indomitable passion and spirit shines through in this true-life novel, written by her granddaughter Jeannette Walls.

JEANNETTE WALLS

HALF BROKE HORSES

Complete and Unabridged

CHARNWOOD
Leicester

First published in Great Britain in 2009 by
Simon & Schuster UK Ltd.
London

First Charnwood Edition
published 2011
by arrangement with
Simon & Schuster UK Ltd.
London

British Library CIP Data

Walls, Jeannette.
Half broke horses.
1. Smith, Lily Casey, *1901 – 1968*- -Fiction.
2. Texas- -Social life and customs- -20th century- -
Fiction. 3. Arizona- -Social life and customs- -20th
century- -Fiction. 4. Biographical fiction.
5. Large type books.
I. Title
813.6–dc22

ISBN 978–1–44480–509–3

Published by
F. A. Thorpe (Publishing)
Anstey, Leicestershire

Set by Words & Graphics Ltd.
Anstey, Leicestershire
Printed and bound in Great Britain by
T. J. International Ltd., Padstow, Cornwall

This book is printed on acid-free paper

This book is dedicated
to all teachers,
and especially to

Rose Mary Walls,
Phyllis Owens, and
Esther Fuchs

And in memory of
Jeannette Bivens and
Lily Casey Smith

ACKNOWLEDGMENTS

My deepest thanks to my mother, Rose Mary Smith Walls. Over hundreds of hours, Mom was unfailingly generous with her stories, memories, and observations, never refusing to answer a question no matter how personal and never trying to restrict or control what I wrote.

I'd also like to thank my brother, Brian, and sisters, Lori and Maureen, as well as my extended family, the Taylor clan. My gratitude goes out as well to my aunt Diane Moody and my Smith cousins, especially Shelly Smith Dunlop, who presented me with a trove of photographs that showed people, places, critters, and a time I knew only through words.

Thanks also to Jennifer Rudolph Walsh, who is a good friend even before she's my agent. At Scribner, Nan Graham brought her precision of words and thoughts to my writing, and Kate Bittman's cheer and hard work are a cherished gift, as is the enthusiastic support of Susan Moldow.

For their horse wisdom and horse sense, I also owe a debt to Joe Kincheloe, Dick Bickel, and especially Susan Homan.

I will never be able to adequately thank my husband, John Taylor, who has taught me so much, including when to pull back and when to let go.

It was the great north wind that made the Vikings.

— *Old Norwegian saying*

Lily Casey Smith, Ashfork, Arizona, 1934

I

SALT DRAW

The KC Ranch on the Rio Hondo

Those old cows knew trouble was coming before we did.

It was late on an August afternoon, the air hot and heavy like it usually was in the rainy season. Earlier we'd seen some thunderheads near the Burnt Spring Hills, but they'd passed way up to the north. I'd mostly finished my chores for the day and was heading down to the pasture with my brother, Buster, and my sister, Helen, to bring the cows in for their milking. But when we got there, those girls were acting all bothered. Instead of milling around at the gate, like they usually did at milking time, they were standing stiff-legged and straight-tailed, twitching their heads around, listening.

Buster and Helen looked up at me, and without a word, I knelt down and pressed my ear to the hard-packed dirt. There was a rumbling, so faint and low that you felt it more than you heard it. Then I knew what the cows knew — a flash flood was coming.

As I stood up, the cows bolted, heading for the southern fence line, and when they reached the barbed wire, they jumped over it — higher and cleaner than I'd ever seen cows jump — and then they thundered off toward higher ground.

I figured we best bolt, too, so I grabbed Helen and Buster by the hand. By then I could feel the ground rumbling through my shoes. I saw the first water sluicing through the lowest part of the pasture, and I knew we didn't have time to make it to higher ground ourselves. In the middle of the field was an old cottonwood tree, broad-branched and gnarled, and we ran for that.

Helen stumbled, so Buster grabbed her other hand, and we lifted her off the ground and carried her between us as we ran. When we reached the cottonwood, I pushed Buster up to the lowest branch, and he pulled Helen into the tree behind him. I shimmied up and wrapped my arms around Helen just as a wall of water, about six feet high and pushing rocks and tree limbs in front of it, slammed into the cottonwood, dousing all three of us. The tree shuddered and bent over so far that you could hear wood cracking, and some lower branches were torn off. I feared it might be uprooted, but the cottonwood held fast and so did we, our arms locked as a great rush of caramel-colored water, filled with bits of wood and the occasional matted gopher and tangle of snakes, surged beneath us, spreading out across the lowland and seeking its level.

★   ★   ★

We just sat there in that cottonwood tree watching for about an hour. The sun started to set over the Burnt Spring Hills, turning the high clouds crimson and sending long purple shadows eastward. The water was still flowing beneath us, and Helen said her arms were getting tired. She was only seven and was afraid she couldn't hold on much longer.

4

Buster, who was nine, was perched up in the big fork of the tree. I was ten, the oldest, and I took charge, telling Buster to trade places with Helen so she could sit upright without having to cling too hard. A little while later, it got dark, but a bright moon came out and we could see just fine. From time to time we all switched places so no one's arms would wear out. The bark was chafing my thighs, and Helen's, too, and when we needed to pee, we had to just wet ourselves. About halfway through the night, Helen's voice started getting weak.

'I can't hold on any longer,' she said.

'Yes, you can,' I told her. 'You can because you have to.' We were going to make it, I told them. I knew we would make it because I could see it in my mind. I could see us walking up the hill to the house tomorrow morning, and I could see Mom and Dad running out. It would happen — but it was up to us to make it happen.

To keep Helen and Buster from drifting off to sleep and falling out of the cottonwood, I grilled them on their multiplication tables. When we'd run through those, I went on to presidents and state capitals, then word definitions, word rhymes, and whatever else I could come up with, snapping at them if their voices faltered, and that was how I kept Helen and Buster awake through the night.

★ ★ ★

By first light, you could see that the water still covered the ground. In most places, a flash flood

5

drained away after a couple of hours, but the pasture was in bottomland near the river, and sometimes the water remained for days. But it had stopped moving and had begun seeping down through the sinkholes and mudflats.

'We made it,' I said.

I figured it would be safe to wade through the water, so we scrambled out of the cottonwood tree. We were so stiff from holding on all night that our joints could scarcely move, and the mud kept sucking at our shoes, but we got to dry land as the sun was coming up and climbed the hill to the house just the way I had seen it.

Dad was on the porch, pacing back and forth in that uneven stride he had on account of his gimp leg. When he saw us, he let out a yelp of delight and started hobbling down the steps toward us. Mom came running out of the house. She sank to her knees, clasped her hands in front of her, and started praying up to the heavens, thanking the Lord for delivering her children from the flood.

It was she who had saved us, she declared, by staying up all night praying. 'You get down on your knees and thank your guardian angel,' she said. 'And you thank me, too.'

Helen and Buster got down and started praying with Mom, but I just stood there looking at them. The way I saw it, I was the one who'd saved us all, not Mom and not some guardian angel. No one was up in that cottonwood tree except the three of us. Dad came alongside me and put his arm around my shoulders.

'There weren't no guardian angel, Dad,' I said.

6

I started explaining how I'd gotten us to the cottonwood tree in time, figuring out how to switch places when our arms got tired and keeping Buster and Helen awake through the long night by quizzing them.

Dad squeezed my shoulder. 'Well, darling,' he said, 'maybe the angel was you.'

We had a homestead on Salt Draw, which flowed into the Pecos River, in the rolling gritty grassland of west Texas. The sky was high and pale, the land low and washed out, gray and every color of sand. Sometimes the wind blew for days on end, but sometimes it was so still you could hear the dog barking on the Dingler ranch two miles upriver, and when a wagon came down the road, the dust it trailed hung in the air for a long time before drifting back to the ground.

When you looked out across the land, most everything you could see — the horizon, the river, the fence lines, the gullies, the scrub cedar — was spread out and flat, and the people, cattle, horses, lizards, and water all moved slowly, conserving themselves.

It was hard country. The ground was like rock — save for when a flood turned everything to mud — the animals were bony and tough, and even the plants were prickly and sparse, though from time to time the thunderstorms brought out startling bursts of wildflowers. Dad said High Lonesome, as the area was known, wasn't a place for the soft of head or the weak of heart, and he said that was why he and I made out just fine there, because we were both tough nuts.

Our homestead was only 160 acres, which was not a whole lot of land in that part of Texas, where it was so dry you needed at least five acres to raise a single head of cattle. But our spread bordered the draw, so it was ten times more valuable than land without water, and we were able to keep the carriage horses Dad trained, the milking cows, dozens of chickens, some hogs, and the peacocks.

The peacocks were one of Dad's moneymaking schemes that didn't quite pan out. Dad had paid a lot of money to import breeding peacocks from a farm back east. He was convinced that peacocks were a sure-fire sign of elegance and style, and that folks who bought carriage horses from him would also be willing to shell out fifty bucks for one of those classy birds. He planned to sell only the male birds so we'd be the sole peacock breeders this side of the Pecos.

Unfortunately, Dad overestimated the demand for ornamental birds in west Texas — even among the carriage set — and within a few years, our ranch was overrun with peacocks. They strutted around screeching and squawking, pecking our knees, scaring the horses, killing chicks, and attacking the hogs, though I have to admit it was a glorious sight when, from time to time, those peacocks paused in their campaign of terror to spread their plumes and preen.

★ ★ ★

The peacocks were just a sideline. Dad's primary occupation was the carriage horses, breeding them and training them. He loved horses despite the accident. When Dad was a boy of three, he

9

was running through the stable and a horse kicked him in the head, practically staving in his skull. Dad was in a coma for days, and no one thought he'd pull through. He eventually did, but the right side of his body had gone a little gimp. His right leg sort of dragged behind him, and his arm was cocked like a chicken wing. Also, when he was young, he'd spent long hours working in the noisy gristmill on his family's ranch, which made him hard of hearing. As such, he talked a little funny, and until you spent time around him, you had trouble understanding what he said.

Dad never blamed the horse for kicking him. All the horse knew, he liked to say, was that some creature about the size of a mountain lion was darting by his flanks. Horses were never wrong. They always did what they did for a reason, and it was up to you to figure it out. And even though it was a horse that almost stove in Dad's skull, he loved horses because, unlike people, they always understood him and never pitied him. So, even though Dad was unable to sit in a saddle on account of the accident, he became an expert at training carriage horses. If he couldn't ride them, he could drive them.

I was born in a dugout on the banks of Salt Draw in 1901, the year after Dad got out of prison, where he'd been serving time on that trumped-up murder charge.

Dad had grown up on a ranch in the Hondo Valley in New Mexico. His pa, who'd home-steaded the land, was one of the first Anglos in the valley, arriving there in 1868, but by the time Dad was a young man, more settlers had moved into the area than the river could support, and there were constant arguments over property lines and, especially, water rights — people claiming their upstream neighbors were using more than their fair share of water, while downstream neighbors made the same claim against them. These disputes often led to brawls, lawsuits, and shootings. Dad's pa, Robert Casey, was murdered in one such dispute when Dad was fourteen. Dad stayed on to run the ranch with his ma, but those disputes kept erupting, and twenty years later, when a settler was killed after yet another argument, Dad was convicted of murdering him.

Dad insisted he'd been framed, writing long letters to legislators and newspaper editors protesting his innocence, and after serving three years in prison, he was set free. Shortly after he was released, he met and married my mom. The prosecutor was looking into retrying the case, and Dad thought that would be less likely if he made himself scarce, so he and my mom left the Hondo Valley for High Lonesome, where they claimed our land along Salt Draw.

Lots of the folks homesteading in High Lonesome lived in dugouts because timber was so scarce in that part of Texas. Dad had made our home by shoveling out what was more or less a big hole on the side of the riverbank, using cedar branches as rafters and covering them over with sod. The dugout had one room, a packed earth floor, a wooden door, a waxed-paper window, and a cast-iron stove with a flue that jutted up through the sod roof.

The best thing about living in the dugout was that it was cool in the summer and not too cold in the winter. The worst thing about it was that, from time to time, scorpions, lizards, snakes, gophers, centipedes, and moles wormed their way out of our walls and ceilings. Once, in the middle of an Easter dinner, a rattler dropped onto the table. Dad, who was carving the ham, brought the knife right down behind that snake's head.

Also, whenever it rained, the ceilings and walls in the dugout turned to mud. Sometimes clumps of that mud dropped from the ceiling and you had to pat it back in place. And every now and then, the goats grazing on the roof would stick a hoof clear through and we'd have to pull them out.

★　★　★

Another problem with living in the dugout was the mosquitoes. They were so thick that sometimes you felt like you were swimming through them. Mom was particularly susceptible to them — her bite marks sometimes stayed swollen for days — but I was the one who came down with yellow jack fever.

I was seven at the time, and after the first day, I was writhing on the bed, shivering and vomiting. Mom was afraid that everyone else might catch the disease, so even though Dad insisted that you got it from mosquitoes, he rigged up a quilt to quarantine me off. Dad was the only one who was allowed behind it, and he sat with me for days, splashing me with spirit lotions, trying to bring the fever down. While I was delirious, I visited bright white places in another world and saw green and purple beasts that grew and shrank with every beat of my heart.

When the fever finally broke, I weighed some ten pounds less than I had before, and my skin was all yellow. Dad joked that my forehead had been so hot he almost burned his hand when he touched it. Mom poked her head behind the quilt to see me. 'A fever that high can boil your brain and cause permanent damage,' Mom said. 'So don't ever tell anyone you had it. You do, you might have trouble catching a husband.'

Mom worried about things like her daughters catching the right husband. She was concerned with what she called 'proprieties.' Mom had furnished our dugout with some real finery, including an Oriental rug, a chaise longue with a lace doily, velvet curtains that we hung on the walls to make it look like we had more windows, a silver serving set, and a carved walnut headboard that her parents had brought with them from back east when they moved to California. Mom treasured that headboard and said it was the only thing that allowed her to sleep at night because it reminded her of the civilized world.

Mom's father was a miner who had struck gold north of San Francisco and became fairly prosperous. Although her family lived in mining boom towns, Mom — whose maiden name was Daisy Mae Peacock — was raised in an atmosphere of gentility. She had soft white skin that was easily sunburned and bruised. When she was a child, her mother made her wear a linen mask if she had to spend any time in the sun, tying it to the yellow curls on the side of her face. In west Texas, Mom always wore a hat and gloves and a veil over her face when she went outdoors, which she did as seldom as possible.

Mom kept up the dugout, but she refused to do chores like toting water or carrying firewood.

'Your mother's a lady,' Dad would say by way of explaining her disdain for manual labor. Dad did most of the outdoor work with the help of our hand, Apache. Apache wasn't really an Indian, but he'd been captured by the Apaches when he was six, and they kept him until he was a young man, when the U.S. Cavalry — with Dad's pa serving as a scout — raided the camp and Apache ran out yelling, '*Soy blanco! Soy blanco!*'

Apache had gone home with Dad's pa and lived with the family ever since. By now Apache was an old man, with a white beard so long that he tucked it in his pants. Apache was a loner and sometimes spent hours staring at the horizon or the barn wall, and he'd also disappear into the range now and then for days at a time, but he always came back. Folks considered Apache a little peculiar, but that's what they also thought of Dad, and the two of them got along just fine.

To cook and wash, Mom had the help of our servant girl, Lupe, who had gotten pregnant and was forced to leave her village outside Juárez after the baby was born because she had brought shame on the family and no one would marry her. She was small and a little barrel-shaped and even more devoutly Catholic than Mom. Buster called her 'Loopy,' but I liked Lupe. Although her parents had taken her baby from her and she slept on a Navajo blanket on the dugout floor, Lupe never felt sorry for herself, and that was something I decided I admired most in people.

Even with Lupe helping her out, Mom didn't really care for life on Salt Draw. She hadn't bargained for it. Mom thought she'd married well when she took Adam Casey as her husband, despite his limp and speech impediment. Dad's pa had come over from Ireland during a potato blight, joined the Second Dragoons — one of the first cavalry units of the U.S. Army — where he served under Colonel Robert E. Lee, and was stationed on the Texas frontier, fighting Comanches, Apaches, and Kiowa. After leaving the army, he took up ranching, first in Texas, then in the Hondo Valley, and by the time he was killed, he had one of the biggest herds in the area.

Robert Casey was shot down as he walked along the main street of Lincoln, New Mexico. One version of the story held that he and the man who killed him had disagreed over an eight-dollar debt. The murderer's hanging was talked about for years in the valley because, once he'd been hanged, declared dead, cut down, and put in his pine box, people heard him moving around, so they took him out and strung him up again.

After Robert Casey's death, his children started arguing over how to split up the herd, which fostered bad blood that lasted for the rest of Dad's life. Dad inherited the Hondo Valley spread, but he felt his elder brother, who'd taken the herd to Texas, had cheated him out of his share, and he was constantly filing lawsuits and appeals. He continued the campaign even after moving to west Texas, and he was also battling away with the other ranchers in the Hondo Valley, traveling back to New Mexico to lodge an endless stream of claims and counterclaims.

★　★　★

One thing about Dad was that he had a terrible temper, and he usually returned from these trips trembling with rage. Part of it was his Irish blood, and part of it was his impatience with folks who had trouble understanding what he said. He felt those people thought he was a lamebrain and were always trying to cheat him, whether it was his brothers and their lawyers, traveling merchants, or half-breed-horse traders. He'd start sputtering and cursing, and from time to time, he'd become so incensed that he'd pull out his pistol and plug away at things, aiming to miss people — most of the time.

Once he got into an argument with a tinker who overcharged to repair the kettle. When the tinker started to mock the way he talked, Dad ran inside to get his guns, but Lupe had seen what was coming and hidden them in her Navajo blanket. Dad worked himself into a lather, hollering about his missing guns, but I was convinced Lupe saved that tinker's life. And probably Dad's as well, since if he'd killed the tinker, he might have ended up swinging, hanged like the man who'd shot his pa.

Life would be easier, Dad kept saying, once we got our due. But we were only going to get it by fighting for it. Dad was all caught up in his lawsuits, but for the rest of us, the constant fight on Salt Draw was the one against the elements. The flash flood that sent Buster, Helen, and me up the cottonwood wasn't the only one that almost did us in. Floods were pretty common in that part of Texas — you could count on one every couple of years — and when I was eight, we were hit by another big one. Dad was away in Austin filing another claim about his inheritance when one night Salt Draw overflowed and poured into our dugout. The sound of thunder awoke me, and when I got up, my feet sank into muddy water up to my ankles. Mom took Helen and Buster to high ground to pray, but I stayed behind with Apache and Lupe. We barricaded the door with the rug and started bailing the water out the window. Mom came back and begged us to go pray with her on the hilltop.

'To heck with praying!' I shouted. 'Bail, dammit, bail!'

Mom looked mortified. I could tell she thought I'd probably doomed us all with my blasphemy, and I was a little shocked at it myself, but with the water rising so fast, the situation was dire. We had lit the kerosene lamp, and we could see that the walls of the dugout

18

were beginning to sag inward. If Mom had pitched in and helped, there was a chance we might have been able to save the dugout — not a good chance, but a fighting chance. Apache and Lupe and I couldn't do it on our own, though, and when the ceiling started to cave, we grabbed Mom's walnut headboard and pulled it through the door just as the dugout collapsed in on itself, burying everything.

Afterward, I was pretty aggravated with Mom. She kept saying that the flood was God's will and we had to submit to it. But I didn't see things that way. Submitting seemed to me a lot like giving up. If God gave us the strength to bail — the gumption to try to save ourselves — isn't that what he wanted us to do?

★   ★   ★

But the flood turned out to be a blessing in disguise. It was all too much for that tenderfoot, Mr. McClurg, who lived up the draw in a two-room wooden house that he had built with timber he carted in from New Mexico. The flood washed away Mr. McClurg's foundation, and the walls fell apart. He said he'd had it with this godforsaken part of the world and decided to return to Cleveland. As soon as Dad got home from Austin, he had us all jump in the wagon and — quickly, before anyone else in High Lonesome got the same idea — we drove over to scavenge Mr. McClurg's lumber. We took everything: siding, rafters, beams, door frames, floorboards. By the end of the summer, we had built ourselves a brand-new wooden house, and after we whitewashed it, you almost couldn't tell that it had been patched together with someone else's old wood.

As we all stood there admiring our house the day we finished it, Mom turned to me and said, 'Now, wasn't that flood God's will?'

I didn't have an answer. Mom could say that in hindsight, but it seemed to me that when you were in the middle of something, it was awful hard to figure out what part of it was God's will and what wasn't.

I asked Dad if he believed that everything that happened was God's will.

'Is and isn't,' he said. 'God deals us all different hands. How we play 'em is up to us.'

I wondered if Dad thought that God had dealt him a bad hand, but I didn't feel it was my place to ask. From time to time, Dad mentioned the horse kicking him in the head, but none of us ever talked about his gimp leg or his trouble speaking.

Dad's speech impediment did make it sound a little like he was talking underwater. If he said, 'Hitch up the carriage,' it sounded to most people like 'Ich'p uh urrj,' and if he said, 'Mama needs to rest,' it sounded like 'Uhmu neesh resh.'

Toyah, the nearest little town, was four miles away, and sometimes when we went there, the kids followed Dad around imitating him, which made me want to thrash them something fierce. A lot of times, particularly when Mom was there, too, Buster, Helen, and I could do little more than glare at them. Dad usually acted like those kids didn't exist — after all, he could hardly run for his gun to shoot them, like he had with that tinker — but once, at the Toyah stable, when a couple of them were especially loud, I saw him glance down with a wounded look. While he and Buster were loading the wagon, I went back to the stable and tried to explain to those kids that they were hurting people's feelings, but all they did was snicker, so I shoved them into the manure pile and ran. I'd never done a bad thing that gave me so much satisfaction. My only regret was that I couldn't tell Dad about it.

What those kids didn't understand about Dad was that, although his speech did sound sort of marbly, he was smart. He'd been taught by a governess, and he was all the time reading books on philosophy and writing long letters to politicians like William Taft, William Jennings Bryan, and Frederick William Seward, who had been Abraham Lincoln's assistant secretary of state. Seward even wrote back, letters Dad treasured and kept in a locked tin box.

When it came to the written word, no one could string together sentences like Dad. His handwriting was elegant, if a little spidery, and his sentences were long and extravagant, filled with words like 'mendacious' and 'abscond' that most of the folks in Toyah would need a dictionary to understand. Two of Dad's biggest concerns in his letters were industrialization and mechanization, which he felt were destroying the human soul. He was also obsessed with Prohibition and phonetic spelling, both of which he saw as cures for mankind's tendency toward irrational behavior.

Dad had come of age seeing too many liquored-up people blazing away at one another. His pa had sold liquor from the store he ran on the Rio Hondo ranch, but his pa also once had to shoot a drunk who tried to shoot him. Alcohol, Dad said, made Indians and Irishmen crazy. After his pa was killed, Dad axed the store's liquor barrels, and to Apache's deep regret, he didn't allow anything stronger than tea on the ranch.

The inconsistent spelling of words in the English language also vexed Dad to no end. Digraphs such as 'sh' and 'ph' infuriated him, and silent letters made him grieve. If words were simply spelled the way they were pronounced, he argued, pretty much anyone who learned the alphabet could read, and that would virtually wipe out illiteracy.

Toyah had a one-room schoolhouse, but Dad thought that the teaching there was second-rate and he could do better tutoring me. Every day after lunch, when the sun was too hot to work outside, we did lessons — grammar, history, arithmetic, science, and civics — and when we were done, I tutored Buster and Helen. Dad's favorite subject was history, but he taught it with a decidedly west-of-the-Pecos point of view. As the proud son of an Irishman, he hated the English Pilgrims, whom he called 'Poms,' as well as most of the founding fathers. They were a bunch of pious hypocrites, he thought, who declared all men equal but kept slaves and massacred peaceful Indians. He sided with the Mexicans in the Mexican-American war and thought the United States had stolen all the land north of the Rio Grande, but he also thought the southern states should have had as much right to leave the union as the colonies had to leave the British Empire. 'Only difference between a traitor and a patriot is your perspective,' he said.

23

I loved my lessons, particularly science and geometry, loved learning that there were these invisible rules that explained the mysteries of the world we lived in. Smart as that made me feel, Mom and Dad kept saying that even though I was getting a better education at home than any of the kids in Toyah, I'd need to go to finishing school when I was thirteen, both to acquire social graces and to earn a diploma. Because in this world, Dad said, it's not enough to have a fine education. You need a piece of paper to prove you got it.

Mom did her best to keep us kids genteel. While I was teaching Buster and Helen, she brushed my hair one hundred strokes, careful to pull backward away from my scalp, putting marrow and lanolin into it to increase its luster. At night, she curled it into ringlets with little pieces of paper she called papillotes. 'A lady's hair is her crowning glory,' she said, and she was always going on about how my widow's peak was my best feature, but when I looked in the mirror, that little V of hair at the top of my forehead didn't seem like much to bank on.

Even though we lived four miles from Toyah and days would go by without seeing anyone outside the family, Mom worked very hard at being a lady. She was dainty, only four and a half feet tall, and her feet were so small that she had to wear button-up boots made for girls. To keep her hands elegantly white, she rubbed them with pastes made from honey, lemon juice, and borax. She wore tight corsets to give her a teeny waist — I helped her lace them up — but they had the effect of causing her to faint. Mom called it the vapors and said it was a sign of her high breeding and delicate nature. I thought it was a sign that the corset made it hard to breathe. Whenever she'd keel over, I'd have to revive her with smelling salts, which she kept in a crystal bottle tied around her neck with a pink ribbon.

Mom was closest to Helen, who had inherited her tiny hands and feet and her frail constitution. Sometimes they read poetry to each other, and in the stifling midafternoon heat, they'd simply lie together on Mom's chaise longue. But while she was close to Helen, she completely doted on Buster, the only son, whom she considered the future of the family. Buster was a rabbity little kid, but he had an irresistible smile, and maybe to compensate for Dad's speech impediment, he was one of the fastest and smoothest talkers in the county. Mom liked to say Buster could charm the sage off the brush. She was always telling Buster there were no limits on what he could become — a railroad magnate, a cattle baron, a general, or even the governor of Texas.

Mom didn't quite know what to make of me. She feared she might have trouble marrying me off because I didn't have the makings of a lady. I was a little bowlegged, for one thing. Mom said it was because I rode horses too much. Also, my front teeth jutted out, so she bought me a red silk fan to cover my mouth. Whenever I laughed or smiled too big, Mom would say, 'Lily, dear, the fan.'

Since Mom wasn't exactly the most useful person in the world, one lesson I learned at an early age was how to get things done, and this was a source of both amazement and concern for Mom, who considered my behavior unladylike but also counted on me. 'I never knew a girl to

26

have such gumption,' she'd say. 'But I'm not too sure that's a good thing.'

★ ★ ★

The way Mom saw it, women should let menfolk do the work because it made them feel more manly. That notion made sense only if you had a strong man willing to step up and get things done, and between Dad's gimp, Buster's elaborate excuses, and Apache's tendency to disappear, it was often up to me to keep the place from falling apart. But even when everyone was pitching in, we never got out from under all the work. I loved that ranch, though sometimes it did seem that instead of us owning the place, the place owned us.

We'd heard about electricity and how some big cities back east were wired with so many glowing lightbulbs that it looked like daytime even after the sun had set. But those wires had yet to reach west Texas, so you had to do everything by hand, heating irons on the stove to press Mom's blouses, cooking cauldrons of lye and potash over the fire to make soap, working the pump, then toting clean water in to wash the dishes and dirty water out to pour on the vegetable garden.

We'd also heard about the indoor plumbing they were installing in fancy houses back east, but no one in west Texas had it, and most people, including Mom and Dad, thought the idea of an indoor bathroom was vile and disgusting. 'Who in the Lord's name would want a crapper in the house?' Dad asked.

Since I grew up listening to Dad, I always understood him completely, and when I turned five, he had me start helping him train the horses. It took Dad six years to train a pair of carriage horses properly, and he had six teams going at all times, selling off one team a year, which was enough to make ends meet. A team had to be perfectly matched in size and color, with no irregularities, and if one horse had white socks, the other needed them as well.

Of the six pairs of horses we'd have, Dad let the yearlings and two-year-olds simply run free in the pasture. 'First thing a horse needs to learn is to be a horse,' he liked to say. I worked with the three-year-olds, teaching them ground manners and getting them to accept the bit, then helped Dad harness and unharness the three pairs of older horses. I'd drive each pair in a circle while Dad stood in the middle, using a whip to drill them, making sure they lifted their feet high, changed gaits in unison, and flexed their necks smartly.

Everyone who spent time around horses, Dad liked to say, needed to learn to think like a horse. He was always repeating that phrase: 'Think like a horse.' The key to that, he said, was understanding that horses were always afraid. The only way they could save themselves from mountain lions and wolves was to kick out and run, and they ran like the wind, racing one another, because it was the slowest horse in the herd that got taken down by the predator. They were all the time looking for a protector, and if you could convince a horse that you'd protect him, he would do anything for you.

Dad had a whole vocabulary of grunts, murmurs, clucks, tocks, and whistles that he used to speak with horses. It was like their own private language. He never flogged their backs, instead using the whip to make a small popping sound on either side of their ears, signaling them without ever hurting or frightening them.

Dad also made tack for the horses, and he seemed happiest sitting by himself, humming at his sewing machine, working the foot pedal, surrounded by hides, shears, cans of neat's-foot oil, spools of stitching threads, and his big saddler's needles, no one bothering him, no one feeling sorry for him, no one scratching their heads trying to figure out what it was he wanted to say.

★   ★   ★

I was in charge of breaking the horses. It wasn't like breaking wild mustangs, because our horses had been around us since they were foals. Most times I simply climbed on bareback — if the horse was too skinny, its spine sometimes rubbed a raw spot on my behind — grabbed a handful of mane, gave them a nudge with my heels, and off we went, at first in awkward fits and starts, with a little crow hopping and swerving while the horse wondered what in tarnation a girl was doing on his back, but pretty soon the horse usually accepted his fate and we'd move along right nicely. After that, it was a matter of saddling him up and finding the best bit. Then you could set about training him.

Still, particularly with a green horse, you never knew what to expect, and I got thrown plenty, which terrified Mom, but Dad just waved her off and helped me up.

'Most important thing in life,' he would say, 'is learning how to fall.'

★ ★ ★

Sometimes you fell in slow motion. The horse stumbled or shied, your weight got thrown forward, and you ended up hugging the horse's neck, your feet losing their lock in the stirrups. If you couldn't right yourself, your best bet was to let go and roll off to the side, then keep rolling once you hit the ground. The dangerous falls were the ones that happened so fast you didn't have time to react.

Dad once bought this big gray gelding for a song. The horse had been in the U.S. Cavalry, and since he was government-issue, Dad named him Roosevelt. Maybe it was because Roosevelt had been fed too much grain, maybe because he'd heard too many bugle calls and too many cannons fired, or maybe he was just born a worrier, but for whatever reason, he was one spooky horse. Roosevelt was beautiful to look at, with dappled hindquarters and dark legs, but sudden noises or movement made him jump up like a jackrabbit.

Shortly after we got Roosevelt, I was riding him back to the barn when a hawk swooped down in front of us. Roosevelt spun around and I was flung off him like a rock out of a slingshot. I tried to break the fall with my arm and ended up snapping my forearm clean in two. The jagged ends of the bones were poking up, making a bulge under my skin. Dad was always telling me I was one tough nut, but with my arm bent and dangling like that, danged if I didn't start bawling like a little girl.

Dad carried me into the kitchen, and when Mom saw me, she got so upset she started gasping for breath, telling Dad when she could get the words out that a little girl like me had no business breaking horses. Dad told Mom she had best leave until she could get control of herself, and she went into the bedroom, closing the door behind her. Dad set the bone and had Lupe cut strips of linen while he made up a paste of chalk, gum, eggs, and flour. Then he wrapped the linen strips around my arm and smeared them all over with the paste.

Dad took me in his arms and we sat on the porch looking at the distant mountains. After a while, I stopped crying because there just wasn't any cry left in me by then. I sat there with my head on my shoulder like a little bird with a broken wing.

'Dumb horse,' I finally said.

'Never blame the horse,' Dad said. 'It's just something he learned along the way. And horses

31

aren't dumb. They know what they need to know. Matter of fact, I always figured horses are smarter than they let on. Kind of like the Indians who pretend they can't speak English because no good ever came from talking with the Anglos.'

★ ★ ★

Dad told me I'd be back in the saddle in four weeks, and I was. 'Next time,' Dad said, 'don't try to break a fall.'

'Next time?' Mom asked. 'I trust there won't be a next time.'

'Hope for the best and plan for the worst,' Dad said. 'Anyway,' he told me, 'once you're going down, accept it and let your rump take the punishment. Your body knows how to fall.'

Meanwhile, Dad enrolled Roosevelt in what he called Adam Casey's School for Wayward Horses. He tied Roosevelt's head to his tail and left him to stand in a stall until he learned patience. He filled empty tin cans with pebbles and tied those to his mane and tail until Roosevelt got used to commotion.

Once Roosevelt was reformed — more or less — Dad sold him at a nice profit to some easterners bound for California. While Dad didn't blame horses for anything, he wasn't sentimental about them, either. If you can't stop a horse, sell him, Dad liked to say, and if you can't sell him, shoot him.

Another one of my jobs was feeding the chickens and collecting the eggs. We had about two dozen chickens and a few roosters. First thing every morning, I'd toss them a handful of corn and some table scraps and add lime to their water to make the eggshells strong. In the spring, when the hens were really fertile, I could collect a hundred eggs a week. We'd set aside twenty-five or thirty for eating, and once a week I drove the buckboard into Toyah to sell the rest to the grocer, Mr. Clutterbuck, a pinched man who wore garters on his sleeves and toted up sales figures on the brown paper he wrapped your goods in. He paid a penny per egg, then sold them for two cents each, which seemed unfair to me since I'd done all the work, raising the chickens, collecting the eggs, and bringing them into town, but Mr. Clutterbuck just said, 'Sorry, kid, that's the way the world works.'

I also brought in peacock eggs, finally giving those showy old birds a way to earn their keep. At first I thought they'd fetch twice as much as chicken eggs, seeing as how they were twice as big, but Mr. Clutterbuck would give me only a penny each for them. 'Egg's an egg,' he said. I thought that danged grocer was cheating me because I was a girl, but there wasn't a whole lot I could do about it. That was the way the world worked.

Dad said it was good for me to go into town and bargain with Mr. Clutterbuck over egg prices. It honed my math and taught me the art of negotiation, all of which was going to help me achieve my Purpose in Life. Dad was a philosopher and had what he called his Theory of Purpose, which held that everything in life had a purpose, and unless it achieved that purpose, it was just taking up space on the planet and wasting everybody's time.

That was why Dad never bought any of us kids toys. Play was a waste of time, he said. Instead of playing house or playing with dolls, girls were better off cleaning a real house or looking after a real baby if their Purpose in Life was to become a mother.

Dad didn't actually forbid us from ever playing, and sometimes Buster, Helen, and I rode over to the Dingler ranch for a game of baseball with the Dingler kids. Because we didn't have enough players for two full teams, we made up a lot of our own rules, one being that you could get a runner out by throwing the ball at him. Once, when I was ten and trying to steal a base, one of the Dingler boys threw the ball at me hard and it hit me in the stomach. I doubled over, and when the pain wouldn't go away, Dad took me into Toyah, where the barber who sometimes sewed people up said my appendix had been ruptured and I needed to get up to the hospital in Santa Fe. We caught the next stagecoach, and by the time we got to Santa Fe,

I was delirious, and what I remember next was waking up in the hospital with stitches on my stomach, Dad sitting next to me.

'Don't worry, angel,' he said. The appendix, he explained, was a vestigial organ, which meant it had no Purpose. If I had to lose an organ, I'd chosen the right one. But, he went on, I'd almost lost my life, and to what end? I'd only been playing a game of baseball. If I wanted to risk my life, I should do it for a Purpose. I decided Dad was right. All I had to do was figure out what my Purpose was.

If you want to be reminded of the love of the Lord, Mom always said, just watch the sunrise.

And if you want to be reminded of the wrath of the Lord, Dad said, watch a tornado.

Living on Salt Draw, we saw our share of tornadoes, which we feared even more than those flash floods. On most occasions, they looked like narrow cones of gray smoke, but sometimes when it had been especially dry, they were almost clear, and you could see tree limbs and brush and rocks swirling at the bottom. From a distance they seemed to be moving slowly, as if underwater, spinning and swaying almost elegantly.

Most weren't more than a dust devil gone a little wild, ripping at the laundry on the clothesline and sending the chickens squawking. But once, when I was eleven years old, a monster came roaring across the range.

Dad and I were working with the horses when the sky turned dark real quickly and the air got heavy. You could smell and taste what was heading our way. Dad saw the tornado first, coming in from the east, a wide funnel reaching from the clouds to the earth.

I set about unharnessing the horses while Dad ran in to warn Mom, who started opening all the windows in the house because she'd been told that would equalize the air pressure and make it less likely that the house would explode. The horses were stampeding like crazy around the corral. Dad didn't want them trapped, so he opened the gate and they galloped through it, heading across the range, away from the tornado. Dad said if we got through this, we could worry about the horses later.

By then the sky overhead was black and streaked with rain, but off in the distance you could see sunlight slanting through golden clouds, and I took that as a sign. Dad had us all, including Apache and Lupe, scramble into the crawl space under the house. As the tornado came closer, it whipped up sand and branches and broken bits of wood in one big swirl around the house, roaring so loud it sounded like we were right under a freight train.

Mom grabbed our hands to pray, and while I didn't usually feel the call, I was scared — scareder than I'd ever been — and I started praying harder than I'd ever prayed, asking God to please forgive my earlier lack of sincere faith and promising that if he spared us, I'd pray to him and worship him every day for the rest of my life.

Right then we heard a crash and the sound of splintering wood. The house seemed to groan and shudder, but the floor above our heads held fast, and very quickly the tornado moved on. Everything grew quiet.

We were alive.

The tornado had missed the house, but it had plucked up the windmill and smashed it down on the roof. The house, made from wood that had already been busted apart once in that flood, was a total wreck.

Dad started cussing up a blue streak. Life, he declared, had cheated him once again. 'If I owned hell and west Texas,' he said, 'I do believe I'd sell west Texas and live in hell.'

Dad predicted that the horses would come back at feeding time, and when they did, he hitched the six-year-olds to the carriage and drove into town to use the telegraph. After some backing and forthing with folks in the Hondo Valley, Dad reckoned he was not going to be tried again on that phony old murder charge and it was safe to return to New Mexico and take up life on the Casey ranch, which he'd been renting out to tenant farmers all these years.

The chickens had disappeared in the tornado, but we had most of the peacocks, the six pairs of horses, the brood mares and cows, and a number of Mom's choice heirlooms, such as the walnut headboard that we'd rescued from the dugout. We packed it all into two wagons. Dad took the reins of one, with Mom and Helen next to him. Apache and Lupe were in the second. Buster and I followed on horseback with the rest of the herd on a string.

At the gate I stopped and looked back at the ranch. The windmill still lay toppled over the caved-in house, and the yard was strewn with branches. Dad was always going on about the easterners who came out to west Texas but weren't tough enough to cut it, and now we were folding our hand as well. Sometimes it didn't matter how much gumption you had. What mattered were the cards you'd been dealt.

Life had been hard in west Texas, but that low yellow land was all I knew, and I loved it. Mom was saying, as she always did, that it was God's will, and this time I accepted it. God had saved us, but he had also taken our house from us. Whether as payment for saving us or as punishment because we didn't deserve it, I couldn't say. Maybe he was just giving us a kick in the behind to say: Time to move on.

II

THE MIRACULOUS STAIRCASE

Lily Casey, age thirteen
at the Sisters of Loretto

We traveled three days to reach the Casey Ranch, which Dad, with his love of phonetic spelling, insisted should officially be renamed the KC Ranch. It was in the middle of the Hondo Valley, south of the Capitan Mountains, and the countryside was so green that when I first laid eyes on it, I could hardly believe what I was seeing. The ranch was really more of a farm, with fields of alfalfa, rows of tomato vines, and orchards of peach trees and pecan trees planted a hundred years ago by the Spanish. The pecan trees were so big that when Helen and Buster and I joined hands, we couldn't reach all the way around.

The house, which Dad's pa had bought from a Frenchman when he first moved to the area, was made of adobe and stone. There were two bedrooms inside — so the grown-ups and kids didn't have to sleep in the same room — and a woodshed outside for Lupe, while Apache took over one of the barn stalls. I couldn't believe we would live in such grandeur. The walls were as thick as Dad's forearm was long. 'No tornado's ever going to knock this feller down,' he said.

★　★　★

The next day, while we were unpacking, Dad hollered for us to come outside. I'd never heard him so excited. We ran out the door, and Dad was standing in the yard, pointing up at the sky. There, floating in the air above the horizon, was an upside-down town. You could see the low, flat stores, the adobe church, the horses tied to the hitching posts, and the people walking in the streets.

We all stared slack-jawed, and Lupe made a sign of the cross. It wasn't a miracle, Dad said, it was a mirage, a mirage of Tinnie, the town about six miles away. To me, the mirage seemed nothing short of a miracle. It was huge, taking up a big hunk of the sky, and I was mesmerized watching those upside-down people silently walking through those upside-down streets.

We all stood staring at the mirage for the longest time, and then it got all fuzzy and faded until it finally disappeared. We'd seen mirages before, patches of blue on the ground that looked for all the world like puddles on the driest days. Dad said that those were ground mirages, and what looked like water on the ground was really the sky. This was a heavenly mirage, he said, which was created when the air closer to the ground was cooler than the air above it.

Even though I was usually good at science, I couldn't grasp what Dad was saying. He drew me a diagram in the dirt, showing how the light was refracted by the cool air, which bent it along the curve of the earth's surface.

The idea of light somehow bending didn't make any sense, until Dad reminded me that when you held up a glass of water, your fingers on the far side of the glass looked like they'd been chopped off and moved. That was because the water was bending the light, and the cold air did the same.

All of a sudden what Dad was saying did make sense, and the knowledge of it truly lit me up.

Dad, who was watching me, said, 'Eureka!' He started telling me about this ancient Greek fellow named Archimedes who ran naked through the streets shouting, 'Eureka!' after he figured out a way to calculate volume while sitting in his bathtub.

I could see why Archimedes got all excited. There was nothing finer than the feeling that came rushing through you when it clicked and you suddenly understood something that had puzzled you. It made you think it just might be possible to get a handle on this old world after all.

Dad relished the notion of being a big landowner but not the headaches that came with it. Instead of the fenced-in range land we had in west Texas, there were now fields to be tilled, planted, and weeded, peaches picked, pecans collected, manure spread, watermelons hauled to market, migrants hired and fed. Because of his gimp leg, some of the work — like pruning peach trees from a ladder — was beyond Dad, and his speech impediment made it hard for the help to understand him, so even though I was still only eleven, I took on the hiring and overseeing.

Also, Dad was never the most practical man in the world, and in New Mexico he started getting caught up in all sorts of projects that had nothing to do with running the farm. We were still training horses, and Dad was still writing politicians and newspapers, railing against modernization. But now he spent hours making two copies of every letter he wrote, filing one in his desk and keeping the other in the barn in case the house burned down.

At the same time, Dad was working on a book arguing the case for phonetic spelling. He called it *A Ghoti out of Water*. 'Ghoti,' he liked to point out, could be pronounced like 'fish.' The 'gh' had the 'f' sound in 'enough,' the 'o' had the short 'i' sound in 'women,' and 'ti' had the 'sh' sound in 'nation.'

Dad also started a biography of Billy the Kid, who had stopped at the Casey Ranch when Dad was a teenager and asked to swap his spent horse for a fresh mount. 'Right polite feller,' Dad always said. 'And sat a horse well.' It turned out the Kid had been on the run, as Dad found out an hour later when a posse stopped and also asked to swap horses. Dad, secretly rooting for the Kid, passed off some old nags on them. Now, in New Mexico, he became so obsessed with the Kid that he put a tintype of him on the wall. Mom hated the Kid, whom she called 'two-bit trash' because he'd killed a man who was engaged to her cousin, and she hung that fellow's picture next to the Kid's.

But Dad felt the cousin must have deserved to die. The Kid, he said, never shot anyone who didn't need shooting. Dad considered the Kid a good American boy with hot Irish blood who'd been vilified by the cattle barons for standing up for the Mexicans. 'History gets written by the winners,' he said, 'and when the crooks win, you get crooked history.'

His biography was going to vindicate the Kid, prove that Dad, despite his speech impediment, was better with words than anyone who'd ever laughed at him, and make us more money than we'd ever make growing peaches, pecans, tomatoes, and watermelons. Westerns sell like hotcakes, he kept saying, and besides, a writer's got no overhead and he never has to worry about the weather.

The fall that I turned twelve, Buster left to go to school, even though he was two years younger than me. Mom said that his education was important for his career — for becoming anything he wanted to become — and they enrolled him in a fancy Jesuit school near Albuquerque. But they'd promised me that when I turned thirteen, I could go to the Sisters of Loretto Academy of Our Lady of the Light in Santa Fe.

I'd wanted to go to a real school for years, and the day finally came when Dad hitched up the buckboard and we set out on the two-hundred-mile journey, camping at night on bedrolls under the stars. Dad was almost as excited about me going off to school as I was, and seeing as how I hadn't spent too much time around girls my age out on the ranch, he gave me an earful of advice about how to get along.

I tended to be a tad bossy, he said, as I was used to ordering around Helen and Buster and Lupe and the migrants. But in school there were going to be a lot of bigger, older girls who'd be bossing me around — not to mention the nuns — and instead of fighting with them, I'd have to learn how to get along. The best way to do that, Dad said, was to figure out what somebody wanted, because everybody wanted something, and make them think you could help them get it.

Dad admitted that, as he put it, he wasn't the best exemplar of his own creed, but if I could find some way to apply it to my life, I'd go a lot further.

★ ★ ★

Santa Fe was a beautiful old place — Dad pointed out that the Spanish arrived here even before the first Poms got to Virginia — with low adobe buildings and dusty streets lined with Spanish oaks. The school was right in the middle of town, a couple of four-story Gothic buildings with crosses on top and a chapel with a choir loft reached by what was known as the Miraculous Staircase.

Mother Albertina, the Mother Superior, showed us around. She explained that the Miraculous Staircase had thirty-three stairs — Jesus's age when he died — and that it went in two complete spirals without any of the usual means of support, such as a center pole. No one knew what type of wood it was made of or the name of the mysterious carpenter who showed up to build it after the original builder failed to include a staircase and the nuns prayed for divine intervention.

'So you're saying it's a miracle?' Dad asked.

I started to explain what Dad was saying, but somehow Mother Albertina understood him perfectly.

'I believe everything is a miracle,' she said.

★ ★ ★

I liked the way Mother Albertina said that, and from the beginning, I liked her, too. Mother Albertina was tall and wrinkled and had walnut-colored skin and thick black brows that formed a single line above her eyes. She always appeared calm even though she was constantly on the move, checking in on the dorms at night, inspecting our fingernails, walking briskly along the paths, her long black robes and white-trimmed headdress billowing in the wind. She treated all of us students — she called us 'my girls' — the same, whether we were rich or poor, Anglo or Mexican, smart or utterly lacking in any talent whatsoever. She was firm without being stern, never raised her voice or lost her temper, but it would have been unthinkable for any of us to disobey her. She would have made a fine horsewoman, but that wasn't her Purpose.

I also really liked the academy. A lot of the girls moped around feeling homesick at first, but not me. I had never had it so easy in my life, even though we rose before dawn, washed our faces in cold water, attended chapel and classes, ate corn gruel, practiced piano and singing, mended our uniforms, swept the dorms, cleaned the dishes and privies, and attended chapel again before going to bed. Since there were no barn chores, life at the academy felt like one long vacation.

I won a gold medal for my high scores in math and another for overall scholarship. I also read every book I could get my hands on, tutored other girls who were having problems, and even helped some of the sisters grade papers and do their lesson plans. Most of the other girls came from rich ranch families. Whereas I was used to hollering like a horse trainer, they had whispery voices and ladylike manners and matching luggage. Some of the girls complained about the gray uniforms we had to wear, but I liked the way they leveled out the differences between those who could afford fancy store-bought clothes and those of us, like me, who had only home-dyed beechnut brown dresses. I did make friends, however, trying to follow Dad's advice to figure out what someone wanted and help her get it, though it was hard, when you saw someone doing something wrong, to resist the temptation to correct her. Especially if that someone acted hoity-toity.

★ ★ ★

About halfway into the school year, Mother Albertina called me into her study for a talk. She told me I was doing well at Sisters of Loretto. 'A lot of parents send their girls here for finishing,' she went on, 'so they'll be more marriageable. But you don't have to get married, you know.'

I'd never thought much about that before. Mom and Dad always talked as if it was a matter of course that Helen and I would marry and Buster would inherit the property, though I had to admit I'd never actually met a boy I liked, not to mention felt like marrying. On the other hand, women who didn't marry became old maids, spinsters who slept in the attic, sat in a corner peeling potatoes all day, and were a burden on their families, like our neighbor Old Man Pucket's sister, Louella.

I wasn't too young to start thinking about my future, Mother Albertina continued. It was just around the bend and coming at me fast. Some girls only a year or two older than me got married, she said, while others started working. Even women who got married should be capable of doing something, since men had such a habit of dying on you and, from time to time, running off.

In this day and age, she went on, there were really only three careers available. A woman could become a nurse, a secretary, or a teacher.

'Or a nun,' I said.

'Or a nun,' Mother Albertina said with a smile. 'But you need to have the calling. Do you think you have the calling?'

I had to admit I wasn't sure.

'You have time to reflect on it,' she said. 'But whether or not you become a nun, I think you'd make a wonderful teacher. You have a strong personality. The women I know with strong personalities, the ones who might have become generals or the heads of companies if they were men, become teachers.'

'Like you,' I said.

'Like me.' She paused for a moment. 'Teaching is a calling, too. And I've always thought that teachers in their way are holy — angels leading their flocks out of the darkness.'

* * *

For the next couple of months, I thought about what Mother Albertina had said. I didn't want to be a nurse, not because I was bothered by the sight of blood but because sick people irritated me. I didn't want to be a secretary because you were always at the beck and call of your boss, and what if it turned out you were smarter than him? It was like being a slave without the security.

But being a teacher was entirely different. I loved books. I loved learning. I loved that 'Eureka!' moment when someone finally figured something out. And in the classroom, you got to be your own boss. Maybe teaching was my Purpose.

I was still getting comfortable with that idea — and in fact, finding it mighty appealing — when one of the nuns told me that Mother Albertina wanted to see me again.

Mother Albertina was sitting behind her desk in her study. She had a solemn expression I'd never seen before, and it gave me an uneasy feeling. 'I've got some unfortunate news,' she said.

Dad had paid the first half of my tuition at the beginning of the year, but when the school billed him for the rest, he'd written back to say that, due to a change in circumstances, he was unable to assemble the funds at this juncture.

'I'm afraid you're going to have to go home,' Mother Albertina said.

'But I like it here,' I said. 'I don't want to go home.'

'I know you don't, but the decision's been made.'

Mother Albertina said she'd prayed on the matter and discussed it with the trustees. Their thinking was that the school was not a charity. If the parents agreed to pay the tuition, as Dad had, the school counted on the money to meet expenses, provide scholarships, and support the order's mission on the Indian reservations.

'I could work for it,' I said.

'When?'

'I'll find the time.'

'Your entire day is full as it is. We make sure of that.'

Mother Albertina told me there was one other option. I could take the cloth. If I joined the

54

order of the Sisters of Saint Loretto, the church would pay my tuition. But that would mean going to the novitiate in California for six months, then living in the convent instead of the dormitory. It would mean marrying the Lord Jesus and submitting totally to the discipline of the order.

'Have you had any chance to reflect on whether you've felt the calling?' Mother Albertina asked.

I didn't say anything right away. The truth was, the idea of being a nun didn't exactly fill me with enthusiasm. I knew I owed God a hefty debt for sparing our lives in the tornado, but I figured there had to be another way of paying him back.

'Can I have the night to think on it?' I asked.

'*May* I have the night,' Mother Albertina said, then added, 'What I tell all the girls is that unless you're certain, it's probably a bad idea.'

★ ★ ★

Much as I wanted to stay in school, I didn't really need a night of contemplation to know I wasn't cut out to be a nun. It wasn't just that you didn't see a lot of nuns on horses. I knew I wasn't called. I didn't have that serenity nuns had, or were supposed to have. I was just too restless a soul. And I didn't like taking orders from anyone, not even the pope.

Dad was a grave disappointment to me. Not only had he welched on the tuition commitment, he didn't have the guts to face the nuns, and so, instead of coming to pick me up, he sent a telegram telling me to take the stagecoach home.

I was sitting in the common room in my home-dyed beechnut brown dress, my suitcase next to me, when Mother Albertina came to take me to the depot. The moment I saw her, my lip started quivering and my eyes welled up with tears.

'Now, don't start feeling sorry for yourself,' Mother Albertina said. 'You're luckier than most girls here — God gave you the wherewithal to handle setbacks like this.'

As we walked up the dusty street to the depot, all I could think was that, my one shot at an education blown, I was going back to the KC Ranch, where I'd spend the rest of my life doing chores while Dad worked on his cockamamie Billy the Kid biography and Mom sat in the chaise longue fanning herself. Mother Albertina seemed to know what I was thinking. Before I boarded the coach, she took my hand and said, 'When God closes a window, he opens a door. But it's up to you to find it.'

When the stagecoach pulled into Tinnie, Dad was sitting in the buckboard outside the hotel, with four huge dogs in the back. As I got out, he grinned and waved. The stagecoach driver tossed my suitcase off the roof, and I lugged it over to the carriage. Dad got down and tried to hug me, but I shrugged him off.

'What do you think of these big fellas?' he asked.

The dogs were black with glistening coats, and they sat there regarding the passersby regally, like they were the lords of the manor even though they were also drooling ropes of slobber. They were the biggest dogs I'd ever seen, and there was hardly any room in the back for my suitcase.

'What happened to the tuition?' I asked Dad.

'You're looking at it.'

Dad started explaining that he'd bought the dogs from a breeder in Sweden and had them shipped all the way to New Mexico. They were not just any dogs, he went on, they were Great Danes, dogs of the nobility. Historically, Great Danes were owned by kings and used to hunt wild boars. Practical and prestigious, Dad said. Can't beat that. And believe it or not, no one west of the Mississippi owned any. He'd checked into it. These four, he said, had cost eight hundred dollars, but once he started selling the

57

pups, we'd make the money back in no time, and from then on it would be pure profit.

'So you took my tuition money and bought dogs?'

'Watch that tone,' Dad said. After a moment he added, 'You didn't need to be going to finishing school. It was a waste of money. I can teach you whatever you need to know, and your mother can add the polish.'

'Did you take Buster out of school, too?'

'No. He's a boy and needs that diploma if he's going to get anywhere.' Dad pushed the dogs over and found a spot for my suitcase. 'And anyway,' he said, 'we need you on the ranch.'

On the way back to the KC, Dad did most of the talking, going on about what great personalities the dogs had and how he was already getting inquiries about them. I sat there, ignoring Dad's prattle about his harebrained schemes. I wondered if buying those dogs had simply given Dad an excuse to stop paying the tuition, so I'd have to come back home. I also wondered where in the blazes was that door Mother Albertina had talked about.

The ranch had fallen into a state of mild disrepair in the months I'd been gone. Fence boards had come loose in a few spots, the chicken coop was unwashed, and tack lay scattered on the barn floor, which needed sweeping.

To help out around the ranch, Dad had brought in a tenant farmer named Zachary Clemens and his wife and daughter, and they were living in an outbuilding on a corner of the property. Mom considered them beneath us because they were dirt-poor, so poor that they used paper for curtains, so poor that when they first arrived and Dad gave them a watermelon, after eating the fruit, they set aside the seeds for planting and then pickled the rind.

But I liked the Clemenses, particularly the daughter, Dorothy, who knew how to roll up her sleeves and get things done. She was a big-boned young woman with ample curves, handsome despite a wart on her chin. Dorothy knew how to skin a cow and trap rabbits, and she tilled the vegetable garden the Clemenses had fenced off, but she spent most of her time at the big kettle that hung over the fire pit in front of the shed, cooking stews, making soap, and washing and dyeing clothes she took in from the townspeople in Tinnie.

Dad let the Great Danes roam free, and one day a few weeks after I'd returned home, Dorothy Clemens knocked on the front door to report to Dad that she'd been out collecting pecans near the property line we shared with Old Man Pucket's ranch and had found all four dogs shot dead. Dad charged into the barn in a fury, hitched up a carriage, and drove off to confront Old Man Pucket.

We were worried about what was going to happen, but talking about your fears only scares you and everyone else even more, so nobody said anything. To keep our hands busy, Dorothy and I sat on the corral fence shucking pecans until Dad drove back up. He was usually careful to avoid overexerting his horses, but he'd pushed that gelding so hard his sides were heaving and his chest was covered in lather.

Dad told us Old Man Pucket had unapologetically admitted killing the Great Danes, claiming they were on his property chasing his cattle and he was afraid they were going to bring one down. Dad was cursing and carrying on about how now he was going to bring down Old Man Pucket. He ran into the house and then came back out with his shotgun and jumped into the carriage.

Dorothy and I raced over. I grabbed the reins as Dad kept trying to crack them. The reins were snaking up and down on the horse's back, and it panicked, starting to bolt, but Dorothy leaped up on the seat and, being a big strong woman, pushed down the brake and wrestled the gun away from Dad. 'You can't go killing someone over dogs,' she said. 'That's how feuds get started.'

When her family was living in Arkansas, she went on, her brother had killed someone in self-defense when a dispute broke out during a game of horseshoes, then he'd been killed by that man's cousin. The cousin, afraid Dorothy's father was going to avenge his son's death, had come after him. They'd had to leave everything behind and take off for New Mexico.

'My brother's dead, and we ain't got two nickels to rub together,' she said, 'because a stupid argument over a damn game of horseshoes got out of hand.'

I thought about how Lupe had stepped in during Dad's spat with the tinker, and how no one with a level head had been there to calm down the man who'd killed Dad's pa when he was shot in a dispute over eight dollars. So I reminded Dad about all that.

Dad eventually settled down, but he kept stewing over the matter and the next day went into town to file a legal case against Old Man Pucket. He prepared obsessively for the hearing, detailing his grievances, researching the case law, taking statements from vets about the value of

Great Danes, and writing the politicians he'd corresponded with over the years to see if they'd file friend-of-the-court briefs. He appointed me to speak for him in court, and he had me rehearse my statements and practice my examination of Dorothy, who was to be a witness testifying about her discovery of the dead dogs.

★   ★   ★

On the day of the trial, we all got up early, and after breakfast we piled into the buckboard. When the circuit judge came to town, he held court in the lobby of the hotel, sitting in a wing-backed chair behind a small desk. The various plaintiffs and defendants leaned against the walls, waiting their turn.

The judge was a rail-thin man who wore a string tie and a jacket with a velvet collar, and he looked at you alertly under his bushy eyebrows, giving the impression that he didn't tolerate fools. The bailiff called each case, and the judge listened to the two sides, then made his decision on the spot, brooking no argument.

Old Man Pucket was there, along with a couple of his sons. He was a stumpy little guy with skin the color of beef jerky and thumbnails he left untrimmed because he used them to pry things open. By way of dressing up for court, he had buttoned the top button of his frayed shirt.

Our case was finally called late in the morning, and I was kind of nervous as I stood to make the presentation Dad had cooked up for me.

'The history of the Great Dane is a proud and storied one,' I began, but the judge interrupted me.

'I don't need a damned history lesson,' he said. 'Just tell me why you're here.'

I explained how Dad had imported the dogs from Sweden, planning to breed them as an investment, but they'd been found shot to death in the pecan grove near the fence line we shared with the Puckets.

'I'd like to call my first witness,' I said, but the judge cut me off again.

'Did you shoot those dogs?' he asked Old Man Pucket.

'Sure did.'

'Why?'

'They was on my property chasing my cattle, and from a distance I thought they was big ol' wolves.'

Dad started arguing, but the judge shushed him.

'Sir, I can't make out what you're saying, and it don't matter anyhow,' the judge said. 'You got no business keeping dogs bigger than wolves in cattle country.'

Turning to Old Man Pucket, he said, 'But those were valuable animals, and he deserves some compensation for their loss. If you're shy of cash, some livestock — horses or cattle — would do it.'

And that was that.

A few days after the trial, Old Man Pucket showed up at the ranch with a string of horses. Dad, still harboring a grudge, refused to leave the house, so I went out to meet Old Man Pucket, who was turning the horses into the corral.

'Just like the judge ordered, miss,' he said.

Even before Old Man Pucket had shot the dogs, we'd had our differences. Like most folks on the Rio Hondo, he did what he could to get by, and if that meant encroaching on someone else's land or diverting a creek onto his property, he was prepared to do it. Dad called him a dirt farmer, but I thought of him as a scrapper who understood that sometimes, instead of asking another person's permission, you were best off doing what needed to be done, defending it with bluster, and then apologizing later — if and when it came to that.

'Payment acknowledged,' I said, and shook his hand. Unlike Dad, I saw no point in carrying a grudge with a neighbor. You never knew when you might need someone's help.

Old Man Pucket handed me a bill listing what he claimed was the value of each horse, then tipped his hat. 'You'd make a mighty fine lawyer,' he said.

★　★　★

After Old Man Pucket left, Dad came out and looked at the horses. When I handed him the bill, he snorted in disgust. 'None of those nags is worth twenty dollars,' he said.

It was true. Old Man Pucket's valuations were wildly inflated. There were eight horses in all, stumpy, tough little mustangs, the kind that cowboys rounded up out in the wild and sat on for a day or two so they'd just barely accept a saddle. I figured that was what Old Man Pucket's sons had done with these critters. None of the males was gelded. They were unshod, with chipped-up hooves in terrible need of trimming, and their manes and tails were matted with burrs. They were also scared, watching us nervously and clearly wondering what sort of dreadful end these humans had in store for them.

The problem with half-broke horses like these was that no one took the time to train them. Cowboys who could ride anything caught them and ran them on fear, spurring and quirting them too hard, taking pride in staying on no matter how desperately they bucked and fishtailed. Not properly broken, they were always scared and hated humans. A lot of times the cowboys released them once the roundup was over, but by then they'd lost some of the instincts that kept them alive out in the desert. They were, however, intelligent and had pluck, and if you broke them right, they made good horses.

One in particular caught my eye, a mare. I always liked mares. They weren't as crazy as stallions but had more fire than your typical gelding. This one was a pinto, no bigger or smaller than the others, but she seemed less scared and was watching me intently, as if trying to figure me out. I cut her out from the herd, lassoed her, and then slowly walked up to her, following Dad's rule around strange horses to keep your eyes on the ground so they won't think you're a predator.

She stood still, and when I reached her, again moving slowly, I raised my hand to the side of her head and scratched behind one ear. Then I brought my hand down the side of her face. She didn't jerk back, like most horses would, and I knew she was something special, not the greatest beauty in the world — being a patchwork of white, brown, and black — but you could tell she could use her brain instead of reacting blindly, and I'd take smarts over looks in a horse any day.

'She's yours, Counselor,' Dad said. 'What are you going to name her?'

I looked at the mare. For the most part, us ranch folks liked to keep names simple. Cattle we never named at all, since it made no sense naming something you were going to eat or ship off to the slaughterhouse. As for other animals, if a cat had socks, we called it Socks; if a dog was red, we called it Red; if a horse had a blaze, we called it Blaze.

'I'll call her Patches,' I said.

★   ★   ★

'I wanted you to finish your education,' Mom told me that night. 'It was your father who had to buy those dogs, and now all we have are these

66

useless range horses.'

I was trying hard not to see it that way. The money was gone, Sisters of Loretto was behind me, I had what I had, and I needed to make the most of it.

The next day we gelded the new males, since, if they were going to be worth anything, they had to be turned into workhorses. It was nasty work, me, Dorothy, Zachary, and his wife, Ellie — who was not quite as big as her daughter but every bit as tough — each holding a rope tied to one of the horse's legs after we'd caught him, knocked him down, and flipped him on his back. Apache tied the horse's two hind legs to his belly, then Dad wrapped his head in a burlap sack and held it down while Apache knelt behind his rump, working first with the cleaver then the knife, blood spraying everywhere, the horse neighing hysterically while farting and kicking and twisting his back.

But it was over pretty quick. When we let the first horse free, he rose and staggered around drunkenly for a few steps. I herded him out of the corral, and after a moment he sighed and put his head into the tall grass to graze like nothing much had happened.

'Don't even miss 'em,' Zachary said.

'We should do Old Man Pucket next,' Dad said.

That got a chuckle out of everyone.

★ ★ ★

I set about breaking Patches properly. That was one smart horse, and in no time she had truly accepted the bit and was moving off the leg at the slightest touch of my spur. After a few months of that, she even started cutting cattle. By fall, she'd become a true packer and was ready for roundup. I told Mom and Dad I wanted to go hire out at the big Franklin ranch across the valley, but they said they wouldn't hear of it, and neither would the Franklins. So I started racing Patches in little amateur quarter-horse races, and from time to time we even returned with the purse.

The following summer Buster came home from school, having completed the eighth grade. Mom and Dad talked about him going on to high school one day when they could afford it, but eighth grade was all the learning lots of folks figured they needed out west — it was more than most got — and Buster wasn't interested in high school. He knew enough math and reading and writing to run a ranch, and he didn't see much point in picking up more knowledge than that. Cluttered the mind, in his view.

Not long after Buster got back, it became clear to me that he and Dorothy were sweet on each other. In some ways it was a strange match, since she was a few years older and he scarcely had hair on his chin. Mom was horrified when she found out, but I thought Buster was lucky. He was always a little unmotivated, and if he was going to run the ranch with any success, he'd need someone determined and hardworking like Dorothy beside him.

★   ★   ★

One day in July, I rode Patches into Tinnie to pick up some dry goods and collect the mail. To my surprise, there was a letter for me, practically the only letter I'd ever received. It was from Mother Albertina, and I sat right down on the steps outside the general store to read it.

She continued to think about me, she wrote, and continued to believe I'd make an excellent teacher. In fact, she went on, she thought I knew enough right now to be a teacher, and that was why she was writing. Because of the war that had started up in Europe, there was a shortage of teachers, particularly in the remote parts of the country, and if I was able to pass a test the government was giving in Santa Fe — it was not an easy test, she warned, the math was particularly tough — I could probably get a job even without a degree and even though I was just fifteen years old.

I was so excited, I had to resist the urge to gallop all the way back to the ranch, but I held Patches at a steady trot, and as I rode along, I kept thinking this was the door Mother Albertina had told me about.

Mom and Dad didn't like the idea at all. Mom kept saying I had a better chance of marriage if I stayed here in the valley, where I was known as the daughter of a substantial property owner. Off on my own, I'd have less to offer in the way of family and connections. Dad kept throwing out one reason after another: I was too young to be on my own, it was too dangerous, training horses was more fun than drilling illiterate kids in their ABCs, why would I want to be cooped up in a classroom when I could be out on the range?

Finally, after raising all these objections, Dad sat me down on the back porch. 'The fact is,' he said, 'I need you.'

I had seen that coming. 'This'll never be my ranch, it's going to Buster, and with Buster marrying Dorothy, you have all the help you need.'

Dad looked out at the horizon. The rangeland rolling toward it was particularly green from a recent rainfall.

'Dad, I got to strike out on my own sometime. Like you're always saying, I've got to find my Purpose.'

Dad thought about it for a minute. 'Well, hell,' he said at last. 'I suppose you could at least go and take the damn test.'

The test was easier than I expected, mostly questions about word definitions, fractions, and American history. A few weeks later, I was back at the ranch when Buster came into the house with a letter for me he'd picked up at the post office. Dad, Mom, and Helen were all there, and they watched me open it.

I'd passed the test. I was being offered the job of an itinerant replacement teacher in northern Arizona. I gave a shriek of delight and started dancing around the room, waving the letter and whooping.

'Oh my,' Mom said.

Buster and Helen were hugging me, and then I turned to Dad.

'Seems you been dealt a card,' Dad said. 'I guess you better go on and play it.'

* * *

The school that was expecting me was in Red Lake, Arizona, five hundred miles to the west, and the only way for me to get there was on Patches. I decided to travel light, bringing only a toothbrush, a change of underwear, a presentable dress, a comb, a canteen, and my bedroll. I had money from those race purses I'd won, and I could buy provisions along the way, since most every town in New Mexico and Arizona was about a day's ride from the next.

I figured the trip would take a good four weeks, since I could average about twenty-five miles a day and would need to give Patches a day off every now and again. The key to the trip was keeping my horse sound.

Mom was worried sick about a fifteen-year-old girl traveling alone through the desert, but I was tall for my age, and strong-boned, and I told her I'd keep my hair under my hat and my voice low. For insurance, Dad gave me a pearl-handled six-shooter, but the fact of the matter was, the journey seemed like no big deal, just a five-hundred-mile version of the six-mile ride into Tinnie. Anyway, you had to do what you had to do.

★ ★ ★

Patches and I left at first light one morning in early August. Dorothy came up to the house to make me johnnycakes for breakfast and wrapped a few extras in waxed paper for me to carry along. Mom, Dad, Buster, and Helen were all up, and we sat down at the long wooden table in the kitchen, passing the platter of johnnycakes and the tin teapot back and forth.

'Will we ever see you again?' Helen asked.

'Sure,' I said.

'When?'

I hadn't thought about that, and I realized I didn't want to think about it. 'I don't know,' I said.

'She'll be back,' Dad said. 'She'll miss ranch life. She's got horse blood in her veins.'

73

After breakfast, I brought Patches into the barn. Dad followed me, and as I saddled up, he started deluging me with all sorts of advice, telling me to hope for the best but plan for the worst, neither a borrower nor a lender be, keep your head up and your nose clean and your powder dry, and if you do have to shoot, shoot straight and be damn sure you shoot first. He wouldn't shut up.

'I'll be fine, Dad,' I said. 'And you will, too.'

''Course I will.'

I swung up into the saddle and headed over toward the house. The sky was turning from gray to blue, the air already warming. It looked to be a dusty scorcher of a day.

Everyone except Mom was standing on the front porch, but I could see her watching me through the blur of the bedroom window. I waved at them all and turned Patches down the lane.

III

PROMISES

Lily Casey with Patches

The dirt road running west from Tinnie was an old Indian trail packed down and widened over the years by wagon wheels and horse hooves. It followed the Rio Hondo through the foothills of the Capitan Mountains north of the Mescalero Apache reservation. The land in those parts of southern New Mexico was easy on the eyes. Cedars grew thick. From time to time I saw antelope standing at the riverbank or bounding down a hillside, and occasionally, a few skinny range cattle wandered by. Once or twice a day Patches and I passed a lone cowboy on a gaunt horse, or a wagonful of Mexicans. I always nodded and said a few words, but I kept my distance.

Late each morning when the sun got high, I looked for a shady spot near the river where Patches could graze on the short grass. I needed rest, too, to keep my wits about me. A walking horse could be as dangerous as a galloping one, since the easy rhythm could lull you into drowsing off just as a rattler darted into your path and your mount spooked.

When it started to cool, we moved on again and kept going until it got dark. I'd make a sagebrush fire, eat some jerky and biscuits, and lie in my blanket, listening to the howling of the distant coyotes while Patches grazed nearby.

At each town — usually a small collection of

wood shacks and adobe huts, a single store, and a little church — I bought the next day's food and chatted with the storekeeper about the road ahead. Was it rocky? Any riffraff I should avoid? Where was the best place to water and camp?

Most of the storekeepers were happy to play the expert, giving me advice and directions, drawing maps on paper bags. They were also happy to have someone to talk to. At one lonely place, the store was deserted except for the owner. The shelves were lined with a few dusty tins of peaches and bottles of liniments. After paying for a bag of hardtack, I asked the storekeeper, 'How many customers have you had today?'

'You're the first this week,' he said. 'But it's only Wednesday.'

*   *   *

I rode from Hondo to Lincoln to Capitan to Carrizozo, where the road wound down out of the hills into the flat, burnt stretch of desert known as the Malpais. There I headed north, the big Chupadera Mesa rising up out of the desert floor to my left. I reached the Rio Grande at a small town called Los Lunas. It wasn't much of a river there, and a Zuni girl ferried me across in a raft, pulling us along with a rope that ran from one bank to the other.

West of the river was a bunch of Indian reservations, and one day I met up with a half-Navajo woman on a donkey. I figured she wasn't much older than me. She wore a cowboy hat, and her thick black hair spilled out from under it like mattress stuffing. She was heading in my direction and we fell in together. She introduced herself as Priscilla Loosefoot. Her mother, she said, had traded her to a settler family for two mules, but they had beaten her and treated her like an animal, so she'd run away and now scratched out a living collecting and selling herbs.

That night we pitched camp in a grove of juniper trees off the road. I took my cornmeal from my saddlebag, and Priscilla got out some fat-back wrapped in leaves. She mixed the cornmeal and fatback with water and some salt she kept in a leather pouch, shaped a short stack of Indian cakes on a flat rock, and fried them on another flat rock she'd placed in the fire.

A lot of Navajos were quiet, but Priscilla was a real talker, and as we sat there licking our fingers while the fire died down, she went on about what a good team we'd make and how maybe we should travel together and she'd teach me how to identify herbs.

After a while we drifted off to sleep, but something woke me in the middle of the night, and I found Priscilla quietly going through my saddlebags.

The pearl-handled revolver was in my boot. I pulled it out and held it up so Priscilla could see it in the moonlight.

'I got nothing worth stealing,' I said.

'I figured you didn't,' Priscilla said. 'But I had to make sure.'

'I thought you said we made a good team.'

'We still could if you don't hold this here against me. Thing is, I don't get a lot of opportunities, and when one comes along, I gots to take it.'

I knew what she meant, but still, I didn't care to wake up and find her gone and Patches with her. I stood up and gathered my bedroll. 'You stay here,' I said.

'Sure thing.'

There was just enough moon to make out the road. I saddled up Patches and moved on alone.

★   ★   ★

I crossed into Arizona at the Painted Cliffs, red sandstone bluffs that rose straight up out of the desert floor. After another ten days of steady riding, I reached Flagstaff. Its hotel advertised a bathtub, and since I was feeling pretty ripe at that point, it was mighty tempting, but I kept going and two days later arrived at Red Lake.

I'd been on the road, out in the sun and sleeping in the open, for twenty-eight days. I was tired and caked with dirt. I'd lost weight, my clothes were heavy with grime and hung loosely, and when I looked in a mirror, my face seemed harder. My skin had darkened, and I had the beginnings of squint lines around my eyes. But I had made it, made it through that darned door.

Red Lake was a small ranch town on a high plateau about thirty miles south of the Grand Canyon. The range sloped away for miles, to both the east and the west, giving you the feeling that you were at one of the world's high points. The land here was greener than the parts of Arizona I'd passed through, with thick grass that grew so high it tickled the bellies of the cattle that grazed there. For as long as anyone could remember, the range around Red Lake wasn't used for much of anything other than grazing, but farmers had recently discovered it, and they came in with their plows and well diggers and high hopes to do the backbreaking work that was needed to bring up crops as green as the grass that grew there. Those farmers brought big families with them, and their kids needed teaching.

Shortly after I arrived, the county superintendent, Mr. MacIntosh, rode up from Flagstaff to explain the situation. Mr. MacIntosh was a slight man with a head so narrow he reminded me of a fish. He wore a fedora and a stiff white paper collar. Because of the war, he explained, men were joining the army and women were leaving the countryside to take the high-paying factory jobs the men had left behind. But even with the shortage of teachers in rural areas, the board wanted the certified teachers to have at least an eighth-grade education, which I didn't have. So I was to teach in Red Lake until they could hire a more qualified person, and then I'd be sent somewhere else.

'Don't worry,' Superintendent MacIntosh said. 'We'll always find a place for you.'

★   ★   ★

Red Lake had a one-room schoolhouse with an oil stove in a corner, a desk for the teacher, a row of benches for the kids, and a slate blackboard that made me especially happy, as a lot of schools lacked them. On the other hand, a lot of one-room schools had a teacherage attached, where the teacher lived, but the one in Red Lake didn't, so I slept on the floor of the school in my bedroll.

Still, I loved my job. Superintendent Mac-Intosh hardly ever came around, and I got to teach exactly what I wanted to teach, in the way I wanted. I had fifteen students of all ages and abilities, and I didn't have to round them up because their parents, eager for them to learn, brought them to the school on the first day and made sure they kept coming back.

Most of the kids were born back east, though some came from as far away as Norway. The girls wore faded floor-length gingham dresses, the boys had chopped-up haircuts, and they all went barefoot in warm weather. Some of those kids were poorer than poor. One day I stopped by the house of one of my Walapai students, and they were cooking up beef with little bugs crawling in it.

'Careful,' I said, 'that meat is full of maggots.'

'Yes,' the mother said, 'but the maggots are full of meat.'

We had no textbooks, so the kids brought whatever they had from home — family Bibles, almanacs, letters, seed catalogs — and we read from those. When winter came, one of the fathers gave me a fur coat he'd made from coyotes he'd trapped, and I wore it in the schoolroom during the day, since my desk was far from the oil stove, which the kids were all huddled around. Mothers made a point of bringing me stews and pies and inviting me to Sunday dinner, when they'd even set out a white tablecloth as a sign of respect. And at the end of every month I picked up my paycheck from the town clerk.

★   ★   ★

Halfway through the year, Superintendent MacIntosh found a certified teacher for Red Lake, and I was sent on to another little town called Cow Springs. For the next three years, that's how Patches and I lived, moving from one town to another — Leupp, Happy Jack, Greasewood, Wide Ruin — after a stay of a few months, never putting down roots, and never getting too close to anyone. Still, all those little rascals I was teaching learned to obey me or got their knuckles rapped, and I was teaching them things they needed to know, which made me feel like I was making a difference in their lives. I never met a kid I couldn't teach. Every kid was good at something, and the trick was to find out what it was, then use it to teach him everything else. It was good work, the kind of work that let you sleep soundly at night and, when you awoke, look forward to the day.

Then the war ended. One day not long after I'd turned eighteen, Superintendent MacIntosh caught up with me to explain that, with the men all returning home, women were being laid off at the factories in favor of the veterans. Many of those women were certified teachers who were looking to get back their old jobs. Some of the boys coming back from overseas were teachers, too. Superintendent MacIntosh said he'd heard glowing things about my work, but I hadn't even finished eighth grade, much less earned a high school diploma, and besides, the state of Arizona needed to give priority in hiring to those who'd fought for their country.

'So I'm getting the boot?' I asked.

'Unfortunately, your services are no longer needed.'

I stared at the fish-faced superintendent. I'd figured this day might come sooner or later, but I still felt like the floor had fallen out from under me. I knew I was a good teacher. I loved it and even loved traveling to all these remote places where no one else wanted to teach. I understood what Mr. MacIntosh was saying about needing to help out the returning troops. At the same time, I'd busted my behind teaching all those wild and illiterate kids, and I couldn't help feeling a little burned about being told by Fish Face that I was now unqualified to do something

I'd spent the last four years doing.

Superintendent MacIntosh seemed to know what I was thinking. 'You're young and strong, and you got pretty eyes,' he said. 'You just find yourself a husband — one of these soldier boys — and you'll be fine.'

The ride back to the KC seemed to take about half as long as that first journey out to Red Lake, but that's the way it always is when you're heading home through familiar territory. The only adventure occurred when a rattler parked itself under my saddle one night, but it reared back and zipped off, doing those wildfire wriggles, before I could get out my gun. And then there was the airplane. Patches and I were heading east near the Homolovi Ruins, some fallen-down pueblos where the Hopis' ancestors had once lived, when we heard the putt-putt of an engine in the sky behind us. I looked back, and a red biplane — the first I'd ever seen — was following the road east a few hundred feet above the ground.

Patches started to scutch about at the strange noise, but I held her in, and as the plane approached, I took off my hat and waved. The pilot dipped the plane's wings in response, and as it passed us, he leaned out and waved back. I kicked up Patches and we galloped after the plane, me flapping my hat and shouting, though I was so excited that I had no idea what I was trying to say.

Never in my life had I ever seen anything like that airplane. It was amazing that it didn't just fall out of the sky, but for the first time it dawned on me — Eureka! — what the word 'airplane' meant. That was what it did. It stayed aloft because it was planing the air.

I only wished I had some students to explain all this to.

All that time I was teaching, I had never gone home, since the trip took so long. People say that when you return to the place where you grew up, it always seems smaller than you remember. That was the case with me when I finally reached the ranch, but I don't know if it was because I had built it up in my memories or I had gotten bigger. Maybe both.

While I was away, I did write the family once a week and in return received long letters from Dad waxing eloquent and purple about his latest political convictions yet providing few details about how they were faring, and I wondered if the family had managed to keep it all together. But the place looked well run, the fences in repair, the outbuildings freshly whitewashed, a new clapboard wing on the main house, a big supply of split firewood neatly stacked under the porch roof, even a bed of hollyhocks and sunflowers.

Lupe was out front scouring a pot when I rode up. She gave a shriek, everyone came running from the house and barn, and there was a whole lot of hugging and happy tears. Dad kept saying, 'You left a girl and you come back a woman.' He and Mom both had strands of gray in their hair, Buster had filled out and grown a mustache, and Helen had become a willowy sixteen-year-old beauty.

Buster and Dorothy had gotten married the

year before. They lived in the new wing of the house, and it soon became clear to me that Dorothy was more or less running the place. She oversaw the kitchen, bossing Lupe around something fierce, and handed out the daily work assignments for Buster, Apache, and even Mom, Dad, and Helen. Mom complained that Dorothy had gotten a tad high-handed, but I could tell they were secretly glad to have someone doing what I used to do.

Mom's biggest concern was Helen. She had reached marrying age, but pretty as she was, that girl just lacked get-up-and-go. Mom worried that Helen might be suffering from neurasthenia, a vague ailment wealthy women got that made them want to lie in a room all day with a wet cloth over their eyes. Helen was happy to sew and bake pies, but she hated any kind of work that made her break into a sweat or gave her hands calluses, and most of the Rio Hondo ranchers looking for wives wanted a woman who could not only cook and clean house but also help out with branding calves and drive the chuck wagon during roundup. Mom's plan was to send Helen to the Sisters of Loretto — hoping that with a little polish, she'd attract a citified man in Santa Fe — but Dorothy argued that all the earnings from the ranch needed to be reinvested in machinery to raise crop yields. Helen herself was talking about how she'd like to move to Los Angeles and become an actress in the movies.

★ ★ ★

The morning after I returned, we were eating breakfast in the kitchen, Mom passing the teapot around. I'd developed a taste for coffee in Arizona, but Dad still allowed nothing stronger than tea on the ranch.

After cleaning up, Dad and I walked out onto the porch. 'You ready to get back in the corral?' he asked. 'I got a couple of new saddlebred fillies that I know you can work wonders with.'

'I don't know, Dad.'

'What do you mean? You're a horsewoman.'

'With Dorothy in charge, I'm not sure there's a place for me here anymore.'

'Don't go talking nonsense. You're blood. She's just an in-law. You belong here.'

But the truth was, I didn't feel I did. And even if there was a place for me, it was not the life I wanted. That plane that had flown overhead at the Homolovi Ruins had got me to thinking. Also, I'd seen a number of automobiles in my years in Arizona, and they gave me a sinking feeling about the future prospects for carriages — and carriage horses.

'You ever think of getting yourself one of those automobiles, Dad?' I asked.

'Consarned contraptions,' Dad said. 'No one'll ever look as smart in one of those fume belchers as they do in a carriage.'

That got him going about how President Taft had taken this country in the wrong direction by getting rid of the White House stables and replacing them with a garage. 'Teddy Roosevelt, now, there was a man, the last president who truly knew how to sit a horse. We'll never see his like again.'

As I listened to Dad, I could feel myself pulling away from him. All my life I'd been hearing Dad reminiscing about the past and railing against the future. I decided not to tell him about the red airplane. It would only get him more worked up. What Dad didn't understand was that no matter how much he hated or feared the future, it was coming, and there was only one way to deal with it: by climbing aboard.

Another thing that airplane made me realize was that there was a whole world out there beyond ranchland that I'd never seen, a place where I might finally get that darned diploma. And maybe I'd even learn to fly an airplane.

So the way I saw it, I had two choices: stay on the ranch or strike out on my own. Staying on the ranch meant either finding a man to marry or becoming the spinster aunt to the passel of children that Dorothy and Buster talked about having. No man had proposed to me yet, and if I sat around waiting for one, I could well end up as that potato-peeling spinster in the corner of the kitchen. Striking out on my own meant going someplace where a young unmarried woman could find work. Santa Fe and Tucson weren't much more than gussied-up cattle towns, and the opportunities there were limited. I wanted to go where the opportunities were the greatest, where the future was unfolding right before your eyes. I wanted to go to the biggest, most boomingest city I could find.

A month later, I was on the train to Chicago.

The railroad ran northeast through the rolling prairie to Kansas City, then on across the Mississippi and into the farmland of Illinois, with its green fields of closely planted corn, tall silos, and pretty white-frame houses with big front porches. It was my first train trip, and I spent much of it with the window down, sticking my face out into the onrushing wind.

We traveled through the night, and even with stops for refueling and to pick up and let off passengers, the trip lasted only four days, whereas it had taken Patches, packer though she was, an entire month to go less than half that distance.

When the train pulled into Chicago, I took down my little suitcase and walked through the station into the street. I'd been in crowds before — county fairs, livestock auctions — but I'd never seen such a mass of people, all moving together like a herd, jostling and elbowing, nor had my ears been assaulted by such a ferocious din, with cars honking, trolleys clanging, and hydraulic jackhammers blasting away.

I walked around, gawking at the skyscrapers going up everywhere, then I made my way over to the lake — deep blue, flat, and as endless as the range, only it was water, fresh and flowing and cold even in the summer. Coming from a place where people measured water by the pailful, where they fought and sometimes killed each other over water, it was hard to imagine, even though I was looking at it, that billions of gallons of fresh water — I figured it had to be billions or even trillions — could be sitting there undrunk, unused, and uncontested.

After gazing at the lake for a long while, soaking up the sight of it, I followed my plan: I found a Catholic church and asked a priest to recommend a respectable boardinghouse for women. I rented a bed — four to a room — then I bought the newspapers and looked at the help-wanted ads, circling possibilities with a pencil.

★   ★   ★

The next day I started searching for a job. As I walked the streets, I found myself staring at people's faces, thinking, So this is what city folk look like. It wasn't so much their features that were different, it was their expressions. Their faces were shut off. Everyone made a point of ignoring everyone else. I was used to nodding when I caught a stranger's eye, but here in Chicago they looked right through you, as if you weren't there at all.

Finding work was considerably harder than I had expected. I had hoped to get a position as a governess or a tutor, but when I admitted that I didn't even have an eighth-grade education, people looked at me like they were wondering why I was wasting their time, even after I told them about my teaching experience. 'That may be fine for sod busters,' one woman said, 'but it won't do in Chicago.'

The sales jobs at department stores all required experience, and mine was limited to my penny-an-egg deals with Mr. Clutterbuck. Businesses were advertising for clerks, but even as I stood in the long lines to fill out the forms, I knew I wasn't going to get the job. With all the soldiers returning home and all the girls like me pouring in from the countryside, there was too much competition. My money started running low, and I had to face the fact that my options were pretty much limited to factory work or becoming a maid.

Sitting in front of a sewing machine for twelve hours a day didn't strike me as much of a way to get ahead, whereas if I worked as a maid, I'd get to know people with money, and if I showed enough initiative, I might be able to parlay that position into something better.

I found a job pretty quickly working for a commodities trader and his wife, Mim, on the North Side. They lived in a big modern house with radiator heat, a clothes-washing machine, and a bathroom with a sunken tub surrounded by mosaic tiles and faucets for hot water, cold water, and icy drinking water. I got there before dawn to make their coffee by the time they woke, spent the day scrubbing, polishing, and dusting, and left after I'd cleaned the dinner dishes.

I didn't mind the hard work. What bothered me was the way that Mim, a long-faced blond woman only a few years older than me, treated me as if I didn't exist, looking off into the distance when she gave me the day's orders. While Mim seemed very impressed with herself, acting terribly grand, ringing a little silver bell for me to bring in the tea when she had visitors, she wasn't that bright.

In fact, I wondered if anyone could really be such a dodo. Once a French woman with a toy poodle came for lunch, and when the dog started barking, the woman spoke to it in French. 'That's a smart dog,' Mim said. 'I didn't know dogs could speak French.'

Mim also did crossword puzzles, constantly asking her husband the answers to simple clues, and when I made the mistake of answering one, she shot me a short, sharp look.

After I'd been there two weeks, she called me into the kitchen. 'This isn't working out,' she said.

I was stunned. I was never late, and I'd kept Mim's house spotless. 'Why?' I asked.

'Your attitude.'

'What did I say?'

'Nothing. But I don't like the way you look at me. You don't seem to know your place. A maid should keep her head down.'

★ ★ ★

I got another job as a maid pretty quickly, and although it was against my nature, I made a point of keeping my mouth shut and my head down. In the evenings, meanwhile, I went to school to get my diploma. There was no shame in doing hard work, but polishing silver for rich

95

dunderheads was not my Purpose.

Busy as I was, and pretty exhausted most of the time, I loved Chicago. It was bold and bawdy and very modern, though bitterly cold in the winter, with a wicked north wind that blew in off the lake. Women were marching for the right to vote, and I attended a couple of rallies with one of my roommates, Minnie Hanagan, a spunky Irish girl with green eyes and luxurious black hair who worked in a beer-bottling plant. Minnie never met a topic she didn't have an opinion on or heard a comment she couldn't interrupt. After working all day as a zip-lipped maid, keeping my thoughts to myself and my eyes on the ground, it was great to unwind with Minnie by arguing about politics, religion, and everything else under the sun. We double-dated a couple of times, factory boys squiring us around to the cheaper speakeasies, but they were usually either tonguetied or loutish. I had more fun talking to Minnie than I did to any of those fellows, and sometimes the two of us went off and danced by ourselves. Minnie Hanagan was the closest thing I'd ever had to a genuine friend.

Minnie asked me what my birthday was, and when it rolled around — I was turning twenty-one — she gave me a tube of dark red lipstick. It was all she could afford, she said, but we could make ourselves up to look like real ladies and go to one of the big department stores, where we'd have fun trying on all the things we'd be able to buy one of these days. I'd never been one for makeup — few women were in ranch country — but Minnie applied it for me, rubbing a dab into my cheeks as well, and darned if I didn't look a bit like a stockbroker's wife.

Minnie led me through the department store. It was as big as a cathedral, with vaulted ceilings, stained glass windows, pneumatic tubes that whooshed the customers' money from floor to floor, and aisle after aisle after aisle of gloves, furs, shoes, and anything else you could possibly imagine buying. We stopped at the hat department, and Minnie had me try on one after another — little hats, big hats, hats with feathers, hats with veils or bows, hats with artificial flowers arranged along the wide brims. As she sat each one on my head, she'd evaluate it — too old-fashioned, too much brim, hides your eyes, this one belongs in your closet — and as the hats piled up on the counter, a salesclerk came over.

'Are you girls able to find anything in your price range?' she asked with a cold smile.

I felt a little flustered. 'Not really,' I said.

'Then maybe you're in the wrong store,' she said.

Minnie stared at the woman square on. 'Price isn't the problem,' she said. 'The problem is finding something up-to-date in this dowdy stock. Lily, let's try Carson Pirie Scott.'

Minnie turned on her heel, and as we walked off, she told me, 'When they get high-handed, all you have to do is remind yourself that they're just hired help.'

After I'd been in Chicago for almost two years, I came home from work on a July evening to find one of my other roommates laying out Minnie's only good dress on her bed.

Minnie, she said, had been at the bottling plant where she worked when her long black hair got caught in the machinery. She was pulled into these massive grinding gears. It was over before anyone nearby even had time to think.

Minnie was supposed to wear her hair up in a kerchief, but she was so proud of those thick, shiny Irish tresses — they made every man in Chicago want to flirt with her — that she couldn't resist the temptation to let them down. Her body was so badly mangled that they had to have a closed-coffin funeral.

I loved that girl, and as I sat through the service, all I could think was that if I'd been there, maybe I could have rescued her. I kept imagining myself chopping her hair off, pulling her back, and hugging her as we sobbed happily, realizing how close she'd come to a gruesome death.

But I also knew that even if I'd been right there — and somehow happened to have had a pair of scissors in my hands — I wouldn't have had time to save her once her hair got tangled up in the machine. When something like that happens, one moment you're talking to the person, and then you blink and the next moment she's dead.

Minnie had spent a lot of time planning her future. She had been saving her money and was confident she'd marry a good man, buy a little house in Oak Park, and raise a boisterous brood of green-eyed kids. But no matter how much planning you do, one tiny miscalculation, one moment of distraction, can end it all in an instant.

There was a lot of danger in this world, and you had to be smart about it. You had to do what you could to prevent disaster. That night at the boardinghouse, I got out a pair of scissors and a mirror, and although Mom always called my long brown hair my crowning glory, I cut it all off just below my ears.

★   ★   ★

I didn't expect to like my new short hair, but I did. It took almost no time to wash and dry, and I didn't have to fuss with curling irons, hairpins, and bows. I went around the boardinghouse with the scissors, trying to talk the other girls into cutting their hair, pointing out that even if they didn't work in a factory, the world today was filled with all manner of machinery — with wheels and cogs and turbines — that their hair could get caught up in. Long curls were a thing of the past. For us modern women, short-cropped hair was the way to go.

Indeed, with my new haircut, I felt I looked the model of the Chicago flapper. Men took more notice of me, and one Sunday while I was walking along the lakefront, a broad-shouldered fellow in a seersucker suit and a straw boater struck up a conversation. His name was Ted Conover, and he'd been a boxer but now worked as a vacuum-cleaner salesman for the Electric Suction Sweeper Company. 'Get a foot in the door, toss in some dirt, and they gotta let you demonstrate your product,' he said with a chuckle.

I knew from the start that Ted was a bit of a huckster. Even so, I liked his moxie. He had quick gray eyes and a lumpy nose — a souvenir from his boxing days. He also had a ruddy-faced vitality and, as Minnie would have put it, the gift of gab. He bought me a snow cone from a street vendor, and we sat on a bench by a pink marble fountain with frolicking copper sea horses. He told me about growing up in South Boston, catching rides on the backs of trolley cars, stealing pickles from the pickle man's wagon, and learning to throw a knockdown punch in street fights with the dagos. He loved his own jokes so much that he'd start laughing halfway through them, and you'd start laughing, too, even though you hadn't heard the punch line yet.

Maybe it was because I was missing Minnie and I needed someone in my life, but I fell hard for that fellow.

The following week, Ted took me to dinner at the Palmer House hotel, and after that we started seeing each other regularly, though he was often out of the city for days at a time because his sales territory stretched all the way to Springfield. Ted always liked to be in a crowd, and we went to ball games at Wrigley Field, movies at the Folly Theater, and prizefights at the Chicago Arena. I smoked my first cigarette, drank my first glass of champagne, and played my first game of dice. Ted loved dice.

Late in the summer, he showed up at the boardinghouse with a bathing suit he'd bought for me at Marshall Field's, and we took the train down to Gary, where we spent the afternoon swimming in the lake and sunbathing in front of these big sand dunes. I didn't know how to swim, since I'd never been in anything much deeper than the puddles left by the flash floods, but Ted taught me how.

'You'll have to trust me,' he said. 'Just relax.'

And he held me in his arms as I floated on my back. It was true, I could do it. When I relaxed my body, I stopped sinking and rose up toward the surface until my face broke through and the water actually supported me. Floating. I'd never known what it was like.

About six weeks after I met Ted, he took

me back to the fountain with the sea horses, bought me another snow cone, and, as he gave it to me, planted a diamond ring on top. 'A piece of ice that I'm hoping will make you melt,' he said.

* * *

We got married in the Catholic church I'd visited when I first came to Chicago. I wore a blue linen dress I borrowed from one of the girls at the boardinghouse. Neither of us could take time off for a honeymoon, but Ted promised me that one day we'd go to the Grand Hotel, this spectacular resort on Mackinac Island at the top of Lake Huron.

That afternoon we moved into a boarding-house that took in married couples, and we celebrated in our room with a bottle of bathtub gin. The next day I went back to my job as a maid, and Ted hit the road.

* * *

I didn't wear my diamond ring to work, keeping it instead in a little silk pouch under our mattress, but I worried about it being stolen. I also worried that Ted had paid more for it than he could afford.

'Relax and learn to enjoy life a little for a change,' he said.

'But it's such an extravagance,' I said.

'It would have been if I'd paid retail,' he said. 'Truth is, it's got a little heat on it.'

Ted assured me he hadn't actually stolen the ring, he just had connections who had connections who knew how to get things through the right channels. In this world, he liked to say, connections were all that mattered.

I had never wanted someone to take care of me, but I found that I liked being married. After so many years on my own, I was sharing my life for the first time, and it made the hard moments easier and the good moments better.

Ted always encouraged people to think big, to dream big, and when he found out that my great ambition had always been not just to finish high school but to go on to college, he told me I might even want to think of getting a Ph.D. When I told him of my dream to fly a plane, he said he could see me becoming a barnstorming stunt pilot. Ted was full of plenty of schemes for himself, too — how he was going to manufacture his own line of vacuum cleaners, build radio antennas out in the prairie, start a telephone company.

We decided we'd put off having kids and squirrel away money while I finished night school. When the future came into better focus, we'd be ready for it.

* * *

Ted was away a lot, but that was fine with me because I was busy with work and night school. To save money, we ate a lot of saltines and pickles, and reused tea bags four times. Busy as we were, the years passed quickly. When I was twenty-six, I finally got my high school diploma. I began looking for a better job but was still working as a maid when, one summer morning, crossing the street while carrying an armload of groceries for the family whose house I kept, a white roadster with wire-spoked wheels came tearing around the corner. The driver slammed on the brakes when he saw me, but it was too late. The grille upended me, and I went rolling across the hood, scattering the apples, buns, and tins that I'd been carrying.

I instinctively went soft as I tumbled off the hood and onto the street. I lay there for a moment, stunned, as people rushed over. The driver jumped out. He was a young man with slicked-back hair and two-tone shoes.

Slick started insisting to everyone that I had stepped out into traffic without looking, which was a darned lie. Then he knelt down and asked if I was okay. The accident looked worse than it was, and lying there, I could tell I had no serious injuries, only bruised bones and some nasty scrapes on my arms and knees.

'I'm fine,' I said.

But Slick was a city boy, not used to seeing women take hard spills, then get up and walk away. He kept asking me how many fingers he was holding up and what day of the week it was.

'I'm okay,' I said. 'I used to break horses. One thing I know how to do is take a fall.'

Slick insisted on taking me to the hospital and paying for the examination. I told the nurse at the emergency room I was fine, but she told me I was a little more banged up than I seemed to believe. While filling out her forms, the nurse asked if I was married, and when I said yes, Slick told me I should call my husband.

'He's a traveling salesman,' I said. 'He's on the road.'

'Then call his office. They'll know how to get in touch with him.'

While the nurse put mercurochrome on my scrapes and bandaged me up, Slick found the number and gave me a nickel for the pay phone. As much to put his mind at rest as anything else, I made the call.

A man answered. 'Sales. This is Charlie.'

'I'm wondering if there's any way you can help me track down Ted Conover on the road. This is his wife, Lily.'

'Ted ain't on the road. He just left for lunch. And his wife's name's Margaret. Is this some kind of prank?'

I felt like the floor was tilting underneath me. I didn't know what to say, so I hung up.

Slick was baffled by the way I rushed out of the phone booth past him, but I had to get away from him and out of the hospital to clear my head and try to think. I kept fighting panic as I made my way to the lake, where I walked for miles, hoping the still blue water would calm me. It was a sunny summer day, and lake water lapped at the promenade's stone wall. Had I misheard Charlie or imagined what he'd said? Was there an explanation? Or had I been two-timed? There was only one way to find out.

The Electric Suction sales office was in a five-story cast-iron building near the Loop. When I got to the block, I fished a newspaper from a trash can and took up a position in a lobby across the street. As five o'clock approached, people began pouring out onto the sidewalks, and sure enough, my husband, Ted Conover, joined them, walking out the door of that cast-iron building wearing his favorite hat — the one with the jaunty little feather — tilted at a rakish angle. He'd clearly fibbed about being out of town, but I still didn't have the full story.

I followed Ted at a safe distance as he made his way through the crowded streets over to the El. He climbed the stairs and so did I. I stood at the far end of the platform with my nose in the newspaper and boarded the train one car behind him. At every stop, I stuck my head out to watch and saw that he got out at Hyde Park. I followed him a few blocks east to a shabby neighborhood with walk-up apartment buildings that had sagging wooden staircases in the back.

Ted went into one of them. I stood outside for a few minutes, but he didn't appear at any of the windows, so I went into the vestibule. None of the mailboxes had names on them. I waited until some kids came out, then slipped through the open door into the hallway. It was dark and narrow and reeked of boiling cabbage and corned beef.

There were four apartments on each floor, and I stopped at every door, pressing my ear against it, listening for the sound of Ted's South Boston accent. Finally, on the third floor, I heard it booming out over a couple of other voices.

Without knowing exactly what I was going to do, I knocked. After a couple of seconds, the door opened, and standing in front of me was a woman with a toddler on her hip.

'Are you Ted Conover's wife, Margaret?' I asked.

'Yes. Who are you?'

I looked at this woman Margaret for a moment. I figured that she was about my age, but she seemed tired, and her hair was going gray before its time. Still, she had a wan, careworn smile, as if life was a struggle but she managed from time to time to find something to laugh about.

Behind her I could hear a couple of boys arguing, then Ted's voice saying, 'Who is it, honey?'

I had an almost overwhelming temptation to push past Margaret and gouge out that lying cheater's eyes, but something held me back — what it would do to this woman and her kids.

'I'm with the census,' I said. 'We just wanted to confirm that a family of four is living here.'

'Five,' she said, 'though sometimes it feels more like fifteen.'

I forced myself to smile and said, 'That's all I need to know.'

I was on the El going back to the boardinghouse, trying to figure out what in the blue blazes to do now, when I suddenly thought about our joint bank account. I stayed up all night, sick with worry about it, and was waiting in front of the bank when the doors opened. Ted and I had salted away almost two hundred dollars in an interest-bearing savings account, but when I got to the teller, he told me there were only ten dollars left.

I got back to the boardinghouse and sat down on the bed. I was surprised by how calm I felt. But as I packed my pearl-handled revolver in my purse, I noticed my hands were trembling.

I took a bus to the Loop and walked up the stairs of the cast-iron building to Ted's office. I pushed open the frosted glass door. Inside was a small, dusty room with several old wooden desks. Ted and another man sat at two of them, their feet up, reading newspapers and smoking.

As soon as I saw Ted, I lost every bit of ladylike decorum my mother had tried to instill in me. I became a wild woman, lighting into that two-timing thief, cursing and screaming — 'You no-good low-down dirty lying scum-sucking son of a bitch!' — and whaling him with my purse, which, since I had my six-shooter in it, meant I was giving him a pretty good pistol whipping.

Ted had his arms up, trying to defend himself,

but I got in some solid blows, and his face was bleeding by the time the other guy pulled me off. I then turned on him with my purse and whacked him good once before Ted grabbed me. 'Calm down or I'll drop you with a roundhouse punch,' he said, 'and you know I can.'

'You go ahead, buster, you hit me and I'll charge you with assault as well as robbery and bigamy.' But I stopped struggling.

The other fellow grabbed his hat. 'I see you two have a few things to discuss,' he said, and slipped out the door.

Everything came exploding out of me then: why had he lied to me, why had he married me when he already had a wife and three children, why had he taken the money that we were supposedly saving for our future together, were there any other lies I hadn't discovered, why hadn't he just left me alone that day he first saw me beside the lake?

As Ted listened, his expression went from defiant to hangdog to downright mournful, and finally, his eyes welled up with tears. He'd taken the money because he'd run up some gambling debts and the dagos were after him, he said. He'd hoped to be able to pay it back before I even noticed. Margaret, he said, was the mother of his children, but he loved me. 'Lily,' he said, 'lying was the only way I could have you.'

The louse was acting as if he expected me to feel sorry for him.

'It's my fault,' he said. Then he reached out and actually touched my hand, adding, 'By loving you, I've destroyed you.'

111

The bum sounded like he was about to blubber up. I pulled my hand away.

'You have a mighty high opinion of yourself,' I told him. 'The fact is, you don't love me, and you haven't destroyed me. You don't have what it takes to do that.'

I shoved past him, slamming the door on my way out, then turned and swung my purse against the frosted glass pane, shattering it, and all the broken little pieces fell in a shower to the floor.

I took another walk along the lake. Sometimes I felt I could see into the future, but I sure as shoot hadn't seen this coming. Things looked pretty bleak right then, but I'd survived a lot worse than a brief marriage to a crumb bum, and I'd survive this, too.

A wind was up, and as I watched it lash the water, I got to thinking how sometimes, as had happened with Minnie, something catastrophic can occur in a split second that changes a person's life forever; other times one minor incident can lead to another and then another and another, eventually setting off just as big a change in a body's life. If that car hadn't hit me and that driver hadn't insisted on taking me to the hospital and hadn't found out I was married and hadn't insisted on my calling Ted, I'd still be happily and obliviously going about my life. But now that life was dead.

I gazed out at the lake, and one thing became crystal-clear. It was over between me and Chicago. The city, for all its beautiful blue water and soaring skyscrapers, had been nothing but heartache. It was time for me to get back to the range.

★ ★ ★

That very day I went over to the Catholic church where I married that heel and told the priest

113

what had happened. He said that if I could prove my husband had been previously married, I could apply to the bishop for an annulment. With the help of a clerk at city hall, I dug out a copy of Ted's other marriage certificate, and the priest said he'd set the wheels in motion.

I thought Ted's wife needed to know what had happened, and I wrote her a letter explaining it all. I decided, however, not to file criminal charges against Ted. It had not been illegal for that weasel to take the money, since it was a joint account; it was just stupid of me to trust him. And if he was sent off to prison as a bigamist, his wife and kids, who had it tough enough already with that Ted Conover in charge of their family, would be worse off than their dad. I also figured the peckerhead had taken up enough of my time and energy, and if he had to wait to get his just deserts from the good Lord himself, that was all right by me.

★   ★   ★

After mailing the letter, I took the ring Ted had given me in to a jeweler. I wasn't going to keep it, but I certainly wasn't going to do something melodramatic, like throw it in the lake. I figured it would fetch a couple hundred dollars, and I was thinking I'd use the money to take some college courses and maybe even splurge on a new dress at Marshall Field's, but the jeweler looked at the diamond with his eyepiece and said, 'It's fake.'

So I threw it in the lake after all.

Once I stopped smacking myself in the head for being so gullible about that crumb bum, I focused on the future. I was twenty-seven years old, no spring chicken. Since I obviously couldn't count on a man to take care of me, what I needed more than ever was a profession. I needed to get my college education and become a teacher. So I applied to the Arizona state teachers' college in Flagstaff. As I waited to hear back — and waited for the annulment — I did nothing but work, scrimp, and save, taking two jobs during the week and another on weekends. The time flew by, and when both the dispensation and the acceptance letter arrived, I had enough money for a year of college.

The day came for me to say good-bye to Chicago. I packed everything I had into the same suitcase I had brought with me. I was leaving the city with about as much stuff as I had arrived with. But I had learned a lot — about myself and other people. Most of those lessons had been hard ones. For example, if people want to steal from you, they get you to trust them first. And what they take from you is not only your money but also your trust.

The train left from Union Station, a spanking-new building with marble floors and hundred-foot ceilings that framed wide skylights. The mayor thought the new station showcased

115

Chicago as a city of the future, the very epitome of technological modernity. I had come to Chicago wanting a slice of that modernity, loving the city for it, but Chicago hadn't loved me back.

The train pulled out of the station, and in a short time we were heading into the countryside. I walked to the back, and from the caboose I watched those massive skyscrapers growing smaller in the distance. Not a single soul in Chicago would miss me. Aside from getting my degree, I'd spent these past eight years in thankless, pointless drudgery, polishing silver that got tarnished again, washing the same dishes day after day, and ironing piles of shirts. Ironing was a particularly galling waste of time. You'd spend twenty minutes pressing one shirt front and back, spraying starch and getting the creases sharp, but once the man of the house put it on, it would wrinkle as soon as he bent an elbow; plus, you couldn't even see whether the danged shirt was ironed or not under his suit coat.

Working in those little desert towns during the war years — teaching illiterate ragamuffins how to read — I had felt needed in a way that I never had in Chicago. That was how I wanted to feel again.

IV

THE RED SILK SHIRT

Helen Casey, Red Lake

You saw plenty of cars in Santa Fe now, and even out in the countryside, but when I got back to the KC, I was surprised by how little things had changed except that Buster and Dorothy had a couple of kids, the third generation of Caseys to be raised on the ranch. Dad had completely abdicated responsibility for the place but was still corresponding with old cowpokes about Billy the Kid's exploits. Mom had grown more frail and complained that her teeth hurt. A couple of years earlier, Helen had moved to Los Angeles to chase her dream of making it in the movies. While she'd yet to get any roles, as she explained in letters home, she'd met a few producers and in the meantime was working as a sales clerk in a millinery.

The first day back, I went out to see Patches, who was standing by herself in the pasture. She was a little whiskery, but she seemed to have aged better than anyone else. I saddled her up and we rode out into the valley. It was late afternoon, and the long purple shadow we cast dipped and swelled across the rolling grassland. Patches was a good seventeen years old, but she still had the juice, and at a rise I clucked her up to a gallop, her hooves clattering over the hard ground while the wind whipped my hair back and whistled in my ears. I hadn't been on a horse since leaving for Chicago, and it just felt right.

* * *

I was a mite concerned about Helen, seeing as how she was not the most self-reliant creature in the world, but Mom, to my surprise, had encouraged her to go to Los Angeles, insisting that with that pretty face and those delicate hands, she was sure to be discovered, and if not, she could find a rich Hollywood husband. Mom also hinted a couple of times that it was good I was going on to college, since with one failed marriage behind me, I'd have trouble landing a good husband and would need something to fall back on. 'A package that's been opened once doesn't have the same appeal,' she said.

Unlike the last time I came home, no one begged me to stay. Even Dad acted as if he assumed I'd be moving on, and that was fine by me. I didn't belong in Chicago, but it had changed me, so I didn't belong on the KC, either. I even felt out of place sleeping in my old bed. Also, if I was going to stay put, I'd need to pitch in on the chores, and after all those years of maid work, cleaning the chicken coop and mucking stalls didn't exactly call to me. I left early for Flagstaff.

* * *

Although I was older than most of the other students, I loved college. Unlike many of the boys, who were interested in football and drinking, and the girls, who were interested in boys, I knew exactly why I was there and what I wanted to get out of it. I wished I could take every course in the curriculum and read every book in the library. Sometimes after I finished a particularly good book, I had the urge to get the library card, find out who else had read the book, and track them down to talk about it.

My only concern was how I was going to pay the next year's tuition. But after I'd been at the university for exactly one semester, Grady Gammage, president of the college, asked to see me. He said he'd been contacted by the town of Red Lake, which was looking for a teacher. He'd been following my performance because he'd also worked hard to put himself through college and admired others who did the same. The folks in Red Lake remembered me from the time I'd taught there. They were willing to sign me up, even though I had just begun college, and Mr. Gammage thought I had what it took as well. 'It's a tough choice,' he said. 'If you start teaching now, you'll give up school, and a lot of people find it hard to come back.'

It didn't seem a tough choice at all. I could either pay money to go to classes or get paid for teaching classes.

'When do I start?' I asked.

I went back to the ranch to get Patches, and for the third time that horse and I made the five-hundred-mile journey between Tinnie and Red Lake. Patches was out of shape, but I easied her along, and she toned up pretty quick. We both enjoyed being on the move in open country.

I ran into more people than I had last time, and every now and again a car would barrel past, the driver white-knuckling the wheel as he bounced over the wagon ruts, trailing a cone of dust. But there were still long stretches of solitude, only me and Patches ambling along, and as I sat by my little fire at night, the coyotes howled just like they always had, and the huge moon turned the desert silver.

★　★　★

The town of Red Lake still felt like it was located at one of the world's high points, the range land sloping away on all sides, but it had changed since I first saw it almost fifteen years before. Arizona, with its wide-open spaces and no one peering over your shoulder, had always been a haven for folks who didn't like the law or other busybodies to know what they were up to, and there were more scoundrels and eccentrics around — Mexican rumrunners, hallucinating

122

prospectors, trench-crazed veterans still wheezing from mustard gas, a guy with four wives who wasn't even a Mormon. One of that guy's kids was named Balmy Gil because when he was born, the guy opened the Bible at random and, eyes closed, planted his finger on the passage about the Balm of Gilead.

More farmers had also put down stakes and more stores had opened, including a new automobile garage with a gasoline pump out front. The grass outside town, which used to be high enough to touch the cattle's underbellies, had been grazed down to the nub, and I wondered if maybe there were more people here than the land could bear.

The schoolhouse now had a teacherage built onto the back, so I had my own room to sleep in. I had thirty-six students of all ages, sizes, and breeds, and I made sure when I entered the classroom that each and every one of them stood up and said, 'Good morning, Miss Casey.' Anyone who talked out of turn had to stand in the corner, and anyone who sassed me was sent out to pluck a willow branch so I could give them a hiding with it. Kids were like horses in that things went a lot easier if you got their respect from the outset rather than trying to demand it after they'd started seeing what they could get away with.

★　★　★

When I'd been in Red Lake a month, I went over to the town hall to pick up my first paycheck. A corral was next to the building, and inside it stood a small sorrel mustang, all veined up and with saddle sweat still on his back. When he saw me, he gave me a baleful look, ears flat, and I could tell right off that was one ornery horse.

Inside the hall, a couple of deputies were lounging by a desk, hats tilted back and pants tucked into their boots. When I introduced myself, one of them — a skinny guy with rooster legs and close-set eyes — said, 'I hear you come all the way from Chicago to teach us hicks a thing or two.'

'I'm just a hardworking gal here for her paycheck,' I said.

'Before you get it, you needs to pass a simple test first.'

'What test?'

'Ride that there little fella out in the corral.'

I could tell from the sidelong glances Rooster Legs and his buddy were giving each other that they thought they were going to play some prank on the greenhorn schoolteacher. I could tell they figured I was a know-it-all about reading, 'riting, and 'rithmetic, so they were going to put this city girl in her place when it came to the fourth R — riding.

I decided to play along with them and we'd see who got the last laugh. Fluttering my eyes and acting all coy, I said this test seemed highly unusual, but I supposed I could give the horse a try since I had ridden before, and I assumed he was a gentle creature.

'Gentle as a baby's fart,' Rooster said.

I had on a loose dress and my sensible

schoolteacher shoes. 'I'm not wearing riding clothes,' I said, 'but if he is as advertised, I guess I could trot him around a bit.'

'You could ride this horse in your pajamas,' Rooster said with a smirk.

I followed the two comedians out to the corral, and while they saddled up the mustang, I went over to a hedge of juniper, broke off a nice limber branch, and stripped the twigs from it.

'Ready to pass your test, ma'am?' Rooster asked. He thought the impending disaster was going to be so hilarious that he could barely contain himself.

The mustang was standing stock-still but watching me out of the corner of his eye. He was just another half-broke horse, and I'd seen plenty of them in my lifetime. I hiked up my skirt and shortened the reins, twisting the horse's head to the right so he couldn't swing his hindquarters away.

As soon as I got my foot into the stirrup, he moved off, but I had him by the mane and I swung into the saddle. He immediately started bucking. By now the two guys were splitting their sides with laughter, but I paid them no mind. The way to stop a horse from bucking was to get his head up — he had to drop it to kick out with his hindquarters — and then send him forward. I popped the horse hard in the mouth with the reins, which jerked his head right up, and whaled his rump with the juniper branch.

That got that little varmint's attention — and the comedians' as well. We set off at a good gallop, but he was still throwing his shoulders around and fishtailing. I was following the motion, riding with my upper body loose, my heels jammed down, and my legs clamped like a vise around his sides. Rooster and his buddy were not going to be seeing any daylight between me and the saddle.

Each time I sensed the small hesitation that meant a buck was coming, I popped the horse's mouth and whaled his rear again, and he soon learned that the only way out for him was to do what I wanted him to do. In no time he settled, and I patted his neck.

I walked the mustang back to the comedians, who were no longer laughing. Both of them had lost their patter. They were even a little slack-jawed. I could tell it was killing them that I could get the best of a horse that must have given them plenty of trouble, but I didn't rub it in.

'Nice little pony,' I said. 'Can I have my paycheck now?'

Word about me breaking that mustang spread around Red Lake, and people began regarding me as a woman to be reckoned with. Both men and women asked for my opinion on problem horses and problem children. Rooster — whose real name was Orville Stubbs but whom I always called Rooster — started acting like my faithful sidekick, as if, since I'd bested him at a game of his own devising, he owed me his utter devotion.

Rooster worked only part-time as a deputy. He lived above the Red Lake stable and also made a little money on the side mucking stalls, shoeing horses, and helping out on roundups. Like most folks out in the country, he didn't have a particular job, much less a career, but got by doing whatever came his way. Rooster turned out to be a likable little guy, even though he had his less than charming habits. He chewed tobacco and was a swallower, not a spitter. 'Spitters just waste good juice,' he declared.

Rooster introduced me to the other horsemen in Red Lake, telling folks I was the former Chicago flapper who'd given up drinking champagne and doing the Charleston to come teach the kids of Coconino County. He encouraged me to enter that mustang, which was his and which he'd named Red Devil, in local races. They were pickup affairs on the weekends, with five to ten horses in quarter-mile heats and a purse of five or ten dollars. I started winning some of those races, and that put around the word about me as well.

I also started playing poker on Saturday night with Rooster and his pals. Our games were in the café, and they involved a fair amount of inebriation. Most folks in that part of Arizona didn't pay much attention to Prohibition, considering it a perverse eastern aberration. All it really meant was that saloon keepers started calling their establishments cafés and stashed their liquor bottles under the counter instead of on the shelf behind the bar. Wasn't no one going to come between a cowboy and his whiskey.

Rooster and the others would put away a good quantity of what they called 'panther piss,' but I'd sit there nursing a single glass all night long. I avoided the elaborate bluffing favored by the cowboys, and always just played the hand I was dealt, folding as soon as the bidding got too rich for my cards, and going for small victories rather than high-stakes table sweepers. Still, on most nights I'd end up ahead of the game, a nice little stack of coins sitting on the table in front of me.

I became known as Lily Casey, the mustang-breaking, poker-playing, horse-race-winning schoolmarm of Coconino County, and it wasn't half bad to be in a place where no one had a problem with a woman having a moniker like that.

★ ★ ★

After a while I could tell Rooster was sweet on me, but before he made his intentions clear, I let him know I'd been married once, it hadn't worked out, and I had no desire to marry again. He seemed to accept this, and we stayed good friends, but one day he came by the teacherage with a shy, sober expression.

'I got something I needs to ask you,' he said.

It sounded like he was going to propose. 'Rooster, I thought you understood we were just friends.'

'It ain't like that,' he said. 'So don't make this any harder.' He hesitated for a moment. 'What I was going to ask was could you show me how to write out 'Orville Stubbs'?'

And that was how Rooster became my secret student.

Rooster started dropping by on Saturday afternoons. We'd work on his reading and writing, then head out for a night of five-card stud. I was still racing Red Devil and winning more often than not. I had spent some of my winnings to buy a crimson-colored shirt of genuine silk, and I wore it whenever I raced. That way even short-sighted spectators could recognize me. I just loved that brilliant, shiny red shirt. Anyone could tell at a moment's glance that it was mail-order, not homemade or home-dyed, and that shirt became my trade-mark.

★   ★   ★

One day in early spring, Rooster and I rode down to a race on a ranch south of Red Lake. It was a bigger meet than usual, with five heats, a final, and a fifteen-dollar purse, and it was held on an actual track, with an inside rail where the spectators had gathered.

Red Devil's legs were on the short side, but that little mustang had fire, and when he got going, he moved so quickly that his hoofbeats sounded like one long drumroll. We took the lead early in the second heat. We were still ahead going into the first turn when a car near the rail backfired with a loud bang. Red bucked and veered sharply to the right, I went left, and before I knew what was happening, I was rolling on the track.

I clamped my hands over my head and lay still, eating dirt, as the other horses thundered by. I'd had the wind knocked out of me, but otherwise, I was fine, and when the sound of the hoofbeats faded, I got up and smacked the dirt off my behind.

Rooster had caught Red and was jogging back toward me with the horse. I climbed into the saddle. I had no chance of catching up with the others, but Red needed to learn that my taking an involuntary dismount didn't mean he got out of doing his job.

When I crossed the finish line, the judge stood up and doffed his Stetson. I raced in a later heat, but Red was off his stride, and we finished toward the back. I had felt that fifteen-dollar purse was within my reach, and afterward, as Rooster watered the horse. I was still cursing about that backfiring car when the judge came over. He was a big man with a deliberate way of moving, a weathered face, and steady pale blue eyes.

'That was quite a tumble you took,' he said. His voice was deep, like he was speaking from inside a bass fiddle.

'No need to be reminding me, mister.'

'Everyone takes spills, ma'am. But I was mightily impressed with how, instead of calling it a day, you got right back on and finished the race.'

I started railing about the backfiring jalopy,

but Rooster cut me off. 'This here is Jim Smith,' he said. 'Some folks call him Big Jim. He owns the new garage in town.'

'Don't much like automobiles, do you?' Jim asked me.

'Just don't like them spooking my horse. Truth is, I always wanted to learn to drive.'

'Maybe I can teach you.'

I wasn't about to pass up an opportunity like that, so Jim Smith taught the teacher how to drive. He had a Model T Ford with a brass radiator, brass headlights, and a brass horn. The car, which Jim called 'the Flivver,' was an ordeal — and sometimes an outright menace — to start. On really cold days you couldn't get it going at all, and even on warm days it helped to have two people, because otherwise you had to crank it by hand, then jump into the front seat to pull out the choke. Sometimes the car lurched forward while you were cranking it, and other times the engine kicked back, causing the crank to suddenly reverse. When that happened, people had been known to break their wrists.

But once you got the Flivver started up, driving it was a hoot. I discovered that I loved cars even more than I loved horses. Cars didn't need to be fed if they weren't working, and they didn't leave big piles of manure all over the place. Cars were faster than horses, and they didn't run off or kick down fences. They also didn't buck, bite, or rear, and they didn't need to be broke and trained, or caught and saddled up every time you needed to go somewhere. They didn't have a mind of their own. Cars obeyed you.

I practiced driving with Jim out on the range, where you didn't have to worry about hitting anything but a juniper tree, and I got the hang of it quickly. In no time at all, I was tootling around the streets of Red Lake at a breakneck twenty-five miles an hour, operating the pedals with my feet and the levers with my hands while honking at the chickens in my way, swerving to avoid hitting the poor foot-bound sodbusters, and startling horses with the occasional backfire.

But they had to get used to it. The automobile was here to stay.

★　★　★

My driving lessons with Jim Smith began to include trips to the Grand Canyon to deliver gas to a filling station near there, then picnics. After I'd learned to drive, we continued the picnics and also took horseback rides out to places like the ice cave near Red Lake, a hole so deep that if you climbed way down into it, you could find ice in the middle of the summer. We used that ice to make cold lemonade to go with our biscuits and jerky.

After a while it became clear that, without saying anything directly, Jim was courting me. He'd been married once before, but his wife — a pretty blond thing — had died in the influenza epidemic ten years earlier. I still wasn't interested in marriage, but there was a lot about Jim Smith that I found to admire. For one thing, unlike my previous crumb-bum husband, he didn't lay down a smooth line of patter. He spoke when he had something to say, and if he didn't, he felt no need to fill the void with hot air.

Jim Smith was a Jack Mormon. He'd been born into the faith but didn't practice it. His father was Lot Smith, a soldier, pioneer, and ranger who had been one of Brigham Young's chief lieutenants when the Mormons went to war with the U.S. government. At one point the federals put a thousand-dollar price on his head, but when they came to arrest him, Lot Smith held off the soldiers at gunpoint. He also helped found the Mormon settlement in Tuba City and was killed there by a Navajo — or by a rival Mormon, depending on which story you believed.

Lot Smith had eight wives and fifty-two children, and those kids learned to fend for themselves. When Jim turned eleven, his father gave him a rifle, some bullets, and a packet of salt and said, 'Here's your food for a week.' Jim became an excellent marksman and horseman and a wrangler at age fourteen. He worked in Canada for a while but fell afoul of the Mounties for using his pistols a little too freely. He returned to Arizona and became a lumberjack and homesteader. After his wife died, he joined the cavalry and, during the Great War, served in Siberia, where American soldiers were protecting the Trans-Siberian Railway in the midst of the fighting between the White Russians and the Red Russians. While he was in Siberia, his homestead was seized for failure to pay taxes, so after being mustered out of the cavalry, he became a prospector before finally opening his garage in Red Lake. The man was no slouch.

Jim Smith was going on fifty, which made him

twenty years older than me, and he had some wear and tear on him, including a star-shaped bullet scar on his right shoulder from an incident he felt wasn't worth discussing. Plus, he was pretty much bald, and all the hair was missing from the left side of his body on account of the time that he was dragged by a horse for two miles. But Jim Smith was hardly worn out. He could spend twelve hours in the saddle, lift a car axle off the ground, and cut, split, and stack enough firewood to keep his stove going all winter.

Jim could see things with those pale blue eyes that other people couldn't see — the quail in the thick brush, the horse and rider on the horizon, the eagle's nest in the side of the cliff. It was what made him a crack shot. He also noticed everything — the small lump below a horse's knee that meant it had a bowed tendon, the hand calluses that only farriers had. He could spot liars, cheaters, and bluffers from the get-go. But while nothing escaped him, he never let on that he knew what he knew.

And nothing ever rattled Jim Smith. He was always calm, never lost his temper, and never flailed about trying to figure out his own mind. He always knew what he thought and how he felt. He was dependable and established. He was solid. He had his own business, and it was a steady and respectable one. He fixed cars that needed fixing. He wasn't trying to sell vacuum cleaners to gullible housewives by throwing dirt on their floors.

Even so, I still wasn't prepared to marry again,

but Jim hadn't yet broached the subject of marriage, so we were enjoying ourselves having picnics, taking horseback rides, and bombing around Coconino County in the Flivver when I got the letter from Helen.

It was postmarked Hollywood.

Helen had been writing me regularly since she moved to California, and her letters always seemed unnaturally cheerful: She was continually on the verge of breaking into the movies, heading off to auditions and narrowly missing out on being cast, taking tap-dance lessons, and sighting stars as they drove around town in their convertibles.

Helen was also always meeting Mr. Wonderful, the man with the connections and wherewithal who treated her like a princess, who was going to open doors for her in this crazy movie business, and whom she might even marry. But after several letters, she'd stop mentioning that particular Mr. Wonderful, and then an even more terrific Mr. Wonderful would come along, so I suspected that, in fact, she was getting involved with a series of cads who used her and then, when they were tired of her, dumped her.

I worried that Helen was in danger of becoming a floozy, and I wrote her letters warning her not to count on men to take care of her and to come up with a fallback plan in case, as seemed pretty obvious by now, the movie career didn't pan out. But she wrote back scolding me for being negative, explaining that this was the way all girls made it in Hollywood. I hoped she was right, since I knew little about the ways of the movie world and hadn't had much luck with men myself.

In this new letter, Helen confessed that she was pregnant by the latest Mr. Wonderful, who had wanted her to get a back-alley abortion. When she told him she was scared of those coat-hanger operations — she'd heard of women dying from them — he claimed the child wasn't his and cut her out of his life.

Helen didn't know what to do. She was a couple of months along. She knew she'd be fired from the millinery shop once she started showing. Auditions would also be out of the question. She was too ashamed to go back to Mom and Dad at the ranch. She was wondering if maybe she should go ahead and get the abortion after all. The whole mess, she wrote, made her want to throw herself out a window.

It was immediately clear to me what Helen needed to do. I wrote her back, telling her not to get an abortion — women did die from them. It was better for her to go ahead and have the child, then decide whether she wanted to keep it or give it up for adoption. She could come to Red Lake, I wrote, and live with me in the teacherage until she figured out what to do.

★   ★   ★

Helen arrived in Flagstaff a week later, and Jim let me borrow the Flivver to drive over and meet her. As she stepped down from the train carrying a raccoon coat that Mr. Wonderful had probably given her, I had to bite my lip. Her slim

139

shoulders seemed thinner than ever, but her face was puffy, and her eyes were red from crying. She'd also peroxided her hair to that shiny white color that a lot of the starlets were favoring. When I gave her a hug, I was startled by how fragile she felt, as if she had a collapsible little bird's body. As soon as we got into the Flivver, she lit a cigarette, and I noticed her hands were shaking.

On the way back to Red Lake, I did most of the talking. I'd spent the last week thinking about Helen's predicament, and as we drove through the range, I laid out what I thought were her options. I could write Mom and Dad, explaining the situation and softening them up, and I was sure they'd forgive her and welcome her home. I'd gotten the name of an orphanage in Phoenix if she wanted to go that route. There were also a lot of men in Coconino County in search of a wife, and she might be able to find someone who'd be willing to marry her even though she was in a family way. Two possibilities that had occurred to me were Rooster and Jim Smith, but I didn't get into specifics.

Helen, however, seemed distracted, almost in a daze. Smoking cigarette after cigarette, she spoke in fragmented sentences, and instead of focusing on practicalities, her mind drifted all over the place. She kept returning to totally ludicrous plans and pointless concerns, wondering if she could get Mr. Wonderful back by putting the child into an orphanage and worrying if childbirth would ruin her figure for bathing-suit scenes in movies.

'Helen, it's time to get realistic,' I said.

'I am being realistic,' she said. 'A girl without a figure is never going to make it.'

I decided this was not the moment to push the point. When someone's wounded, the first order of business is to stop the bleeding. You can figure out later how best to help them heal.

My bed was small, but I scooted over so Helen and I could sleep side by side, just as we had done when we were kids. It was October, and the desert nights were turning cold, so we snuggled together, and sometimes late at night, Helen would start whimpering, which I took as a good sign because it meant that at least once in a while she seemed to understand how grim the situation was. When that happened, I held her close and reassured her that we'd get through this, just the way we'd survived that flash flood in Texas when we were kids.

'All we need to do,' I'd say, 'is find us that cottonwood tree to climb up in, and we'll make it.'

* * *

During the day, while I was teaching, Helen kept to herself in that little room. She never made any noise and spent a lot of time sleeping. I'd hoped that once she'd gotten some rest, her mind would clear, and she'd be able to start thinking about her future in a constructive fashion. But she continued to be vague and listless, talking about Hollywood in a dreamy way that, quite frankly, irritated me.

I decided Helen needed fresh air and sunshine. We went for a stroll through town

142

every afternoon, and I introduced her to people as my sister from Los Angeles who'd come out to the desert to cure the vapors. The next time I had a race scheduled, Jim Smith brought Helen along in the Flivver. He was courteous and considerate, but as soon as I saw them together, I could tell they were not meant for each other.

Rooster, however, immediately took a shine to Helen. 'She's real purty,' he confided to me.

But Helen had no interest in Rooster. 'He swallows his tobacco juice,' she said. 'I get sick every time I see his Adam's apple bobbing up and down.'

I didn't think Helen could afford to be picky at this particular juncture, but it was true that a part-time deputy who'd only just learned to write his name wouldn't make the best husband for her.

Helen loved my crimson shirt. When she saw me in it, she smiled for the first time since coming to Red Lake. She asked to try it on and seemed so excited while she was buttoning it up that I thought maybe she had shaken off her blues. But as she was tucking the shirt into her skirt, I saw that she was beginning to show. Our story about her coming here to take the desert air wasn't going to wash much longer, I realized, and regardless of her mood, her problems weren't going to go away.

Helen and I started attending the Catholic church in Red Lake. It was a dusty little adobe mission, and I didn't particularly cotton to the priest, Father Cavanaugh, a gaunt, humorless man whose scowl could peel the paint off a barn. But a lot of the local farmers went there, and I thought Helen might meet someone nice.

One day about six weeks after Helen had arrived, we were in the stuffy church, standing then kneeling then sitting then standing again as we listened to the mass. Incense wafted up to the ceiling. Helen had been wearing baggy dresses and a loose coat to hide her condition, but suddenly, she fainted dead away. Father Cavanaugh rushed down from the altar. He felt her forehead, then looked at her for a moment, and something made him touch her stomach. 'She's with child,' he said. He glanced at her ringless fingers. 'And unmarried.'

★ ★ ★

Father Cavanaugh told Helen she must make a full confession. When she did, instead of offering her forgiveness, he warned her that her soul was in mortal danger. Because she had committed the sin of lust, he said, the only place for her in this world was one of the church's homes for wayward women.

Helen came back from the visit with Father Cavanaugh more distraught than I'd ever seen her. She had no intention of going to any home — and I wouldn't have let her — but now her secret was out, and the townspeople of Red Lake began regarding both of us differently. Women stared at the ground when they passed us on the street, and cowboys felt free to give us the eye, as if the word had gone around that we were loose women. Once when we walked by a Mexican grandmother sitting on a bench, I looked back, and she was making the sign of the cross.

Early one evening a couple of weeks after Helen made her confession, I heard a knock on the teacherage door. Superintendent MacIntosh — the same man who had given me the boot from my teaching job when the war was over — was standing there.

He tipped his fedora, then looked past me into the room, where Helen was washing the supper plates in a tin pan. 'Miss Casey, may I have a word with you in private?' He asked me.

'I'll go for a walk,' Helen said. She wiped her hands on her apron and made her way past Mr. MacIntosh, who, making a great show of civility, tipped his hat a second time.

Since I didn't want Mr. MacIntosh looking at the dirty dishes as well as Helen's suitcase lying open on the floor, I led him through the connecting door into the classroom.

Looking out the window and fingering the brim of his fedora, Mr. MacIntosh cleared his throat nervously. Then he began what was obviously a prepared speech about Helen's

145

condition, moral standards, school policy, impressionable schoolchildren, the need to set a good example, the reputation of the Arizona Board of Education. I started arguing that Helen had no one else to turn to and stayed well away from the students, but Mr. MacIntosh said there was no room for discussion, he was getting pressure from a lot of the parents, the matter was out of his hands, and while he was sorry he had to say it, the fact was, if I wanted to keep my job, Helen had to go. Then he put on his fedora and left.

I still felt stung and humiliated, and I sat down for a moment at my desk. For the second time in my life, that fish-faced pencil pusher Mr. MacIntosh was telling me I wasn't wanted. The parents of my schoolkids included cattle rustlers, drunks, land speculators, bootleggers, gamblers, and former prostitutes. They didn't mind me racing horses, playing poker, or drinking contraband whiskey, but my showing some compassion to a sister who'd been taken advantage of and then abandoned by a smooth-talking scoundrel filled them with moral indignation. It made me want to throttle them all.

I walked back into the teacherage. Helen was sitting on the bed smoking a cigarette. 'I didn't really go for a walk,' she said. 'I heard everything.'

I spent the night holding Helen in my arms, trying to reassure her that it was all going to work out. We'd write Mom and Dad, I told her. They'd understand. This sort of thing happened to young women all the time, and she could go live at the ranch until the baby was born. I'd start racing horses every weekend, and I'd save all my winnings for her and the baby, and when it was born, Buster and Dorothy could raise the child as theirs and Helen would have money to go start a new life in some fun place like New Orleans or Kansas City. 'We have all sorts of options,' I said. 'But this one makes the most sense.'

Helen, however, was inconsolable. She was convinced that Mom in particular would never forgive her for bringing shame on the family. Mom and Dad would disown her, she believed, the same way our servant girl Lupe's parents had kicked her out when she got pregnant. No man would ever want her again, Helen said, she had no place to go. She wasn't as strong as me, she said, and couldn't make it on her own.

'Don't you ever feel like giving up?' Helen asked. 'I just feel like giving up.'

'That's nonsense,' I said. 'You're much stronger than you think. There's always a way out.' I talked again about the cottonwood tree. I also told her about the time I was sent home

147

from the Sisters of Loretto because Dad wouldn't pay my tuition, and how Mother Albertina had told me that when God closes a window, he opens a door, and it was up to us to find it.

Helen finally seemed to find some comfort in my words. 'Maybe you're right,' she said. 'Maybe there's a way.'

★ ★ ★

I was still awake and lying in bed with Helen when the first gray light of dawn began to appear in the window. Helen had finally fallen asleep, and I studied her face as it emerged from the shadows. That silly platinum hair had fallen forward, and I tucked it behind her ear. Her eyes were swollen from all the crying she'd been doing, but her features were still delicate, her skin still pale and smooth, and as the light filled the room, her face seemed to glow. She looked to me like an angel, a slightly bloated, pregnant angel, but an angel nonetheless.

All of a sudden I felt a lot better about things. It was Saturday. I got out of bed, put on my trousers, and brewed some strong coffee. When it was ready, I brought Helen a cup and told her it was time to rise and shine. A new day was beginning, and we had to get out in the world and make the most of it. What we'd do, I said, was borrow the Flivver from Jim and go for a picnic up to the Grand Canyon. Those mighty cliffs would give us some perspective on our puny little problems.

Helen smiled as she sat there drinking her coffee. I told her I'd go get the car while she got dressed, and we'd get an early start to make the most of the day. 'Back in a jiffy,' I said at the door.

'Okay,' Helen said. 'And Lily, I'm glad you asked me to come out here.'

It was a beautiful morning, the air so clear and crisp in the sharp light of the November sun that every twig and blade of grass stood out. The range had turned the color of hay. There was not a wisp of cloud to be seen anywhere, and mourning doves were cooing in the cedars. I walked past the old adobe houses and the newer frame houses, past the café and the gas station, past the farm families in town for market day, then all at once I felt like something was choking me.

I put my hand to my throat, and in that instant I was overtaken with a horrible feeling of dread. I turned and ran back as fast as I could, the stores and houses and puzzled farmers all flying by in one big blur, but when I flung open the door, I was too late.

My little sister was dangling from a rafter, a kicked-over chair beneath her. She'd hanged herself.

Father Cavanaugh wouldn't let me bury Helen in the Catholic cemetery. Suicide was a mortal sin, he said, the worst of all sins, because it was the only one for which it was impossible to repent and receive forgiveness; therefore, suicides were not allowed to be buried in hallowed ground.

So Jim, Rooster, and I drove out onto the range, far from town. We found a beautiful site at the top of a rise overlooking a shallow forested valley — so beautiful that I knew in God's eyes it must be sacred — and we buried Helen there, in my red silk shirt.

V

LAMBS

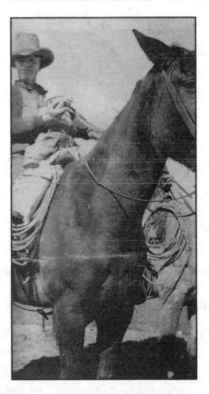

Big Jim holding Rosemary

When people kill themselves, they think they're ending the pain, but all they're doing is passing it on to those they leave behind.

For months after Helen's death, pain laid so dark and heavy on me, like a big slab of lead, that most days I wouldn't have gotten out of bed if I hadn't had kids to teach. The idea of riding horses — much less racing — playing cards, or driving the Flivver out into the country seemed so pointless as to be repulsive. Everything got on my nerves: kids yelling or even just laughing in the school yard, church bells ringing, birds chirping. What the hell was there to chirp about?

I thought of quitting my job, but I was under contract, and anyway, I couldn't blame the kids for what the parents had done. But I was through with Red Lake, and when the school year was over, I was moving on. I wasn't even sure I wanted to be a teacher anymore. I felt like I'd given everything I had to the kids of this town, and when I'd needed a little understanding, their families hadn't cut me any slack. Maybe I should stop devoting myself to other people's kids and instead have some kids of my own. I had never particularly wanted kids, but when Helen killed herself, she also killed the little baby inside her, and something about that made me want to bring another baby into the world.

153

As time passed, and without my even realizing it, this idea of having a baby of my own eased my grief. One day in the spring, I got up early, as usual, and sat on the front step of the teacherage, drinking my coffee as the sun rose over the San Francisco Mountains to the east. The shafts of light gliding across the plateau had that golden color that they get in the spring, and when they reached me, they warmed my face and arms.

I realized that in the months since Helen had died, I hadn't been paying much attention to things like the sunrise, but that old sun had been coming up anyway. It didn't really care how I felt, it was going to rise and set regardless of whether I noticed it, and if I was going to enjoy it, that was up to me.

★   ★   ★

And if I was going to have a baby, I needed to find a husband. I started looking at Jim Smith in a different light. He had plenty of good qualities, but the most important one was that I felt I could trust that man inside and out. Once I'd made up my mind about this, I didn't see the need to beat around the bush or make any grand gestures. It was late afternoon in early May with school over for the day when I saddled up Patches and rode over to the garage. Jim was on his back underneath a car, and all I could see were his legs and boots sticking out. I told him I needed to talk to him, so he slowly pushed himself out and stood up, wiping the grease off his hands with a rag.

'Jim Smith, do you want to marry me?' I asked.

He stared at me a moment and then broke into a big grin. 'Lily Casey, I wanted to marry you ever since I saw you take that fall off that mustang and then get right back on him. I just been waiting for a good time to ask.'

'Well, this is it,' I said. 'Now, I only got two conditions.'

'Yes, ma'am.'

'The first is that we've got to be partners. Whatever we do, we'll be in it together, each sharing the load.'

'Sounds good to me.'

'The second is, I know you were raised a Mormon, but I don't want you taking any more wives.'

'Lily Casey, from what I know of you, you're just about as much woman as any man can handle.'

When I told Jim how my crumb-bum first husband had given me a fake ring, he got out a Sears, Roebuck catalog and we chose a ring together so I'd know I was getting the genuine article. We got married in my classroom once school was out for the summer. Rooster was the best man. Before the ceremony, he gave me a kiss.

'I knew I was going to smooch you one day, but I didn't think it would be because you were marrying my buddy,' he said. 'Still, I'll take what I can get.'

Rooster had a friend with an accordion, and since I still had a soft spot for teaching, instead of Mendelssohn's 'Wedding March,' I asked him to play the PTA anthem.

The year was 1930, and I was twenty-nine. A lot of women my age had children who were practically grown, but getting a late start didn't mean that I wouldn't enjoy the journey every bit as much — maybe even more. Jim understood why I wanted to leave Red Lake, and he agreed to move his garage to Ash Fork, about thirty miles west, just over the Yavapai County line. Ash Fork was a bustling little town on Route 66 at the base of Williams Mountain. It was a stop on the Santa Fe Railroad, with a roundhouse, and some days the streets were filled with sheep being shipped to market. Ash Fork had a general store run by a descendant of George Washington's brother, not one but two churches, and a Harvey House restaurant for the railroad passengers, where Harvey Girls in white aprons served you an entire quarter of a pie when you ordered a slice, and diners wiped their mouths with elegant linen napkins.

At the Ash Fork bank, Jim and I took out a loan and built a garage made of Coconino sandstone, laying the stones and spreading the mortar ourselves. We hung the GARAGE sign from Red Lake over the door. With money from the loan, we sent off for a tire pump, a ball-bearing handle jack, and a stack of ribbed tread tires from the same Sears catalog that we'd used to order my ring.

We had also brought the gas pump with us from Red Lake. The big glass cylinder on top was filled with gasoline — dyed red so you could tell it apart from kerosene — and every time you filled a car, air bubbles gurgled up through it.

Business was brisk. Since we were partners, Jim taught me to pump gas. The pump was hand-operated. I'd pump, pump, pump, and the gas would go glug, glug, glug. I also changed oil and fixed flat tires. By that winter, I was pregnant, but I was still pitching in every day, filling up gas tanks and making change while Jim worked on cars.

We built a little house — also made of Coconino sandstone — right on Route 66, which was still a dirt road, and in the dry season, dust kicked up by the wagon wheels and automobile tires sometimes drifted through the windows,

157

coating the furniture. But I loved that house. We ordered the plumbing system from Sears and installed it ourselves. In the kitchen we had running water that gushed out of shiny nickel-plated faucets, and a chain flush toilet — just like the rich people I cleaned for in Chicago — with a porcelain enamel bowl and a lid of mahogany veneer.

When the house was finished, Rooster paid us a visit. Like my dad, he couldn't believe that anyone would ever want a crapper in the house. 'Ain't it unsanitary?' he asked.

'Everything goes down the pipe,' I said. 'If you want to freeze your behind off in an outhouse, that's fine by me.'

Rooster was just one of those people who didn't like change regardless of how it might improve his lot. As for me, I was so danged proud of my indoor plumbing that if someone looking for directions knocked at the door, I couldn't resist the temptation to say, 'Would you like a glass of fresh tap water?' or 'Do you, by chance, need to use the toilet?'

By the time I was eight and a half months pregnant, I had swelled up pretty big. I was happy to continue working at the garage, but Jim thought that in my condition, it might be dangerous. I could slip on an oil spill, he said, or faint from gasoline fumes, or break my water trying to twist off a rusted radiator cap. So he insisted I stay at home, where I'd be safe. For a lot of women, it didn't get any better than that, lounging around in a housecoat with nothing to do. But after a few days, I started getting cabin fever, cooped up by myself reading books and mending clothes, and maybe that was why I got so irritated with the Jehovah's Witness who stopped by.

I was usually friendly to folks like Jehovah's Witnesses, admiring their genuine conviction, but this fellow was particularly persistent, lecturing me, giving me a lot of poppycock about how Armageddon was imminent and for the sake of my unborn baby I needed to seek salvation and convert. Who the hell was he to tell me what I had to believe? I asked. All folks needed to find their own way to heaven. One of the problems of the world today was all the muttonheads — like those Bolshies in Russia — going around convinced they were the only ones who had the answers and killing everyone who didn't agree with them.

I got so steamed up, pacing back and forth and arguing with the fellow, that without thinking about what I was doing, I sat down on my sewing, and a needle stuck me in my behind. I let out a yelp, started cussing, and tried to work the needle out of my rear, while the Jehovah's Witness wagged his finger and argued that this was a sure sign from Jesus that I needed to see the error of my way and get right with the Lord.

'What it's a sign of, mister,' I said, 'is that I shouldn't be staying at home by myself, getting in theological arguments with harebrained strangers.'

I headed back to the garage, where I told Jim what had happened. 'I don't care if I only man the cash register,' I said, 'but I'm working until I go into labor. Sitting at home is just too dangerous.'

* * *

The baby came two weeks later, on a scorching-hot July day. I gave birth at home with the help of Granny Combs, the best midwife in Yavapai County. One of Granny Combs's legs was shorter than the other, and she walked with an even worse limp than my dad. She also chewed tobacco, though she was a spitter and not a swallower like Rooster. Still, all the women in the county swore by her. If Granny Combs couldn't bring your baby into this world, they said, it wasn't meant to be here.

When I went into labor, the pain started coming in waves. Granny Combs told me that I couldn't stop the pain, but she could teach me how to get the best of it. What I needed to do was separate the actual pain from the fear that something terrible was happening to my body. 'The pain is your body complaining,' she said. 'If you listen to the pain and tell your body, 'Yeah, I hear you,' then you won't be so afraid of it. I'm not saying the pain goes away, but it ain't gonna make you crazy, either.'

My labor lasted only a couple of hours, and Granny Combs's advice did help keep the pain in check — sort of. When the baby came out, Granny Combs said, 'It's a girl,' and held her up. She was purple, and I felt a stab of alarm. But Granny Combs started slapping and kneading her, and the baby let out a cry and gradually turned pink. Granny Combs cut the cord and rubbed the baby's navel with a burned cork to close up the wound.

Granny Combs had a sixth sense — the way I sometimes felt I did — and could read minds and tell fortunes. While I held the baby and nursed her, Granny Combs tore herself a plug of tobacco and laid out cards to see what the future had in store for my newborn.

'She will have a long life, and it will be eventful,' Granny Combs said.

'Will she be happy?' I asked.

Granny Combs chewed her tobacco and studied the cards. 'I see a wanderer.'

I named the baby Rosemary. Roses were my favorite flower, Mary was a good Catholic girl's name, and Rosemary was a darned useful herb. I was hoping the kid would have a practical side. Most babies looked to me like monkeys or Buddhas, but Rosemary was a beautiful thing. When her hair came in, it was so pale and fine it looked white. By the time she was three months old, she had a wide smile to match her merry green eyes, and even early on it seemed to me she looked a lot like Helen.

Helen's beauty, as far as I was concerned, had been a curse, and I resolved that I would never tell Rosemary she was beautiful.

★　★　★

A boy followed a year and a half later. A big new hospital had just opened in the town of Williams, forty miles to the east, and I was determined to have my baby there, but as I went into labor, a hellacious winter storm blew in from Canada, covering the roads with drifting snow. We almost didn't make it through, the Flivver spinning and skidding, but Jim got out the jack and put the chains on the wheels, hunkering down against the driving snow while I sat there taking deep breaths behind the steamed-up windows. We arrived just as my contractions were becoming severe.

Granny Combs's mind-over-matter method of getting through pain was pretty good when it came to a stubbed toe, and it had helped me get through my first childbirth, but it couldn't compare to the marvelous modern anesthesia they used to knock me out at the hospital this time.

The doctor put that mask over my face, and I just drifted off to dreamland. When I woke up, I had a son. He was a big bruiser of a boy, the first baby born in that hospital, and the nurses and doctors were as proud as Jim and me. We named him after his dad and from the outset called him Little Jim.

*   *   *

It was around then that hard times hit northern Arizona. A big part of the problem was that too many farmers and greenhorn ranchers had moved into the area. They didn't understand that Arizona wasn't like the land back east, where thousands of years of decaying trees had built up a deep loam. This land had just a thin layer of topsoil that, if plowed, would blow away with the first strong wind. The greenhorns had all made fun of the Navajos for planting each stalk of corn in a little hole three feet from the next, instead of a foot apart in plowed rows, but the Indians understood that was all the soil could bear. Land that God had never intended for the till had been farmed beyond its limit, and too many cattle had grazed the once green range into hard, dry stubble. The grass couldn't reseed,

163

and when it rained, there wasn't enough grass to hold the water, so it would run off, eroding the good soil, and the fine land would be ruined forever. When a long drought hit, stretches of countryside all around the state turned to swirling dust, which rose a half mile into the air.

At the same time, the country was a few years into the Depression. At first that seemed like a problem afflicting mostly the big cities. But it soon hurt the cattle market because so many folks back east couldn't afford to eat steak anymore. Some of the littler ranches in Arizona started going under, and ranch hands joined the stream of Okies making their way past our house on Route 66 in the hopes of finding work in California.

A lot of people could no longer afford gas, and they began selling off the tractors and cars they'd been persuaded to buy, leaving many of them wishing they'd kept their plow horses. Business at the garage dwindled. Jim was also too generous for his own good, undercharging people who were poor and even doing repairs for free.

I sat down at the kitchen table with pencil and paper, working the numbers, looking for ways to cut expenses, but no matter what angle I came at it from, the bottom line was inescapable: We had more going out than coming in, and it was just a matter of time before we went broke. With the loans we'd taken out, that meant bankruptcy. I took the babies to the garage and helped out as much as I could, but I figured there must be something else we could do to bring in a little extra cash.

One day Mr. Lee, the Ash Fork Chinaman, knocked on our door. Mr. Lee ran a chop-suey joint in a tent near the garage and made enough money from it to drive a Model A that Jim repaired. Mr. Lee was usually one happy, beaming Chinaman, but that day he was in a panic. Prohibition had ended a few years earlier, but a lot of people had gotten used to the easy money that came from selling bootleg liquor, and Mr. Lee was one of them, offering his customers shots of home brew to wash down their noodles. But he'd heard that the revenuers were onto him, and he was looking for a place to hide a few cases of booze.

Mr. Lee and Jim had hit it off because Mr. Lee had been a soldier in Manchuria when Jim was seeing service in Siberia, and they'd lived through the same bitter winters, picking icicles out of their hair and gnawing on frozen meat. Mr. Lee trusted Jim. We agreed to take the booze and stashed the cases under Little Jim's crib, where they were hidden by the skirt.

That night I lay awake thinking about Mr. Lee's hooch, and a plan occurred to me. I could bring in extra money by selling bootleg booze out the back door. Although Dad had been a staunch prohibitionist, his pa had sold booze from the store on the KC Ranch, so I had family tradition going for me. Also, I never saw anything wrong with an honest man taking a well-deserved drink. I even had one myself from time to time.

When I proposed the idea to Jim at the breakfast table the next morning, he wasn't so

165

keen on it. Although he had stopped drinking years ago, after shooting up some Canadian town while on a bender, he didn't have any problem with booze itself. He just didn't want to see the mother of his two children wind up in jail for rum-running.

It was because I was a mother with two kids, I said, as well as a respected former schoolteacher, that the revenuers would never suspect me. There was a definite market out there, since everyone was looking to save pennies wherever they could. It wasn't like we'd be running a speakeasy, just a little retail operation with absolutely no overhead. And we'd even be striking a blow for the little guy, giving a hardworking cowboy a chance to have a drink without being forced to fork over a nickel to Uncle Sam every time he did so.

I kept hammering away at Jim, pointing out that I couldn't see any other way to keep us afloat, and because I would give him no peace on the matter, he reluctantly agreed. Since we'd done him a favor, Mr. Lee also agreed, promising to provide me two cases a month from his boot-legger if we split the profit.

I was a good liquor lady. I discreetly put the word out, and soon local cowboys were knocking at the back door. I sold only to people I knew or those who came recommended. I kept things friendly but businesslike, inviting them in briefly but not allowing anyone to linger around or drink on the premises. I began to get regular customers, including the Catholic priest, who always blessed the babies on the way out. My regulars got a discount, but I never gave credit and I never sold to anyone I thought was drinking the rent money. After Mr. Lee got his cut, I made a quarter on each bottle I sold. Soon I was averaging three bottles a day, and that extra twenty dollars or so a month balanced the books.

One day that spring, when Rosemary was three and Little Jim was starting to talk, the Camel brothers drove their huge flock of sheep past our house and into town toward the depot. The Camel brothers had bought a big ranch west of Ash Fork in Yavapai County with the idea of raising sheep for wool and mutton. They were from Scotland and knew a lot about sheep but precious little about conditions on the Arizona range. The Camel brothers had decided that the forage in Yavapai County was too dry for sheep, especially with the drought, and they'd made up their minds to sell off their flock, as well as the ranch, rather than watch their sheep grow gaunt and weak while more and more of them got picked off by wolves and hungry hobos.

It was a dry, hot day, and the sheep filled the streets of Ash Fork, kicking up the dust so bad you had to cover your mouth with a bandana. The ewes were bleating and the lambs were mewing as the Camel brothers' hands rode back and forth, driving the flock toward the shipping station, cracking whips at wandering strays.

The Camel brothers weren't there — they were back at the ranch, rounding up the remaining sheep — and when the flock reached the shipping pen, some numbskull hand got the brilliant idea of separating the lambs from their mothers. As soon as they'd accomplished that, bedlam broke loose. The lambs were still nursing and were hungry from the journey, so they started scrambling around, crying for their mothers. The ewes, for their part, were frantically calling out for their babies.

The hands, realizing their mistake, opened the gate separating the ewes from the lambs, and the sheep all mingled together, mothers looking for babies and babies looking for mothers. That was when things got really bad. The more frantic the lambs became, the more energy they burned, which made them all the hungrier, but the flock was so big and so jumbled up that none of them could find their mothers. After a couple of hours of this, the lambs grew weak from hunger. They tried to nurse from any ewe they could, but the ewes wanted to save the milk for their own babies. They put their noses up to the lambs, and if the smell was unfamiliar, the ewes kicked them away and continued searching for their own.

The hands, frantic themselves, were wading around in the flock, trying to force the ewes to let any lamb nurse, but the ewes weren't cooperating. They were kicking and bawling and squirming, making a god-awful racket and filling the air with even more dust as the cowboys cursed and the townspeople who had gathered around stood there watching, some calling out advice, others chuckling, shaking their heads, and waiting to see how it was all going to play out.

I was there with Little Jim and Rosemary, who was fascinated by the idea that a ewe could smell its own lamb and was running around shoving her nose into the lambs' wool. 'They all just smell like sheep to me,' she announced.

The Camel brothers finally showed up, but they were at a loss about what to do, and the situation was getting desperate, with lambs starting to drop from heat and hunger.

'You should talk to my husband,' I said. 'He knows animals.'

The Camel brothers sent for Jim, who was at the garage. When he arrived, the hands explained what had happened.

'What we got to do,' Jim said, 'is get those ewes to accept any lamb as her own for the time being. Then we can worry about straightening out the flock.'

Jim sent me back to the house for an old bedsheet while he fetched two cans of kerosene from the garage. He had the Camel hands tear the sheet into rags, dip the rags in the kerosene, and wipe the ewes' noses with them. That blocked their sense of smell, and they let whatever lamb was at hand nurse their milk.

Once the lambs had been fed and the immediate crisis had passed, Jim had the hands separate the lambs and the ewes again. One by one they brought each lamb into the ewe pen and carried it around until its mother recognized it. The flock was so big that this took the better part of two days, with stops to douse the mothers' noses again whenever the remaining lambs got hungry.

Little Rosemary was riveted by the scene and terribly concerned that all the lambs find their mothers, and she stayed there watching the entire time. When it was finally done, there was one little lamb that no ewe had claimed. Its black eyes were frightened, its white wool thick with dust, and it ran around on its spindly legs, bleating mournfully.

The Camel brothers told Jim to do whatever he thought best with the lamb. Jim scooped it up in his arms and carried it over to Rosemary. He knelt down and set the lamb in front of her. 'All animals are meant for something,' he said. 'Some to run wild, some for the barnyard, some for market. This little lamb was meant to be a pet.'

Rosemary loved that creature. She shared her ice cream cones with it, and it followed her everywhere. So we decided to name it Mei-Mei, which Mr. Lee told us was Chinese for 'little sister.'

A couple of weeks after Jim straightened out the flock, I heard the sound of a car pulling around the house and then a knock on the back door. A man was standing outside, smoking a cigarette. He'd left his car door open, and a girl and a young woman were sitting inside, watching us. He was a good-looking fellow with a lock of sandy hair falling across his forehead, and although his teeth were crooked and stained, he had the easy smile of a charmer. Even before he said anything, I could tell from the slightly off-balance way he was standing that he was a little potted.

'I'm a friend of Rooster's,' he said. 'And I heard this is where a man could get his hands on a good bottle of shellac.'

'Looks to me like you're already pretty shellacked,' I said.

'Well, I'm working on it.'

His smile became even more charming, but I looked over at the woman and the girl, and they weren't smiling at all.

'I think you've had enough to drink as it is,' I said.

His smile disappeared and he got all indignant, the way drunks do when you point out that they're drunk. He started telling me his money was as good as anyone else's, and who was I to go around deciding who had and hadn't had too much to drink, I was just some two-bit moon-shine madam. But I didn't budge, and when he realized I wasn't giving in and he'd be leaving empty-handed, he really lost it, telling me I was going to regret crossing him and calling me nothing but the sister of a whore who'd hanged herself.

'Wait right there,' I said. Leaving the door open, I walked into the bedroom, got my pearl-handled revolver, walked back out, and pointed it at the man's face. The end of the barrel was about six inches from his nose. 'The only reason I don't shoot you right now is because of those two women in that car,' I said. 'But you get out of here and don't ever come back.'

★　★　★

That night I told Jim what had happened.

He sighed and shook his head. 'We probably haven't seen the end of it,' he said.

Sure enough, two days later, a car pulled around the house, and when I opened the door, two men in khaki uniforms and cowboy hats were standing there. They had badges on their shirt pockets, guns in their holsters, and handcuffs dangling from their belts. They tipped their hats. 'Afternoon, ma'am,' one of them said.

173

He hitched up his pants and stuck his thumbs in his belt. 'Mind if we come in?' he asked.

I didn't see that I had much choice in the matter, so I led them into the living room. Little Jim was asleep in the crib, and under it, behind the white cotton skirt, were two cases of bootleg hooch.

'Would you fellows like a nice cool glass of tap water?' I asked.

'Thank you, ma'am, no,' the talker said. They were both glancing around, trying to suss the place out.

'We received a report,' he went on, 'that liquor is being illegally sold from these premises.'

At that moment Rosemary came running into the room with Mei-Mei right behind. It must have been the sight of all that gleaming metal and shiny leather, but as soon as Rosemary saw the two lawmen, she gave out a shriek that could have woken the dead. Howling, she flung herself at my feet and grabbed my ankles. I tried to pick her up, but she'd become truly hysterical and was flailing her arms, screaming, and blubbering.

Mei-Mei was bleating, and all the noise woke Little Jim, who stood up in the crib and started wailing.

'Does this look like a speakeasy?' I asked. 'I'm a schoolteacher! I'm a mother! I got my hands full here just taking care of these kids.'

'I can see that,' he said. All the screaming was discombobulating the two of them. 'We have to check these things out, but we'll be on our way.'

The lawmen were happy to be out of there, and as soon as they left, Rosemary stopped her howling. 'You sure saved my chestnuts, little girl,' I said.

★　★　★

When Jim came home, I told him about the visit from the law and how the chorus of howling youngsters had driven those deputies right out the door. It already seemed to me like a pretty funny story, and it got Jim laughing, too, but then he stopped and said, 'Even so, they were putting us on warning. It's time we get out of the bootleg business.'

'But Jim,' I said, 'we need the money.'

'I'd rather see you in the poorhouse than behind bars.'

Selling liquor had kept us afloat for a year. But we shut the operation down, and six months later, the bank foreclosed on us.

Fall was usually my favorite time of year, when the air turned cool and the hills were green from the August rains. But I didn't have much time to enjoy the September sunsets and the crisp, starry nights. Jim and I had decided to auction off everything — the furniture, his tools, the tires, the tire pump, the handle jack, and the gas pump with its pretty glass cylinder. Once we'd done that, we would strap our suitcases on the roof of the Flivver and join the stream of Okies heading to California for work.

Mulling our prospects made us feel both ground down and wound up. One morning we were in the garage, tagging tools and arguing about what we should take with us, when Blackie Camel, the older of the two Camel brothers, stopped by. Blackie was a swag-bellied man with a bushy black beard who wore his embroidered vest everywhere. He was kind of a mathematical genius when it came to sheep, and he could glance at a flock and tell you not only how many animals were in it but also how many pounds of wool they were carrying.

Ever since Jim had saved the lambs, Blackie had taken to dropping by the garage to shoot the breeze. The more he got to know Jim, the more he liked him. Jim, he was fond of telling people, knew not only sheep, he also knew cattle and horses and just about every creature with fur or feathers. Jim never bragged about himself, which Blackie also liked, and Blackie was particularly impressed with a story he'd heard from a local Hopi about how, when Jim was a young man, an eagle was going after a newborn calf and Jim actually lassoed the bird in midair.

That morning, as we sat at the wobbly linoleum table Jim used as his desk, Blackie told us that he and his brother had sold their ranch to a group of investors in England who wanted to run cattle there. They had asked him and his brother to recommend someone to manage the ranch, and Blackie said that if Jim was so inclined, he and his brother would put Jim's name forward.

Jim reached under the table and squeezed my hand so hard that my knuckles cracked. We both knew the only jobs out in California were picking grapes and oranges, and the Okies were fighting over what little work existed, while the Daddy Warbucks owners kept cutting everyone's wages. But there was no way we were going to acknowledge to Blackie Camel how desperate we were.

'Sounds like something worth considering,' Jim said.

Blackie sent a telegram to London, and a few days later, he dropped by to tell Jim the job was his. We called off the auction, and Jim kept most of his tools, but we did sell the gasoline pump and tires to a mechanic from Sedona. Rooster brought a buckboard down from Red Lake, and we loaded our furniture onto it, put the kids and Mei-Mei in the back of the Flivver, and then, with Jim behind the wheel, Rooster on the wagon, and me bringing up the rear on Patches, we set out on our little procession for Seligman, the town nearest the ranch.

That part of the journey was smooth and passed quickly because Route 66 was being paved for the first time with a layer of shiny black asphalt. Seligman wasn't as big as Ash Fork, but it had everything a ranch town needed: a building that served as both the jail and post office, a hotel, a bar and café, and the Commercial Central, a general store where pairs of Levi's were stacked four feet high on the wide-planked floor next to shovels, spools of rope and wire, water buckets, and tins of crackers.

From Seligman we headed west for fifteen miles through rolling rangeland covered with rabbitweed, prairie grass, and juniper trees. The Peacock Mountains in the distance were dark green, and overhead the sky was iris blue. After fifteen miles, we turned off Route 66 and followed a narrow dirt road for another nine miles. It took a full day to get from Seligman to the ranch by wagon. Finally, late in the afternoon, we came to a gate where the road just ended.

To the right and left of the gate, barbed-wire fencing, held up by neatly trimmed juniper saplings, stretched away into the distance. There was no sign on the gate, which was closed, but we were expected, so the gate was dummy locked — the chain that kept it shut was held together by a padlock that had been left unsnapped. Beyond the gate was a long driveway. We followed it another four miles and finally reached a fenced-in compound with a collection of unpainted wood buildings shaded by enormous cedar trees.

The buildings were at the foot of a hill dotted with pinyon and scrub cedar. Facing east, you looked out over miles and miles of rolling range-land that gradually sloped down toward a flat grassy basin known as the Colorado Plateau. It stretched out all the way to the Mogollon Rim, big blush-colored bluffs where the earth had shifted along a single fault line that ran all the way to New Mexico. From where we stood, you could see to forever, and there wasn't a single other house, human being, or the slightest sign of civilization, only the huge sky, the endless grassy plain, and the distant mountains.

The Camel brothers had let most of the hired help go, and the place was deserted except for one remaining hand, Old Jake, a grizzled, stogie-chewing coot who came limping out of the barn to greet us. Old Jake had a lopsided walk because, to avoid serving in the Great War, he had put his foot on a railroad track and let a train run over his toes. 'Won't win any dancin' contests,' he said, 'but don't need toes to ride — and it beats spittin' up mustard gas.'

Old Jake showed us around. There was a main house with a long porch, its unpainted wood siding a sun-bleached gray. The barn was huge, and next to it were four small log buildings: the grainery and the smithy; the meat house, where hides and sides of beef were cured; and the poison house, which had shelves full of bottles containing medicines, potions, spirits, and solvents, all with corks or rags stuffed in their tops. Old Jake kept pointing out various details — the bags of sulfur and jars of tar used for treating injured livestock, the knife sharpener in the smithy, the troughs that collected runoff rainwater from the roofs.

He took us into the other outbuildings, including a toolshed, chicken coop, and bunk-house. Then we came to a garage filled with twenty-six carriages, wagons, and vehicles — brogans, surreys, phaetons, an old Conestoga covered wagon, a few beat-up cars, a rusty Chevy pickup. Old Jake proudly named every one. He showed us the pit in the garage that you could climb down into, then have someone drive the car over it when you needed to work on the undercarriage.

Finally, Old Jake led us back through the barn to a double corral: one made of six-foot-high saplings posted vertically and used to break horses, the other made of standard post-and-wire fencing with a small herd of tough little ponies inside it.

Jim walked around nodding and taking it all in. We could both see that although the buildings were weathered, they were solid and true. There was nothing fancy about the place, it was a real working ranch, but tools were hung in their place, ropes were coiled neatly, harnesses mended, fence posts stacked in tidy bundles, and the barn floor was swept. On a ranch you had to be able to find a given tool in a hurry when there was an emergency, and you had to hand it to the Camel brothers. They knew the importance of keeping things shipshape.

Rooster was visibly impressed. 'A fellow could do a lot worse than this,' he said. 'Jim, you old hound dog, you got lucky.' He glanced at me. 'Again,' he added.

I swatted Rooster on the arm, but Jim just shook his head and grinned. Then he looked out across the range. 'I think we can make this work,' he said.

'I think we can,' I said.

I could tell life at the ranch was going to be a lot of hard work. We were too far from town to count on anyone else for anything. Jim and I would have to be our own veterinarian, farrier, mechanic, butcher, cook, as well as cattle driver, ranch manager, husband and wife, and mother and father of two little children. But Jim and I both knew how to roll up our sleeves, and in times like these, I knew how lucky we were not just to have work but to be our own bosses doing something we were good at doing.

I felt nature calling and asked Old Jake where I could find the facilities. He pointed toward a little wooden shed in the north corner of the compound. 'It's nothing fancy, just a one-holer,' he said. 'No moon cut in the door to advertise it, either, 'cause we all knows what it is.'

Inside the outhouse, once you'd closed the door that didn't have a moon, enough light came through the cracks in the wood so that you could see. Spiderwebs dangled in the roof corners, a sack of lime sat on the dirt floor, and there was a scoop to sprinkle it into the hole to keep the flies down. A distinctly malodorous aroma arose from the hole, and for a moment I missed my snazzy mail-order toilet with the shiny white porcelain bowl, the mahogany lid, and the nifty pull-chain flush. As I sat down, though, I realized that you can get so used to certain luxuries that you start to think they're necessities, but when you have to forgo them, you come to see that you don't need them after all. There was a big difference between needing things and wanting things — though a lot of people had trouble telling the two apart — and at the ranch, I could see, we'd have pretty much everything we'd need but precious little else.

Next to the seat was a stack of Sears, Roebuck catalogs, and I picked one up and leafed through it. I came to a page advertising silk bodices and lacy chemises. I won't be ordering from this page, I thought, and when I was done with my business, that was the one I tore out and used.

The following morning, as Rooster was getting ready to head back to Red Lake, he caught me alone in the kitchen.

'Thank you for helping us move,' I said, and handed him a cup of coffee.

He looked at me for a moment. 'You know I always been carrying a torch for you,' he said.

'I know.'

'Funny,' he said. 'Just can't help it.' He paused and then asked, 'You think I'll ever get married?'

'I do,' I said. I had just been being polite, but suddenly I saw it clearly. The right woman was out there for him. 'I do,' I said again. 'You just got to look in unexpected places.'

After Rooster left, Jim said our first order of business was to tour the ranch. It was a big place, with a little over a hundred thousand acres — almost 160 square miles — and it would take us at least a week just to ride the outer fence line. We loaded one pony with supplies. Jim and Old Jake mounted up two others, and I was on Patches, with Little Jim in my lap, while Rosemary climbed on with her dad.

We headed west until we reached white and yellow limestone foothills, then swung south. A hot, dry wind blew across the valley. We passed pinyon and juniper trees and now and then saw a herd of white-tailed antelope on distant slopes, grazing on the gama grass. Old Jake showed us

Tres Cruces, a group of rocks on which someone had carved stick figures of horses and riders carrying three crosses to depict — according to ranch lore — an early Spanish expedition. Late in the afternoon, we reached a high point below the Coyote Mountains. From there we could see south toward the Juniper Mountains and east to the Mogollon Rim.

'Lot of land,' Jim said. 'Not a lick of water.'

'Drier than a crone's dugs,' Old Jake said.

There were a few dirt ponds, small sad things dug out to collect rain, but the water disappeared during dry spells, and the ponds were now empty, cracked pits.

After ten days, we'd made a big circle, covering most of the ranch, although there were large stretches of territory we didn't have time to see. And while we passed any number of gullies and draws that you could tell ran with water during flash floods, there wasn't a single stream, spring, or natural source of water on the whole spread. 'No wonder the Camel brothers threw in the towel,' Jim said.

Jim sent to Flagstaff for a water witch, and the two of them set out on another tour of the ranch, stopping at clumps of trees and spots where the grass was green. The water witch walked around holding a forked branch in his outstretched arms, waiting for the branch to dip, a sign that there was water underground. But the branch never dipped.

I kept thinking about all those gullies and draws we'd passed during our trip around the ranch. The only water this land would ever see was going to come from the sky. During flash floods, thousands and thousands of gallons of water would roar through all those gullies and draws only to soak through the range floor. If we could figure out how to trap that water for ourselves, we'd have plenty.

'What we really need to do is build a dam,' I told Jim.

'How?' he said. 'You'd need an army.'

I thought about it for a while, and then it came to me. I'd read magazine articles about the building of the Boulder Dam, as it was called by those of us who hated Herbert Hoover and refused to call it the Hoover Dam. Alongside the articles were photographs of some of the newfangled earthmoving machines used in the construction. 'Jim,' I said, 'let's rent us a bulldozer.'

At first Jim thought I was nuts, but I decided we at least needed to look into the idea. I drove into Seligman, and someone knew someone in Phoenix who had a construction company with a bulldozer. Sure enough, when I tracked him down, he said that if we were willing to pay for it, he could send his bulldozer and its operator up to Seligman by rail. We'd need to find a flatbed truck to haul it out to the ranch. It wouldn't be cheap, but once the bulldozer was here, it could build a good-sized earth dam in a matter of days.

Jim said we needed to present the idea to the English investors. A group of them was headed our way in a few weeks to meet us and survey their property.

* * *

The Poms arrived by wagon after taking a steamer from England to New York and a train to Flagstaff — a three-week trip. They had clipped accents and wore bowler hats and suits with vests. None of them had ever pulled on a pair of cowboy boots or cracked a bullwhip, but that was just fine with Jim and me. They were businessmen, not dudes out to play cowboy. And they were polite and smart. You could tell from the questions they asked that they knew what they didn't know.

The first night they arrived, Old Jake built an open fire and roasted a shoulder of beef. He kept making fun of the investors under his breath, saying things like 'Rather cheeky' and 'Jolly good' in an English accent, and rolling up his cowboy hat to look like a bowler, so I had to bop him in the back of the head. I prepared a few range specialties like rattlesnake stew and prairie oysters to give them something to talk about when they got back to their London clubs.

Afterward we sat around the fire eating tins of sliced peaches. Jim took out his little cotton sack of Bull Durham, rolled himself a cigarette, closing the sack by pulling on the yellow string with his teeth like he always did, then made his pitch.

Only two things really mattered to a rancher, he said: land and water. We had plenty of land in these parts, but not enough water, and without water, the land ain't worth nothing. Water made the difference. Water out here was precious, he said, more precious than you gentlemen, living on that rainy island of yours, can possibly imagine. That was why, for centuries, the Indians and the Mexicans and the Anglos had all been fighting over it, why families were torn apart over it, why neighbors killed each other over it.

One of the Poms piped up to say he knew firsthand how precious water was, because at the hotel in Seligman, he'd been charged an extra fifty cents to take a bath. Everyone got a laugh out of that, and it made me hope that Jim's pitch would receive a sympathetic hearing.

Seeing as how the ranch had no natural source of water, Jim said, one had to be created if it was going to support a sizable herd. Some ranchers went drilling for water, but you might drill all sorts of dry holes before you actually found water, and there was no guarantee of how long it would last. When the Santa Fe Railroad had needed water for its steam engines, it had drilled a hole half a mile deep in these parts and come up dry.

What made the most sense, Jim went on, was to build a big dam to trap rainwater. He described my plan to bring up a bulldozer from Phoenix. When Jim mentioned the cost, the Poms looked at one another, and a few raised their eyebrows, but then Jim pulled out a column of numbers I'd drawn up and explained that without the dam, they could run only a few thousand head on the ranch; with it, they could go to twenty thousand, and that meant bringing five thousand head to market every year. The dam would pay for itself in no time.

The next day the Poms went into Seligman to cable the rest of the investors. After some backing and forthing about engineering details, we got the go-ahead. The Poms wrote a check before they left, and in no time, a flatbed truck was pulling up to the ranch with a big yellow bulldozer on the back. It was the first bulldozer to be seen in these parts, and people came from all over Yavapai County to marvel at it chugging away.

Since we had the darned contraption there, we decided to build dams all over the ranch, the operator scraping out the sides of gullies and draws, lining the bottoms with packed-down clay, and using the fill to build up the walls that would hold back the water from the flash floods. By far the biggest dam we built — so big you needed five minutes to walk around it — was the one in front of the ranch house.

When the rains came that December, the water coursed through the gullies and draws and poured right into the ponds created by the dams. It was just like filling a bathtub. That winter was unusually wet, and by the spring, the water was three feet deep in the big pond — the finest body of water I'd seen since Lake Michigan.

In one sense, that pond was nothing more than a hole in the ground, but Jim treated it like our proudest possession, and that was what it was. He checked the dam every day, measuring the depth of the water and inspecting the walls. In the summer, folks drove from miles away to ask if they might take a dip, and we always let them. Sometimes during dry spells, neighbors without as much water would come over with wagonloads of barrels and ask, as they'd put it, to borrow from our pond, though there was no way they were ever going to repay us, and we never charged for it, since, as Jim liked to say, the heavens had given it to us.

The dam and its pond came to be known as Big Jim's Dam, and then just Big Jim. People around the county measured the severity of dry spells by the amount of water in Big Jim. 'How's Big Jim doin'?' people in town might ask me, or 'I hear Big Jim's low,' and I always knew they were talking about the water level in the pond, not my husband's state of mind.

The Ranch's official name was the Arizona Incorporated Cattle Ranch, but we always called it the AIC, or just The Ranch. It was only dudes and greenhorns — people who got their ideas about ranching from western movies and dime-store novels — who gussied up their ranches with highfalutin names like Acres of Eden or Rancho Mirage or Paradise Plateau. A fancy name, Jim liked to say, was a sure sign that the owner didn't know the first thing about ranching.

With the Depression still going strong, owners like that — as well as plenty of owners who did know a thing or two about ranching — were going out of business. That meant more people were selling than buying cattle, and Jim traveled around Arizona picking up entire herds for rock-bottom prices. He hired about a dozen cowboys, mostly Mexican and Havasupai, to drive the cattle to the ranch and brand them before sending them out to the range. Cowboying was rough, and so were those kids — misfits, most of them, runaways and boys who'd been whipped too hard. For these young fellows, it was a question of joining the roundup or joining the circus — not a lot of other options out there for them — and they took life day by day. The one thing they knew how to do better than anything else was stick a horse, and they took great pride in that.

When the cowboys arrived, the first thing they did was head out into open country and round up a herd of range horses, which they proceeded to break — after a fashion — in the palisaded corral. The horses bucked and fishtailed like rodeo broncs, but those hard-assed boys would just as soon bust every bone in their bodies before calling it quits. They weren't much more than half-broke horses themselves.

I stood there watching them with Rosemary. 'I feel bad for the horses,' she said. 'They just want to be free.'

'In this life,' I said, 'hardly anyone gets to do what they want to do.'

Once the cowboys each had a string of horses, they started bringing in the cattle and branding them. They were all living in the bunkhouse, and I had my hands full cooking for everyone, in addition to helping out with the branding. The cowboys got steak and eggs for breakfast and steak and beans for dinner, with as much salt and roof water as they wanted. Anyone who asked for one could have a raw onion, as good as an orange for staving off scurvy. Most of the boys peeled those onions and ate them like apples.

I didn't particularly trust them around Rosemary, who wasn't allowed to go near the bunkhouse — where there was nonstop cussing, drinking, brawling, card play, and knife play — and that was when I got in the habit of sleeping with her in the bedroom of the ranch house while Big Jim and Little Jim slept in the main room.

Rosemary was also a little like a half-broke

horse. She was happiest running around out of doors, without a stitch of clothing if I'd let her. She climbed the cedar trees, splashed in the horse trough, peed in the yard, swung from vines, and jumped from the barn rafters onto the hay bales, yelling at Mei-Mei to stand clear. She loved spending the day on horseback, holding on behind her father. The saddles were too heavy for her to lift, so she rode her little mule, Jenny, bareback, mounting her by grabbing mane and toe-walking up the animal's leg.

Jim once told Rosemary that she was so tough, any critter that took a bite of her would spit it out, and she just loved that. Rosemary was never afraid of coyotes or wolves, and she hated to see any animal caged, tied up, or penned in. She even thought that the chickens should be freed from the coop, that the risk of being eaten by a coyote was a price worth paying for freedom, and besides, she said, the coyotes needed food, too. That was why I always blamed Rosemary for what happened to Bossie the cow.

The Poms were so thrilled with Jim's work on the ranch that they sent us a pure-blooded Guernsey. Bossie was dun-colored, big and beautiful, and she gave us two gallons a day of rich milk with good cream. She was such a good milk cow that I planned to breed her in the fall, sell the calf in the spring, and sock away the proceeds. I had already begun to think about saving for the day when we could afford a ranch of our own.

But one day someone left Bossie's stall unlatched, and she broke into the granary, where she devoured almost an entire bag of feed. When Old Jake came upon her, she had bloated and was leaning against the barn wall, her stomach swollen while she groaned in pain.

Jim and Old Jake did everything they could. To get her to throw up, they made a mixture of the worst stuff they could think of: tobacco and milk of magnesia and whiskey and soapy water. They put it in a whiskey bottle and tried to pour it down her throat, but Bossie wouldn't swallow, and it dribbled out the sides of her mouth. So then Old Jake held her jaws apart while Jim stuck the bottle so far down inside her gullet that his arm disappeared up to his elbow.

He poured the concoction directly into her stomach, and she did throw up a little, but she was so far gone by then that it made no difference. Her knees buckled, and she collapsed slowly to the ground. In desperation, Jim punctured her gut with his pocketknife to let the gas out. But that didn't work, either, and in another hour, our big, beautiful Guernsey was gone, lying glass-eyed and heavy on the barn floor.

I was furious, heartbroken about the death of Bossie, but beside myself about the loss of what I hoped we'd earn come calving season. I was sure that it was Rosemary, with her misguided notions about animals and freedom, who had let Bossie out. The girl had been too horrified to watch Jim and Old Jake ministering to the cow, and I found her on the long porch, sobbing about Bossie's end. I felt like smacking her good, but she insisted she hadn't let the cow out, that it was Little Jim who'd done it, and since I didn't have any proof one way or another, I had to let the matter go.

'Just you remember,' I said, 'that this is what could happen when an animal gets freedom. Animals act like they hate to be penned up, but the fact is, they don't know what to do with freedom. And a lot of times it kills them.'

Shortly after the herd arrived, Jim set out to repair all the fencing on the ranch. The job took a month. He brought Rosemary along with him in the pickup, and they were gone for days at a time, sleeping in the bed of the truck, cooking over campfires, and returning only for resupplies of food and wire. Rosemary adored her father, and he was completely unfazed by her wild streak. They were happy to spend hours in each other's company, Rosemary talking nonstop and Jim barely saying a word, just nodding and smiling — with an occasional 'That so?' or 'Sounds good' — as he dug holes, trimmed posts, and tightened wire.

'Doesn't that kid ever shut up?' Old Jake once asked.

'She's got a lot to say,' Jim told him.

While they were gone, I settled in to life on the ranch. There was always more to do on any given day than you could get done, and I quickly established a few rules for myself. One was to dispense with any unnecessary cleaning — no maid's work. Arizona was a dusty place, but a little dirt never killed anyone. That bit about cleanliness being next to godliness was a lot of balderdash as far as I was concerned. In fact, I considered it downright insulting. Anyone who worked the land got dirty, and in Chicago I'd seen my share of less than godly people living in squeaky-clean mansions. So I gave the house a going-over only once every few months, working myself into a frenzy and blazing through all the scrubbing and dusting in a single day.

As for clothes, I flatly refused to wash them. I made sure we all bought loose-fitting clothes that let us do squats and windmill our arms — none of that tight buttoned-up stuff like my mother favored. We wore our shirts till they got dirty, then we put them on backward and wore them until that side got dirty, then we wore them inside out, then inside out backward. We were getting four times more wear out of each shirt than persnickety folks did. When the shirts reached the point where Jim was joking about them scaring the cattle, I'd take the whole pile into Seligman and pay by the pound to have them all steam-cleaned.

Levi's we didn't wash at all. They shrank too much, and it weakened the threads. So we wore them and wore them until they were shiny with mud, manure, tallow, cattle slobber, bacon fat, axle grease, and hoof oil — and then we wore them some more. Eventually, the Levi's reached a point of grime saturation where they couldn't get any dirtier, where they had the feel of oilskin and had become not just waterproof but briar-proof, and that was when you knew you had really broken them in. When Levi's reached that degree of conditioning, they were sort of like smoke-cured ham or aged bourbon, and you couldn't pay a cowboy to let you wash his.

I kept the cooking basic as well. I didn't make dishes the way fancy eastern housewives did

— soufflés and sauces and garnished this and stuffed that. I made food. Beans were my specialty. I always had a pot of them on the stove, and that usually lasted two to five days, depending on how many cowboys we had around. My recipe was fairly simple: Boil beans, salt to taste. What I liked most about beans was that as long as you added water from time to time, you couldn't overcook them.

When we weren't having beans, we had steak. My recipe for steak was also fairly simple: Fry on both sides, salt to taste. With the steak came potatoes: Boil unpeeled, salt to taste. For dessert, we'd have canned peaches packed in tasty syrup. I liked to say that what my cooking lacked in variety, it made up for in consistency. 'No surprises,' I'd tell the cowboys, 'but no disappointments, either.'

Once when some milk had spoiled and I was feeling ambitious, I did make cottage cheese the way my mother made it when I was growing up. I boiled the clabbered milk and cut up the curds with a knife. Then I wrapped it in a burlap sugar sack and hung it overnight to let the whey drain out. The next day I chopped it again, salted it, and passed it out at supper. The family loved it so much they wolfed it down in under a minute. I couldn't believe I'd worked so long over something that was gone so quickly.

'That was the biggest waste of time,' I said. 'I'll never make that mistake again.'

Rosemary was eyeing me.

'Let that be a lesson to you,' I told her.

★ ★ ★

Jim never had it in him to raise his hand to his daughter, and when he and Rosemary returned from fixing fences, she was more rambunctious than ever. Even though Rosemary was still just a little girl, I could sense the beginnings of a fundamental difference of opinion between her and me. I felt there was a lot I needed to teach her. I wanted to give her an early grounding in the basics of arithmetic and reading, but even more important, I wanted to get across the idea that the world was a dangerous place and life was unpredictable and you had to be smart, focused, and determined to make it through. You had to be willing to work hard and persevere in the face of misfortune. A lot of people, even those born with brains and beauty, didn't have what it took to knuckle down and get the thing done.

From the time she was three, I drilled Rosemary on her numbers. If she asked for a glass of milk, I told her she could have it only if she spelled out 'milk.' I tried to make her see that everything in life — from Bossie to the cottage cheese — was a lesson, but it was up to her to figure out what she'd learned. Rosemary was a bright little kid in a lot of ways, but math and spelling confused her, and answering questions on cue bored her, as did the routine of daily chores. Jim told me to lighten up, she was just four, but by four I'd been gathering eggs and taking care of my baby sister. I began to worry that Rosemary was unfocused and that if we didn't stamp it out early, it could become a permanent part of her character.

'She'll outgrow it,' Jim said, 'and if she don't, that means it's her nature, not something we can change.'

'It's up to us to set her straight,' I said. 'I turned illiterate Mexican kids into readers. I can make my own daughter shape up.'

★　★　★

Rosemary was always getting caught up in dangerous situations, almost as if she was drawn to them. She was constantly falling into draws and out of trees. It was always the buckingest horse that caught her eye. She loved to catch snakes and scorpions, keeping them in a jar for a while, but then she'd grow worried that they were lonely and missed their families, so she'd turn them loose.

That first October on the ranch, we bought a pumpkin in Seligman and carved it into a jack-o'-lantern to celebrate Halloween. Rosemary had dressed for Halloween in a tattered old silk dress she'd found in a trunk in the storage barn, and she held it up over the jack-o'-lantern, fascinated by the patterns that the flame made through the thin fabric. Jim and I weren't paying much attention when she lowered the dress too close to the candle and it caught fire, the dry silk bursting into flames.

Rosemary was screaming while Jim grabbed his horsehide duster and wrapped it around her to smother the flames. It was all over in an instant. We carried her into the bedroom, and Jim quietly talked her down from hysteria while I cut off the remains of the silk dress. Rosemary had a wide burn across her stomach, though it wasn't too deep. The nearest hospital was over two hours away, and besides, I didn't care to splurge on a doctor, so I lathered her burn in Vaseline, which cured everything from boils to rashes, and bandaged her up. When I was finished, I looked down at her and shook my head.

'Are you mad at me, Mommy?' Rosemary asked.

'Not as mad as I should be,' I said. I just didn't believe in molly-coddling kids when they hurt themselves. Fussing over her wasn't going to help her realize the mistake she'd made. 'You're the most accident-prone little girl I've ever known. And I hope at least you've learned what happens when you play with fire.'

Still, she'd been pretty brave about it all — she was always a brave little kid, you had to hand it to her — and I softened up.

'Same thing happened to my brother, Buster, when he was small, and to my grandfather,' I said. 'So I guess it runs in the family.'

That first winter, Jim and I paid fifty dollars for a marvelous long-range radio from Montgomery Ward. It had a big wire antenna that a couple of the cowboys helped us rig up, stringing it between two of the tall cedars outside the house. 'Brings the twentieth century to Yavapai County,' I told Jim.

Since we had no electricity, we ran the radio off two massive batteries that cost another fifty dollars and weighed about ten pounds apiece. When the batteries were fresh, we could get stations all the way from Europe with announcers jabbering away in French and German. Adolf Hitler had taken over in Germany, and a civil war was brewing in Spain, but we weren't particularly interested in European affairs. The reason we shelled out so much money was to get the weather report, which was much more important to us than what the Krauts were up to.

Every morning we got up before dawn and Jim turned the radio on low, crouching down next to it to listen to the weather report from a station in California. The fronts that came our way usually started there, though sometimes we were hit by winter storms that traveled all the way down from Canada. With water so scarce and severe storms so dangerous — drowning or freezing cattle, flattening barns, washing away entire families, the lightning electrocuting horses with steel shoes — we lived and died by those forecasts. You could say we were true aficionados of the weather. We'd follow a storm that started out in Los Angeles and moved east. The clouds usually ended up getting caught by the tip of the Rockies, where they'd dump most of their moisture, but sometimes that storm drifted south, making its way east through a passage above the Gulf of California, and that was when we got our big rains.

Rosemary and Little Jim loved the storms more than just about anything else. When the skies turned dark and the air grew heavy, I called them onto the porch and we all watched as the storm, with its boiling clouds and cannonading thunder, its white claws of lightning and drifting sheets of black rain, rolled across the range.

A distant storm sometimes seemed small in the huge sweep of the plateau, darkening one patch of land while everything else remained bathed in sunlight. Sometimes the storm veered off and missed us altogether. But if it hit the yard, the excitement really began, the thunder and lightning splitting the sky, the water hammering on the tin roof and pouring off the sides, filling the cisterns, the draws, and the dams.

To live in a place where water was so scarce made the rare moments like this — when the heavens poured forth an abundance of water and the hard earth softened and turned lush and green — seem magical, almost miraculous. The kids had an irresistible urge to get out and dance in the rain, and I always let them go and sometimes joined them myself, all of us prancing around, arms upraised, as the water beat down on our faces, plastering our hair and soaking our clothes.

Afterward, we all ran down to the draws that led to Big Jim the dam, and once the first rush of water had passed, I'd let the kids strip off their clothes and go swimming. They'd stay out there for hours, paddling around, pretending to be alligators or dolphins or hippopotamuses. They had a heck of a time playing in the rain puddles, too. When the water sank through the soil and all that was left was mud, they'd keep playing, rolling around until everything but the whites of their eyes and their teeth was plastered with mud. Once the mud dried, which didn't take long, it sheared right off, leaving them pretty clean, and they got back into their clothes.

Sometimes over supper, when Jim got home after a storm, the kids would describe their escapades in the water and mud, and Jim would recount his vast store of water lore and water history. Once the world was nothing but water, he explained, and you wouldn't think it to look at us, but human beings were mostly water. The miraculous thing about water, he said, was that it never came to an end. All the water on the earth had been here since the beginning of time, it had just moved around from rivers and lakes and oceans to clouds and rain and puddles and then sunk through the soil to underground streams, to springs and wells, where it got drunk by people and animals and went back to rivers and lakes and oceans.

The water you kids were playing in, he said, had probably been to Africa and the North Pole. Genghis Khan or Saint Peter or even Jesus himself might have drunk it. Cleopatra might have bathed in it. Crazy Horse might have watered his pony with it. Sometimes water was liquid. Sometimes it was rock hard — ice. Sometimes it was soft — snow. Sometimes it was visible but weightless — clouds. And sometimes it was completely invisible — vapor — floating up into the sky like the souls of dead people. There was nothing like water in the world, Jim said. It made the desert bloom but also turned rich bottomland into swamp. Without it we'd die, but it could also kill us, and that was why we loved it, even craved it, but also feared it. Never take water for granted, Jim said. Always cherish it. Always beware of it.

The rains usually arrived in April, August, and December, but in our second year on the ranch, April came and went without rain. So did August and so did December, and by the following year, we were in the midst of a serious drought. The range turned sandy and windblown, and the mudflats became dry and cracked.

Every day Jim listened grim-faced to the weather report, hoping in vain for a forecast of rain, and then we'd go down and check the water level of Big Jim. The days were beautiful, with endless deep blue skies, but all that fine weather only gave us a desperate, helpless feeling as we stood there, watching the water level sink and sink until the bottom of Big Jim became visible. And then the water disappeared altogether and there was nothing but mud, and then the mud dried out with cracks so big you could stick your arm into them.

Early into the drought, Jim had sensed it coming on. He'd grown up in the desert, so he knew that one came along every ten or fifteen years, and he had culled the herd deeply, selling off steers and heifers and keeping only the healthiest breeding cattle. Even so, once the drought was in full swing, we had to bring in water. Jim and I hitched up the Conestoga wagon to the pickup and hauled it into Pica, a stop twenty miles away on the Santa Fe Railroad where they were shipping in water. We loaded old fuel drums with as much water as the Conestoga could hold and hauled it — the wagon's suspension groaning under all that weight — back to the ranch, where we drained it into Big Jim.

We made that trip a couple of times a week. We darned near broke our backs loading those fuel drums, but we saved the herd, whereas many ranchers around us went bust.

★ ★ ★

The following August, the rains returned. And when they came back, they came with a vengeance, a terrific deluge the likes of which I'd never seen. We sat at our kitchen table, a long wooden thing with patterned linoleum nailed to the top, listening to the rain drum on the roof. Unlike other storms, this one didn't peter out after half an hour. Instead, it kept raining and raining, striking the tin roof so loud and incessant that it began to get on my nerves. After a while Jim started worrying about Big Jim. If too much water flooded into the dam, he said, its walls might burst and we'd lose it all.

The first time Jim went out to check the dam, he reported back that it was holding, but an hour later, with the rain still coming down in sheets, he checked it again and realized that if nothing was done, it would give. He had a plan, which was to go out in the middle of the storm and dig furrows in the draws and the wash approaching the dam, to drain off the water before it reached

Big Jim. To dig the furrows, he was going to harness old Buck, our Percheron draft, to the plow.

Jim had on his horsehide duster, waterlogged and dripping. I put on my canvas coat and we headed out into the rain, which was coming down so furiously that within moments it had worked its way past my turned-up coat collar, down my sleeves, and was soaking through my shoes. I felt it trickling all over me, and even before we got to the barn, I had reached the point where you give up trying to stay dry.

The barn was dark from the storm, and we couldn't find the harness, which no one had used in years. Old Jake, who had sprained his good foot falling off a horse and was hobbling around worse than ever, started getting panicky at the idea of the dam giving out and washing away the cattle, but I told him to hush his mouth. We all knew what was at stake, and if we were going to save the ranch, we needed clear heads.

What we could do, I said to Jim, was hitch the plow to the pickup. If he handled the plow, I could drive. Jim liked the idea. Old Jake was useless, so we left him to fret in the barn, but we brought the kids with us. The water out in the yard was more than ankle-deep by then, the rain coming down so hard that the force of it practically knocked Rosemary to the ground. Jim scooped her up in his arms. I followed with Little Jim, who was still a baby, grabbing a wooden carton so we'd have something to keep him in, and we sloshed out to the Chevy.

At the equipment shed, Jim jumped out and threw the plow, together with some ropes and chains, into the pickup bed. Once we reached the wash above the dam, we rigged up the plow to the Chevy's hitch, and I got behind the wheel, putting Little Jim in the carton on the floor so he wouldn't slide around too much.

I looked in the rearview mirror, but the rain was splattering so hard on the window that Jim was just a blur. I had Rosemary stand up on the seat and stick her head out the window and take directions from him. Jim was gesturing and shouting, but the rain was making such a racket that it was hard to figure out what he wanted.

'Mom, I can't hear him,' Rosemary said.

'Do the best you can,' I said. 'That's all anyone can do.'

I needed the pickup to creep along at a walking pace, but the Chevy wasn't geared to go that slow, and it kept stalling and lurching, jerking the plow out of Jim's hands and sending Rosemary tumbling off the seat and into Little Jim's box. Making matters worse, the earth around the dam was that godforsaken malpais rock, and the tires would spin on it, then catch, and we'd pop forward.

We knew we didn't have much time, and Jim and I were both cussing like sailors while Rosemary, her hair plastered, scrambling back onto the seat every time she was knocked off, did her best to read Jim's gestures and shouts and relay them to me. Finally, I figured out that by engaging the clutch, easing up on it ever so slightly, then reengaging it, I could send the truck forward just a few inches at a time, and that was how we got the job done, digging four furrows off the sides of the wash that drained the rising water away from the dam.

It was still raining furiously. Jim heaved the plow into the pickup bed and climbed in beside me. He was as wet as if he'd fallen into a horse trough. Water sloshed in his boots and dripped from his hat and sopping horsehide coat, pooling on the seat.

'We did a good job — good as we could,' he said. 'If she breaks, she breaks.'

She didn't break.

While our place was spared, not everyone fared as well. The rains washed away a few bridges and several miles of railroad track. Ranchers lost cattle and outbuildings. Seligman was flooded, several houses were swept off, and the rest had mud lines five feet high, which was so astounding that no one wanted to paint over them. For years afterward, folks who'd lived through the storm pointed out those mud lines in a combination of disbelief and pride. 'Water come clean up to there,' they'd say, shaking their head.

But a few hours after the rain stopped, the plateau turned bright green, and the next day the ranch was covered with the most spectacular display of flowers I had ever seen. There were crimson Indian paint-brushes and orange California poppies, white mariposa poppies with their magenta throats, goldenrod and blue lupines and pink and purple sweet peas. It was like a rainbow you could touch and smell. All that water must have churned up seeds that had been buried for decades.

Rosemary, who was ecstatic over it, spent days collecting flowers. 'If we had this much water all the time,' I told her, 'we might have to break down and give this ranch some greenhorn name like Paradise Plateau.'

VI

TEACHER LADY

Lily Casey Smith before a flying lesson

The water we bought during the drought cost a fortune, but the Poms knew that ranching was a long-term proposition only for people with wallets fat enough to tough out the bad times and then make a killing in the good. They actually saw the drought, and all the bankruptcies it was causing, as a buying opportunity. So did Jim. As much land as we had, he realized that if the ranch was going to make it through the next drought, we needed even more land — land with its own water. He convinced the investors to buy the neighboring ranch, called Hackberry. It had some hilly terrain with a year-round spring, and out on the flat range, there was a deep well with a windmill that pumped water up to the cattle troughs.

Jim's plan was to move the herd back and forth between the two ranches, keeping the cattle in Hackberry during the winter and bringing them back to the high plateau around Big Jim in the summer. When the two ranches were combined, they totaled 180,000 acres. It was a big spread — one of the biggest in Arizona — and in good years, we could bring some ten thousand head of cattle to market. When the Poms saw those numbers, they were more than happy to pony up for Hackberry.

The first time we rode out to Hackberry, I flat-out fell in love with the place. It was down off the plateau, between the Peacock and the Walapai mountains, the range dotted by chaparral. Runoff from the mountains fed the plain, and there was also that spring in the granite foothills. The house, nestled in a hollow, was a former dance hall that had been taken apart, moved to the spot, and reassembled, with a swank linoleum floor and the walls painted with signs saying NO ROUGH STUFF and TAKE THE FIGHT OUTSIDE.

The first time I saw the windmill, I took a drink of its well water, which came from deep beneath us and had been there for tens of thousands of years waiting for me to taste it. That well water tasted sweeter than the finest French liqueur. Some folks, when they struck it rich, liked to say that they were in the money, and that was how I felt — rich — only we were in the water. Our days of busting our humps hauling fuel drums over dirt roads were gone for good.

★   ★   ★

After the Poms bought Hackberry, one of the first things Jim did was to drive all the way to Los Angeles in the Chevy and return with a truck-load of half-inch lead pipe. It was a mile from the spring to the house, and we laid pipe the entire length, running strips of inner tube between the interconnecting pipe ends and tying it up with bailing wire. It wasn't indoor plumbing — and it wasn't exactly pretty — but it brought a constant supply of spring water to our

214

back door, spurting forth clear and fresh when you opened the spigot.

Next to the spigot, we kept a metal cup, and few things were finer than coming back from a hot, dusty ride and filling that cup with a cold, wet drink, then pouring what was left over your head.

★ ★ ★

We moved the herd over to Hackberry in the fall and stayed there until the spring. I always loved bright colors, and at Hackberry, I decided to really go to town. I painted each room a different color — pink, blue, and yellow — put Navajo rugs on the floors, and got some red velvet curtains for the windows, using several books of S&H green stamps that I'd saved over the years.

Rosemary loved the colors even more than I did. She was already showing some artistic talent, tossing off perfect little line drawings without once lifting the pencil from the paper. Both kids were crazy about Hackberry, its green mountains, the lilacs, the birds of paradise, the tamarack trees around the chicken coop. There were several deep canyons running down out of the mountains, and after it rained, I'd rush with the kids up to the lip of one of them and we'd watch and cheer as the flash floods came thundering down the dry creek beds, shaking the ground beneath us.

Rosemary and Little Jim were also fascinated by the story of Hackberry's ghosts. Years earlier, a fire had broken out in the house when two children were inside. The mother rushed in and saved the boy, then returned to get her baby girl, but they both died in the flames and the little boy standing outside could hear their anguished cries. A few months later, the boy was on his swing, and he started going higher and higher, pumping his legs, trying to get up to heaven to be with his mother and sister, but he swung so high that he fell off and died as well.

All three of them supposedly haunted the ranch, and Rosemary, instead of being frightened, couldn't stop looking for them. She'd wander around at night, calling out their names, and whenever she heard a sudden noise — a distant bobcat, a rustling in the tamarack trees, oil drums expanding with a bang in the heat — she'd get excited thinking maybe it was the ghosts. She was particularly intrigued by the little boy ghost, and she wanted to explain to him that since he was with his mother and sister, everything was in fact okay, and they were all free to go to heaven.

★   ★   ★

Ever since moving to the ranch, Jim and I had talked on and off about buying it, or at least buying a place of our own one day, but we'd had our hands full getting the ranch up and running, and buying had seemed a distant dream. Now that I'd spent time at Hackberry — a beautiful spread with good water — I wanted it and was determined to turn my dream into a plan.

We needed cash. We were never going to go

into debt again, I swore, we were not going to lose this place the way we'd lost the house and the filling station in Ash Fork. I worked up the figures and decided we might be able to swing it in ten years if I started bringing in money and we scrimped and saved, pinching every penny till old Abe Lincoln yelped.

We'd always been frugal — Jim made the Poms a lot of money, but he made it a nickel at a time, reusing nails, saving old barbed wire, building fences with juniper saplings rather than milled posts. We never threw away anything. We saved bits of wood in case we needed shims. When our old shirts finally frayed to pieces, we cut off the buttons and put them in the button box; the shirts we either used as rags or gave to a seamstress in Seligman who turned them into patchwork quilts.

But now I came up with additional ways to save money. We made the children chairs out of orange crates. Rosemary drew on used paper bags — both sides — and painted on old boards. We drank from coffee cans with wire tied around them for handles. Whenever possible, I drove behind trucks so their slipstream pulled me along and I saved on gas.

I also came up with all sorts of moneymaking schemes, some more successful than others. I sold encyclopedias door-to-door, but that didn't go over so well, seeing as how there were not a lot of bookish ranch hands in Yavapai County. I did a lot better visiting neighbors to solicit orders for Montgomery Ward, and I didn't even have to resort to tricks like throwing dirt on the floor the way my crumb-bum first husband did. I also stayed up late writing short stories about cowboys and gunslingers for pulp magazines — using the nom de plume Legs LeRoy because I figured those pulp editors wouldn't buy western tales from a lady — but I got no takers. I collected scrap metal in the Chevy and sold it by the pound. I also started playing poker with the hands, but Jim put a stop to that after I cleaned a couple of them out. 'We don't pay them enough as it is,' he said. 'We can't go taking what little they get.'

On weekends, I drove down Highway 66 with the kids, sending them out to pick up bottles that people had thrown out their car windows. Rosemary would take one side of the road, Little Jim the other, each of them dragging a burlap bag. The deposit was two cents for Coke bottles, five cents for cream bottles, ten cents for milk bottles, and a quarter for gallon jugs. One day we collected thirty dollars' worth of bottles.

Sometimes other drivers would stop to see if we were okay. 'You folks need any help there?' they'd call out.

'We're just dandy,' I'd say. 'Got any empties?'

Rosemary loved our scavenging expeditions. One day all four of us were over paying a call on our neighbors, the Hutters. After dinner, we were heading back to the Chevy, parked near their barn, when Rosemary spotted a bottle in the fuel drum that they used to hold trash. She ran to fetch it.

'Lily, this is getting a little out of hand,' Jim said. 'We're not so darned broke that we need to have our daughter digging around in someone's garbage for a two-cent bottle.'

Rosemary held up the bottle. 'It's not a two-center, Dad,' she said. 'It's a ten-center.'

'Good girl,' I said, and turned to Jim. 'Ten cents adds up. And anyway, I'm teaching them resourcefulness.'

By then I was closing in on my thirty-ninth birthday, and there was still one thing I'd never done and had always wanted to do. One summer day Jim and the kids and I had driven the Flivver over to Mohave County to look at a breeding bull Jim was interested in buying when we passed a ranch with a small plane parked near the gate. A hand-painted sign in the windshield read: FLYING LESSONS: $5.

'That's for me,' I said.

I had Jim pull into the driveway, and we stopped to look at the plane. It was a two-seater, one behind the other, with an open cockpit, a faded green paint job, rust rings around the rivets, and a rudder that creaked in the wind.

I remembered the first time I'd seen an airplane, when I was riding Patches through the desert back from Red Lake. I loved Patches, but that had been one long, rump-numbing journey. On an airplane, it wouldn't have been much more than a little hop.

A fellow came out of a shack behind the plane and sauntered up to the Flivver. He had a windburned face, a cigarette dangling from his mouth, and a pair of aviator goggles pushed up on his forehead. He rested his elbows on Jim's open window and said, 'Looking to learn her?'

I leaned across the gearbox. 'Not him,' I said. 'Me.'

'Whoa,' Goggles said. 'Ain't never taught a woman before.' He looked at Jim. 'Think the little lady's up to it?'

'Don't you 'little lady' me,' I said. 'I break horses. I brand steers. I run a ranch with a couple dozen crazy cowboys on it, and I can beat them all in poker. I'll be damned if some nincompoop is going to stand there and tell me that I don't have what it takes to fly that dinky heap of tin.'

Goggles stared at me for a moment, then Jim patted him on the arm. 'No one's ever won betting against her,' Jim said.

'That don't surprise me,' Goggles said. He pulled out a fresh cigarette and lit it with the old one. 'Ma'am, I like your spirit. Let's take 'er up.'

Goggles brought out a flight suit for me, along with a leather aviation helmet and a set of goggles. As I pulled them on, he walked me around the plane, checking the struts, pointing out the ailerons, explaining basics such as lift and tailwind, and showing me how to operate the copilot's stick. But Goggles wasn't much for theory, and soon he was climbing aboard and having me climb in behind him. As I did, I realized that the fuselage wasn't made of metal after all, but canvas. That airplane was a right spindly contraption.

Then we were taxiing down the driveway, bumping along, gathering speed. The bumping stopped, but at first I wasn't even aware that we were airborne — it was that smooth — then I saw the ground falling away beneath us and I knew I was flying.

We circled around. The kids were running back and forth waving like mad, and even Jim was enthusiastically flapping his hat. I leaned out and waved. The sky was a royal blue, and as we gained altitude, I saw the Arizona range rolling away in all directions, the Mogollon Rim to the east, and in the distant west, beyond a serpentine river, the Rockies, with some thin high clouds hovering above them. Route 66 threaded its way like a ribbon through the desert, a few tiny cars moving along it. Living in Arizona, I was used to long views, but still, the sight of the earth spread out far below made me feel huge and aloof, like I was beholding the entire world, seeing it all for the first time, the way I figured angels did.

Goggles operated the controls for most of the lesson, but by keeping my hand on my stick, I was able to follow the way he banked, climbed, and dived. Toward the end, he let me take over, and after a few heart-stopping jerks, I was able to put the plane into a long, steady turn that brought us right into the sun.

Afterward, I thanked Goggles, paid him, and told him he'd be seeing me again. As we walked back to the car, Rosemary said, 'I thought we were supposed to save money.'

'Even more important than saving money is making it,' I said, 'and sometimes, to make money, you have to spend it.' I told her if I got a pilot's license, I could bring in cash dusting crops and delivering mail and flying rich people around. 'This lesson was an investment,' I said. 'In me.'

Working as a freelance bush pilot struck me as one glorious way of earning a living, but I knew it would take a while to get my pilot license, and we needed money now. I finally decided that the smartest way for me to bring in the bucks was to put my most marketable skill — teaching — back into use. I wrote Grady Gammage, who had helped me get the job at Red Lake, to ask if he knew of any opportunities.

He replied that there was a town called Main Street with an opening. It was up in the Arizona Strip, and I'd be welcome there, he said, because Main Street was so remote and, quite frankly, so peculiar that no teacher with a college degree wanted the job. Truth be known, he went on, the people in the area were almost all Mormon polygamists who'd moved all the way out there to escape government harassment.

Neither remoteness nor peculiarity troubled me, and as for Mormons, I'd married one, so I figured I could handle a few polygamists. I wrote back telling Grady Gammage to sign me up.

★ ★ ★

What made most sense was to take Rosemary and Little Jim with me, so one day late in the summer, we packed the Flivver, which was still running but on its last legs, and headed for the

Arizona Strip. Jim followed in the Chevy to help us get settled.

The Arizona Strip was in the northwest corner of Mohave County, cut off from the rest of the state by the Grand Canyon and the Colorado River. To get there, we had to drive into Nevada, then Utah, then turn back south to Arizona.

I wanted my children to see the awesomeness of modern technology, so we stopped off at the Boulder Dam, where four enormous turbines generated electricity that was sent all the way to California. It was Jim's idea to also visit one of the ruined cities of the Hohokams, an ancient and extinct tribe that had built elaborate four-story houses and a complex irrigation system. We stood there for a while, looking at those collapsed sandstone buildings and the troughs that had carried water directly to the Hohokams' houses.

'What happened to the Hohokams, Daddy?' Rosemary asked.

'They thought they could civilize the desert,' Jim said, 'and it was their undoing. The only way to survive in the desert is to recognize that it is a desert.'

★ ★ ★

The Arizona Strip was desolate but beautiful country. There were grassland plateaus where distant mountains sparkled with mica, and sandstone hills and gullies that had been carved into wondrous shapes — hourglasses and spinning tops and teardrops — by wind and water. The sight of all that time-worn stone, shaped grain by grain over thousands and thousands of years, made it seem like the place had been created by a very patient God.

The town of Main Street was so small that it didn't appear on most maps. In fact, the main street of Main Street was the only street, lined with a few ramshackle houses, one general store, and the school, which had a teacherage. It was nothing fancy, one tiny room with two box windows and a single bed that Little Jim, Rosemary, and I would share. The water barrel outside the kitchen was swimming with pollywogs. 'At least we know it's not poison,' Jim said. 'Just drink with your teeth closed.'

Many of the people in the area herded sheep, but the land had been overgrazed, and it was startling how threadbare the local folks were. None of them had cars. Instead, they drove wagons or, too poor to afford saddles, rode horses with just blankets on their backs. Some lived in chicken coops. The women wore bonnets, and the children came to school barefoot and in overalls or dresses stitched from feed sacks. Their underwear — if they had any — was also made of feed sacks. Some Mormons were sewed into ceremonial undergarments during a special church ritual, and since the garments were supposed to protect them from harm, snide folks referred to them as Mormon wonder underwear.

When we first arrived, the people around Main Street were polite yet guarded, but after they found out my husband was the son of the great Lot Smith, who fought the federals with Brigham Young and founded Tuba City and had eight wives and fifty-two children, they warmed right up. As a matter of fact, they started treating us like visiting dignitaries.

I had thirty students of all ages, and they were a sweet and well-behaved lot. Because they were polygamists, they were almost all related in one way or another and talked about their 'other mothers' and 'double cousins.' The girls doted on Rosemary, who was now six, and Little Jim, who was four, fussing over them, combing their hair, dressing them up, and practicing mothering skills. The girls were all listed in the 'Joy Book,' meaning they were eligible for marriage and were waiting for their 'uncle' to decide whom they would marry.

The houses they lived in, I came to see, were essentially breeding factories where as many as seven wives were expected to churn out a baby a year. The way the Mormons saw it, God had populated earth with beings in his likeness, so if Mormon men were going to follow the path of God, they had to have their own brood of kids to populate their own heavenly world in the hereafter. The girls were raised to be docile and submissive. In the first few months I was there, a couple of my thirteen-year-old girls simply disappeared, vanishing into their arranged marriages.

Rosemary was fascinated by these kids with all their multitudes of moms, and these dads with all their sets of wives, and she kept asking me to explain it. She was particularly intrigued with

Mormon underwear and wondered if it really gave the Mormons special powers.

'That's what they believe,' I told her, 'but that doesn't mean it's true.'

'Then why do they believe it?'

'America is a free country,' I said. 'And that means people are free to believe whatever cockamamie thing they want to believe.'

'So they don't have to believe it if they don't want to?' Rosemary asked.

'No, they don't.'

'But do they know that?'

Smart kid. That, I came to see, was the heart of the matter. You were free to choose enslavement, but the choice was a free one only if you knew what your alternatives were. I began to think of it as my job to make sure the girls I was teaching learned that it was a big world out there and there were other things they could do besides being broodmares dressed in feed sacks.

In class, I spent the bulk of my time on the basics of reading and writing and arithmetic, but I also peppered my lessons with talk of nursing and teaching, the opportunities in big cities, the Twenty-first Amendment, and the doings of Amelia Earhart and Eleanor Roosevelt. I told them how, when I was no older than they were, I was breaking horses. I talked about going to Chicago and learning to fly an airplane. Any of them could do all that, too, I said, long as they had the gumption.

Some of them — both boys and girls — looked shocked, but more than a few seemed genuinely intrigued.

I hadn't been in Main Street for long when I got a visit from Uncle Eli, the patriarch of the local polygamists. He had a long graying beard, scraggly eyebrows, and a beaklike nose. His smile was practiced and his eyes were cold. I gave him a drink of pollywog water, and as we talked, he kept patting my hand and calling me 'Teacher Lady.'

Some of the mothers, he said, had told him their little girls were coming home from school talking about suffragettes and women flying airplanes. What I needed to understand was that he and his people had moved to this area to get away from the rest of the world, and I was bringing that world into their very schoolroom, teaching the children things their mothers and fathers considered dangerous and even blasphemous. My job, he went on, was to give them just enough arithmetic and reading to manage the household and make their way through the Book of Mormon.

'Teacher Lady, you're not preparing these girls for their lives,' he said. 'You're only upsetting and confusing them. There will be no more talk of worldly ways.'

'Look, Uncle,' I said, 'I don't work for you. I work for the state of Arizona. I don't need you telling me my job. My job is to give these kids an education, and part of that is letting them know a little bit about what the world is really like.'

Uncle's smile never wavered. Rosemary was sitting at the table drawing, and he walked over and stroked her hair. 'What are you drawing?' he asked.

'That's my mom riding Red Devil,' Rosemary said. It was one of her favorite stories about me, and she was always making drawings of it. She looked up at Uncle Eli. 'My daddy used to be a Mormon.'

'But he's not any longer?'

'No. He's a rancher.'

'Then he is lost.'

'Dad never gets lost — and he doesn't even need a compass. He just says Mom made him throw away his wonder underwear. Do you wear wonder underwear?'

'We call it the temple garment,' Uncle said. 'You'll make some man a fine wife one day soon. Shall we put you in the Joy Book?'

'Leave her out of this,' I said. 'And leave her out of that darned book.'

'I'm done talking to you,' he said. 'If you don't obey me, we will all shun you as the devil.'

The next day I gave an especially impassioned lesson on political and religious freedom, talking about the totalitarian countries where everyone was forced to believe one thing. In America, by contrast, people were free to think for themselves and follow their hearts when it came to matters of faith. 'It's like one of the wonderful department stores in Chicago,' I said. 'You can go around trying on different dresses until you find one that suits you.'

That night when I went to throw out the dishwater, Uncle Eli was standing in the yard, his arms crossed, staring at me.

'Evening,' I said.

He didn't reply. He just kept staring at me, like he was giving me the evil eye.

The next night I looked up from fixing dinner, and there he was again, standing framed in the window, staring out from under his unruly eyebrows with the same baleful expression.

'What's he want, Mommy?' Rosemary asked.

'Oh, he's just hoping I'll have a staring contest with him.'

The teacherage didn't have curtains, but the next day I sewed together some feed sacks and tacked them over the window. That evening there was a knock at the door. When I opened it, Uncle Eli was standing there.

'What do you want?' I asked.

230

He just stared at me, and I closed the door. The knocking started up again, slow and persistent. I went into the room where we slept and loaded my pearl-handled revolver. Uncle Eli was still knocking on the door. I opened it, and as I did, I swung the gun up and across so that by the time he saw me, the gun was pointed dead at him.

The last time I'd pointed the gun had been at that drunk in Ash Fork who'd called Helen a dead whore when I wouldn't sell him any hooch. I hadn't fired then, but this time I aimed just to the left of Uncle Eli's face and pulled the trigger.

When the shot rang out, Uncle Eli barked in fright and instinctively jerked his hands up. The bullet had whizzed by his ear, but the barrel had been close enough that his face was sprayed with soot. He stared at me, speechless.

'You come knocking around here again, you better be wearing your wonder underwear,' I said, ''cause next time I won't aim to miss.'

★ ★ ★

Two days later, the county sheriff showed up at the school. He was an easygoing country fellow with a goiter. Investigating a schoolmarm for shooting at a polygamous elder wasn't something he did every day, and he seemed uncertain how to handle it.

'We received a complaint, ma'am, alleging you took a potshot at one of the townspeople.'

'There was a menacing intruder, and I was defending myself and my children. I'll be happy to stand up in court and explain exactly what happened.'

The sheriff sighed. 'Around here, we like people to work out their differences amongst themselves. But if you can't get along with these folks, and there's many that can't, you probably don't belong here.'

After that, I knew it was only a matter of time. I continued to teach in Main Street, telling those girls what I thought they needed to know about the world, but I stopped getting dinner invitations, and a bunch of the parents took their kids out of the school. In the spring I got a letter from the Mohave County superintendent saying that he didn't think it would be a good idea for me to continue teaching in Main Street come next fall.

I was unemployed again, which really fried my bacon because I'd been acting in the best interests of my students. Fortunately, that summer a teaching job opened up in Peach Springs, a tiny town on a Walapai reservation about sixty-five miles from the ranch. It paid fifty dollars a month, but in addition, the county had set aside ten dollars a month for a part-time janitor, ten dollars a month for a bus driver, and another ten dollars a month for someone to cook lunch for the kids. I said I'd do everything, which meant eighty dollars a month, and we'd be able to sock away almost all of it.

The old school bus had died, so the county had also budgeted money to buy another one — or at least some form of transportation — and after scouting around, I found the perfect vehicle at a used-car lot in Kingman: a terrifically elegant dark blue hearse. Since it had only front seats, you could jam a whole passel of kids in the back. I took some silver paint and, in big block letters, wrote SCHOOL BUS on both sides.

Despite my fancy silver sign, people in those parts, including my husband, were pretty literal-minded, and they all kept calling it the hearse.

'It's not a hearse,' I told Jim. 'It's a school bus.'

'Painting the word 'dog' on the side of a pig

don't make the pig a dog,' he said.

He had a point, and after a while I started calling it the hearse, too.

★ ★ ★

I'd get up around four in the morning and cover upward of two hundred miles a day between traveling to and from Peach Springs and picking up and dropping off the kids at the different stops all over the district. I'd teach the whole bunch by myself, take them all home, return to the school and do the janitoring, then head back to the ranch. I farmed out the cooking at five dollars a week to our neighbor Mrs. Hutter, who made pots of stew that I took to the school. Those were some long days, but I loved the work, and the money started piling up pretty quickly.

Rosemary was seven by then and Little Jim was five, so I took them with me in the morning, and they became part of the class. Rosemary hated being taught by her mother, particularly because I sometimes gave her paddlings in front of other students to set an example and show I wasn't playing favorites. Little Jim had also become a handful, and he got his share of paddlings as well, though a spanking never kept either of those rascals out of mischief for long.

I had to make two trips to collect all the kids, and I left Rosemary, Little Jim, and the kids from the town of Yampi at the school while I made my usual second run to pick up the kids from Pica. One morning when I got back to the school, Little Jim was lying on his back on my desk, stone-cold unconscious. The other kids explained that he'd fallen out of the swing, trying to make it all the way to heaven like the little ghost boy.

I was in a bind. I needed to take Little Jim to the hospital, but the nearest one was in Kingman, thirty-five miles away, and I couldn't leave the kids unsupervised for that long. I packed as many of them as I possibly could into the hearse and had the rest stand on the sideboards, hanging on through the open windows. With Rosemary holding limp Little Jim in her lap beside me, I set out to take all the kids home, going to Yampi and then Pica — the kids on the sideboards having the time of their lives, hooting and hollering, treating it like a carnival ride — before heading for Kingman.

We were barreling down Route 66 when Little Jim suddenly sat up. 'Where am I?' he asked.

Rosemary, thinking this was hilarious, burst into laughter, but I was furious. I wanted to take Little Jim to the hospital anyway, but he insisted he was fine and even stood up on the car seat and started dancing around to prove it, which got me even more furious. I'd done all that driving around for nothing, canceling class for no good reason, and I was worried I'd be docked a day's pay.

'We're just going to go round up all those kids a second time,' I said.

'But they've already gone home,' Rosemary said. 'They'll be out playing and won't want to come back.'

'I've told you before, life's not about doing what you want.'

Rosemary looked a little pouty. Then she started saying she didn't feel so well, she was dizzy and needed to go home.

'Oh, so you're the sick one now?' I said.

'That's right, Mommy.'

'Well, I'm going to take you to the hospital, then,' I said.

'I just want to go home.'

'Not another word,' I said. 'If you're sick, you don't need pampering, you need treatment.' Whenever she tried to protest, I repeated myself.

I drove straight to the Kingman hospital. After a talk with one of the nurses about a daughter who wanted to play hooky, I arranged for Rosemary to spend the night in a room by herself where she could ponder truth and consequences. If I was going to be docked a day's pay, someone, at the very least, was going to learn a lesson from the experience.

★　★　★

'Feeling better?' I asked Rosemary when I picked her up the next day.

'Yep,' she said.

And we both left it at that. But the kid never tried to play hooky again.

One Saturday morning that fall, when I went out into the yard, I looked over at the hearse parked next to the barn. It was just sitting there, and that struck me as a real waste. Unlike a horse, a car didn't need a day off every now and then. If I could put the hearse to work for me on the weekends, it would — after gas — be pure profit. I decided to start up a taxi service.

On the side of the hearse, under SCHOOL BUS, I used the same silver paint to add AND TAXI. Jim came up with the idea of strapping some old buggy seats in the back when we had paying passengers.

There weren't exactly a lot of people standing by the road trying to hail taxis in that part of Arizona, but there were folks without cars who from time to time needed to get to the courthouse in Kingman or be picked up at the train depot in Flagstaff, and they'd hire me. They'd leave word in advance with Deputy Johnson in Seligman, and every day or two I'd stop by his office to see if I had any customers.

Most of the money went into our savings, but I kept some aside for the occasional flying lesson.

★ ★ ★

I was an excellent driver. I didn't particularly like city driving, with all the stoplights and street

237

signs and traffic cops, but out in the country I was in my element. I knew the shortcuts and the back roads and had no hesitation heading out cross-country, barreling through the sagebrush and startling the roadrunners out of the undergrowth.

If we got stuck in a ditch while I was ferrying around the schoolkids, I had them get out and push while we all chanted Hail Marys. 'Push and pray!' I'd holler while gripping the steering wheel and gunning the engine, sand and rocks spraying behind the spinning tires as the car fish-tailed its way out of the ditch. My paying passengers were also expected to help push if we got stuck. I didn't make them say Hail Marys, but I used the same line: 'Push and pray!'

When Jim heard it, he said, 'Probably should paint that on the hearse, too.'

★   ★   ★

One weekend that December, three ladies from Brooklyn were staying with our neighbor Mrs. Hutter, the woman who cooked the stews for the school and who was their cousin, and they hired me to take them all up to see the Grand Canyon. I stored a picnic lunch in the hearse and brought Rosemary along with me.

I expected these Brooklyn gals to be tough and smart, and maybe even practicing socialists, but instead they were all ninnies who wore too much makeup and kept complaining about the Arizona heat, the hearse's uncomfortable buggy seats, and the fact that there was no place in the entire state to get a good egg cream. They had these thick Brooklyn accents, and I had to fight the temptation to correct their atrocious pronunciation.

While I tried to keep up a positive line of chatter, pointing out that the town of Jerome was named after Winston Churchill's mother's family, they kept saying things like 'But whatta youse people *do* out here?' and 'How do youse *live* wit-out electricity?'

They also kept going on about Christmas in New York, about the tree in Rockefeller Center, the window displays at Macy's, the gifts, the lights, the kids lining up to talk to the red-suited Santas.

'What's Santa Claus gonna bring youse dis year?' one of the ladies asked Rosemary.

'Who's Santa Claus?' she asked.

'Youse never heard of Santa Claus?' The woman sounded bewildered.

'We don't pay much heed to that sort of thing around here,' I said.

'Well, dat's a crying shame.'

'So, who's Santa Claus?' Rosemary asked again.

'Saint Nicholas,' I said. 'The patron saint of department stores.'

Near Picacho Butte, I noticed that the emergency brake had been on the entire time, and without saying anything, I reached down and quietly released it. Just then we came to a long downward slope at the edge of the plateau. The hearse began picking up speed, and when I pressed down on the brake pedal, it went all the way to the floor with no resistance. We had no brakes.

I started swerving the car on and off the road, hoping the sand and loose gravel on the shoulder would slow us down. The Brooklyn women got all overwrought, telling me to slow down, asking me what was happening and demanding that I let them out. 'Stop duh car!'

'Now, calm yourselves, girls,' I said. 'We just got us a little runaway taxi, but everything's under control. I'll get us out of this.'

I looked over at Rosemary, who was staring at me wide-eyed, and gave her a big wink to show her just how much fun we were having. The little creature grinned. She was positively fearless, unlike those honking lace-panties in the back.

But the swerving hadn't slowed the car, and I realized the situation called for more drastic measures. We reached a stretch of the road that was cut into the side of the mountain. On our side it sloped down, and on the far side it rose upward.

'Ready for some hijinks?' I shouted.

'I am,' Rosemary said, but the Brooklyn ladies continued to wail.

'Hang tight!' I shouted.

I cut the car across the road and angled up the hillside, bouncing over holes and rocks, but the slope was steep, and while we started losing momentum, we also started tipping sideways, and then the car rolled once, landing upside down, exactly like I'd planned.

We got knocked around a bit, but no one was seriously hurt, and we all scrambled out through the open windows. The Brooklyn ladies were in a tizzy, cussing my driving and threatening to sue or have me arrested and my license revoked. 'Youse almost got us kilt!'

'All that's happened to you is that you've had the lace knocked off your panties,' I said. 'Instead of carrying on, you should be thanking me, because my driving skills just saved all your necks. You ride, you got to know how to fall, and you drive, you got to know how to crash.'

Those Brooklyn broads were a bunch of sissies, but they got me thinking about Christmas. For the most part, pioneers and ranchers didn't have the time or money for gift giving and tree trimming, and they tended to treat Christmas like Prohibition, another eastern aberration that wasn't of much concern to them. A couple of years back, when some missionaries were trying to dazzle the Navajos into converting, they had a gift-bearing Santa Claus jump out of a plane, but his parachute didn't open, and he landed with a thud in front of the Indians, convincing them — and most of the rest of us — that the less we had to do with jolly old Saint Nick, the better off we'd be.

Still, I got to wondering if maybe I was depriving my kids of a special experience, and that week I bought some of those fancy new electric Christmas lights in Kingman and a couple of small toys from the Commercial Central, the general store in Seligman.

On Christmas morning I had Jim secretly climb up on the roof and start shaking a string of old carriage bells while I explained to the kids that it was Saint Nick and his flying reindeer visiting all the children in the world, bringing them toys that he and his elves in the North Pole had spent the year making. Rosemary's expression went from bewildered to doubtful, then she started shaking her head and grinning. 'What are you talking about, Mom?' she asked. 'Any dummy knows deer can't fly.'

'The deer are magic, for crying out loud,' I said. I explained that Santa Claus himself was magic, and that was how he was able to visit every child in the world, leaving them all gifts in socks, in the course of one evening. Then I held up two socks and passed them over to Rosemary and Little Jim.

Rosemary pulled out an orange, some hazelnuts, a roll of LifeSavers, and a small packet with a set of jacks inside. 'These aren't from the North Pole,' she said as she examined the jacks. 'These are from the Commercial Central. I saw them there.'

I walked over to the window and stuck my head out. 'Come on down, Jim,' I hollered. 'They're not buying it.'

* * *

Even though I couldn't sell the kids on Santa Claus, they were beside themselves with excitement about the Christmas lights. We all drove up into the hills and cut down a short pine that the kids picked out. Jim dug a hole in the front yard and we set it in that, tamping down the dirt and stringing the lights around its branches. All afternoon Rosemary and Little Jim danced around the tree and shouted at the sun to hurry up and set.

Once it grew dark, we called the cowboys out from the bunkhouse, and Jim pulled the hearse

243

up next to the tree. He opened the hood, attached a cable to the battery, and as we all stood in a circle around the tree, he raised the cable and the light cord above his head, and with a flourish, brought them together. The tree burst into color and we all gasped at the red, yellow, green, white, and blue lights boldly glowing in the cold night, the only lights for miles around in the immense darkness of the range.

'It's magic!' Rosemary shrieked.

A number of the ranch hands had never seen electric lights, and a few of them took off their hats and held them over their hearts.

And those Brooklyn broads thought we didn't know how to celebrate Christmas in style.

In my second year at Peach Springs, I had twenty-five students in my one-room schoolhouse. Six of them — almost a quarter of the class — were the children of Deputy Johnson, a rawboned chain-smoker who wore an old fedora and had a droopy mustache. For the most part, I liked Deputy Johnson. He turned a blind eye to minor infractions and tended to give folks the benefit of the doubt as long as they acknowledged that he was the law, deciding what was right and wrong. But he could come down on you hard if you took issue with him. He had a total of thirteen children and, their daddy being one of the county lawmen, they did pretty much as they pleased, letting air out of people's tires, throwing cherry bombs down outhouse holes, and leaving the babysitter tied to a tree all night.

One of the deputy's sons was Johnny Johnson, who was a couple of years older than Rosemary. He'd been a handful ever since I started teaching at Peach Springs. Maybe it was because he had older brothers who sat around telling dirty stories about girls, but Johnny couldn't keep his hands off them — a regular tomcat in the making. He had kissed Rosemary on the mouth, something I learned a few days later from one of the other students. Rosemary said it was just a yucky thing that had happened, nothing she wanted anyone to get in any trouble over.

Johnny, for his part, called Rosemary and the other student lying finks and said I couldn't prove anything.

It wasn't worth holding a court of inquisition over, but I was still simmering about the matter a couple of weeks later when, one day during class, the little punk reached over and stuck his hand up the dress of a sweet Mexican girl named Rosita. That boy needed to be taught to keep his grimy hands to himself, so I put my book down, walked up to him, and slapped him hard in the face. He looked at me, bug-eyed with shock, and then he reached up and slapped me in the face.

For a second I was speechless. A smile started creeping across Johnny's face. The little squirt thought he had the best of me. It was then that I hauled him up and threw him against the wall, backhanding him again and again, and when he cowered down in a ball on the floor, I grabbed my ruler and started whaling his butt.

'You'll be sorry!' he kept screaming. 'You'll be sorry!'

I didn't care. Johnny Johnson needed to learn a lesson he'd never forget, and you couldn't spell it out on the blackboard, you had to beat it into him. Also, he was clearly in danger of becoming a crumb-bum heel like my first husband and the producer who seduced Helen, and he needed to realize there could be consequences for mistreating girls. So I kept whaling on him, maybe even beyond the call of duty, and truth be told, I got more than a little satisfaction from it.

Just as I expected, Deputy Johnson showed up at school the next day.

'I'm not here to have a conversation,' he said. 'I'm here to tell you to keep your hands off my boy. Got it?'

'You deputies may think you run Yavapai County, but I run my classroom,' I said, 'and I'll discipline wayward kids as I see fit. Got it?'

* * *

When Jim came home that night, I told him what had happened.

'This is getting almost predictable,' he said.

'What are you talking about?' I said.

'These showdowns. It's becoming a pattern.'

'It would be either a pattern of me standing up for myself or a pattern of me getting pushed around.'

* * *

Deputy Johnson couldn't get me fired outright, since they'd have trouble replacing me in the middle of the school year, but a few months later, I received another one of those blasted letters saying my contract was not going to be renewed. At this point I'd practically lost count of the number of times I'd been fired, and I was

247

getting pretty sick of it.

The day the letter arrived, I sat at the kitchen table thinking about my situation. If I had it all to do over again, I'd have done the same thing. I wasn't in the wrong. The rules were. I was a darned good teacher and had been doing what was necessary, not only for Rosita but also for Johnny Johnson, who needed to be reined in before he wound up in serious trouble. Even so, I'd been booted once again, and there was nothing I could do about it.

As I sat there brooding about all this, Rosemary walked into the kitchen, and when she saw me, a look of alarm swept her face. She started stroking my arm. 'Don't cry, Mom,' she said. 'Stop it. Please stop it.'

It was only then that I realized tears were running down my cheeks. I remembered how disturbed I'd been as a little girl, watching my mother cry. Now, by letting my own daughter see me all weak and pitiful, I felt that I'd failed her in a big way, and I was furious with myself.

'I'm not crying,' I said. 'I just got dust in my eyes.' I pushed her hand away. 'Because I'm not weak. You'll never have to worry about that. Your mother is not a weak woman.'

And with that I headed out to the woodpile and went on a tear splitting logs, setting each one up on the chopping block and using every ounce of strength I had to bring the ax down on it, sending the split pieces of white wood flying apart while Rosemary stood watching. It was almost as satisfying as whaling Johnny Johnson.

Deputy Johnson made sure everybody knew I'd been let go, and he also made no secret as to who was behind it. When I ran into people at the Commercial Central, they figured they couldn't ask me how things were going at school, the way they usually did, and there were the awkward silences that everyone who's been given the boot knows all too well.

But I was bound and determined to show folks that Deputy Johnson hadn't broken my spirit, and I was looking for a way to do that when it was announced that a special premiere of *Gone with the Wind* would be held in Kingman. I decided to attend, in the fanciest dress this county had ever seen.

Gone with the Wind was by far and away my favorite book — after the Bible — and I thought it had about as many lessons in it. I'd read it when it first came out, then I'd sat down and read it again. I'd also read most of it aloud to Rosemary. Scarlett O'Hara was my kind of gal. She was tough, she was sassy, she knew what she wanted, and she never let anything or anyone get in her way.

Like most people in the country, I'd been looking forward to the movie for years. It was the most expensive movie ever made — shot entirely in Technicolor — and magazines and newspapers had been following all the details of the casting and production. Now that it was finally finished, the studio was holding premieres around the country, including the one in Kingman, and charging five dollars for a ticket — an astronomical amount compared to the nickel that a ticket usually cost.

Women were expected to wear gowns and men to wear tuxedos, or at least their Sunday best, to the premiere. Since I'd never owned a gown and wasn't about to splurge on one — the ticket being enough of an extravagance — I decided that I'd take my inspiration from Scarlett herself: I'd fashion my own gown using the living room curtains. The way I saw it, having curtains in the bedrooms made sense, but you didn't really need them in the living room. Those red velvet curtains I'd bought with the S&H green stamps were just hanging there in the living room at Hackberry, gathering dust and starting to fade from the Arizona sun. And red was my favorite color.

My gown wasn't going to be the sort of fitted, wasp-waisted getup that Scarlett had to be laced into. It would be floor-length but simple and free-flowing, more Grecian than antebellum. I borrowed a sewing machine from my neighbor Mrs. Hutter, who was an accomplished seamstress. She helped me design the pattern and assisted in the fittings, but I did all the actual sewing. For a belt, I used the curtain sash.

I didn't have a full-length mirror, but I could tell when I finished it and put it on for the first time that the gown was, quite frankly, a masterpiece.

'You look like a movie star,' Rosemary said.

'That's a lot of dress,' Jim said. 'They'll sure see you coming.'

★   ★   ★

Jim refused to go to the premiere with me. He had no use for movies. We'd been to a few westerns, and he'd actually walked out of a couple of them, completely disgusted by what he considered the phony depiction of cowboy life — the way movie cowboys sat by the campfire singing after a supposedly rough day on the trail, the way they hung around the corral doing rope tricks instead of mending fences, the way they wore clean white hats and fringy vests and fluffy sheepskin chaps, and most of all, the way they jumped from rooftops onto their horses.

'That's not the way it is at all,' Jim said.

''Course it's not,' I told him. 'Who would pay good money to see an actual smelly cowboy? You go to movies to escape from the way things really are.'

'I guess gangsters complain about gangster movies, too,' he said.

★   ★   ★

But Jim agreed to be my *Gone with the Wind* chauffeur, and the night of the premiere, he drove me in the hearse — a little dented after the crash with the Brooklyn broads — into Kingman. When we pulled up to the theater, spectators were milling around on the sidewalk, watching everyone arrive in their finery. Deputy Johnson stood out front in his uniform, directing traffic. Jim got out and opened the hearse door for me, and I stepped onto the red carpet, waving grandly to the crowd — and to Deputy Johnson — as the photographer's flashbulb popped.

VII

THE GARDEN OF EDEN

Rosemary and Little Jim on Old Buck

I told Rosemary and Little Jim that I didn't want them making friends with the other schoolkids, because if they did, those kids would expect special treatment from me. Even if they didn't, the other students might believe they had if they got good grades. 'I have to be like Caesar's wife,' I told Rosemary and Little Jim. 'I have to be above suspicion.'

We were also pretty isolated on the ranch, there being no other kids within walking distance, but Rosemary and Little Jim got along fine by themselves. In fact, those two little scamps were each other's best friend. After morning chores, if there was no school, they were free to do whatever they wanted. They loved to rummage around in all the outbuildings. Once they found a couple of old whalebone corsets in a trunk in the garage and wore them around for weeks. They also hiked out to the Indian graveyard, collected arrowheads, swam in the dam and the horse troughs, threw their pocketknives at targets, and worked in the blacksmith shop, heating up pieces of metal and, on one occasion, fashioning something they called the Wagon Wheel Express: two wagon wheels with an axle and a central iron tongue that they'd welded to the axle and that dragged behind the wheels. They'd pull the Wagon Wheel Express to the top of hills and then sit on the tongue as the contraption barreled down.

What they loved most of all was riding. Both of them had been on horseback since before they could walk and rode as naturally as any Indian kids. The Poms, in gratitude to Jim for his success with the ranch, had sent Rosemary and Little Jim a Shetland pony. It was the meanest creature on the whole place, always wanting to unhorse whoever was on him, but Rosemary had great fun trying to hang on as the Shetland bucked away or veered under a low-hanging branch, hoping to knock her off.

Most days she and Little Jim saddled up Socks and Blaze, two chestnut quarter horses, and set out into the range. One of their favorites pastimes was racing the train. A set of tracks for the Santa Fe Railroad cut across the ranch, and every afternoon they'd wait for the two-fifteen. When it came chugging up, they'd gallop alongside it, the passengers leaning out and waving and the engineer sounding the whistle until the train inevitably pulled ahead.

It was a race they never minded losing, and they'd return hot and sweaty, with the horses all lathered up.

★ ★ ★

The kids took their share of knocks. They were always falling out of trees and off roofs and horses, getting scraped and bruised, but Jim and I never put up with any tears. 'Tough it out,' we'd always tell them. They rolled boulders down hills at each other. They ate horse feed and

256

pissants on dares. They fired at each other with slingshots and BB guns. Cattle charged them and horses stepped on their toes. Once when Rosemary and Little Jim were playing in the pond, he stepped into a sinkhole and was sucked underwater. Big Jim, who was working on the dam, dove in without taking off his boots. He kept plunging down to the pond floor, feeling around for Little Jim, and finally found one of his arms sticking up through the muck. He pulled Little Jim's limp body to the side and, with Rosemary kneeling beside him, kept squeezing on Jim's chest until the muddy water upgushed out of his mouth and he started gasping for air.

★   ★   ★

One day in the middle of the summer when Rosemary turned eight, she and I were driving off-road across the Colorado Plateau in the pickup, bringing supplies out to Jim and some of the hands who were riding the northern fence line, checking for breaks. Since it had rained a few days earlier, a mudflat we had to cross was soggier than I'd expected, and darned if we didn't get stuck. We tried pushing but couldn't budge her. I didn't relish the five-hour walk in the hot sun back to the ranch house, and as I leaned against the hood, trying to figure my options, I noticed a herd of wild horses grazing in a copse of cottonwoods about a quarter mile off.

'Rosemary, we're going to catch us a horse,' I said.

'How, Mom? We don't even have a rope.'

'Just you watch.'

In the back of the pickup was a sack of feed for the ranch hands' horses and a bucket with some rusting fence nails in it. I emptied the nails onto the flatbed and poured some feed into the bucket, dumping the rest next to the nails. Then I cut the empty feed bag into strips with my pocketknife, tied them together, and made a small loop with one end. I had me a hackamore.

I gave the bucket to Rosemary, and we set out toward the horses. There were six of them, and as we drew near, they all raised their heads and looked at us warily, trying to decide if it was time to bolt. They were scruffy little buggers, with chipped hooves, long bedraggled manes, and bite marks on their rumps, but a lot of the horses on the range had been ridden at one point in their lives and, with the right coaxing, could be brought back around.

I had Rosemary rattle the grain in the bucket, and when one of the horses, a red mare with black legs, pricked her ears forward at the sound, I knew I had a candidate. I reminded Rosemary of my dad's old rule about keeping your eyes to the ground so the horse wouldn't think you were a predator. Instead of approaching the mare directly, we circled around her, Rosemary rattling the bucket constantly. When we got close, the other horses moved off, but the mare stayed where she was, watching. We turned our backs to her. There was no way we could catch her by chasing her, but I knew if we could get her to approach us, we'd won.

The mare took a step toward us and we took a step away, which encouraged her to take another step. After several minutes of this, she drew close enough to touch, and I had Rosemary hold out the bucket, letting the horse feed a little, then I slipped the hackamore around her neck. She looked up, startled, and pulled her head back, but then she understood we had her, and instead of fighting it, she went back to the grain.

I let her finish, then had Rosemary give me a leg up and hoisted her aboard behind me.

'Mom, I can't believe we caught a wild horse without even a rope,' she said.

'Once they've tasted grain, they never forget it.'

★ ★ ★

Rosemary loved the idea that this wild animal had come up to her so willingly. Once we got back to the ranch, I told her to let the horse go, and she opened the gate, but the horse just stood there. She and Rosemary were both looking at each other, all daffy-eyed.

'I want to keep her,' Rosemary said.

'I thought you wanted all these animals to run free.'

'I want them to do what they want to do,' she said. 'This one wants to stay with me.'

'The last thing we need around here is another half-broke horse,' I said. 'Smack her on the rump and send her off. She belongs on the range.'

As much fun as ranch life was for the kids, I felt they needed more civilizing than it could provide. Jim and I decided to send them both to boarding school. While they were away, I was going to finally earn that darned diploma, get a permanent teaching job, and join the union, so beetleheads like Uncle Eli and Deputy Johnson couldn't have me fired just because they didn't like my style.

Since the hearse was pretty dinged up after the rollover — and because Little Jim had branded the seats with the dashboard lighter — the county let us buy it for a song. We packed it up and I drove the kids south, first dropping Little Jim, who was eight, at a boys' school in Flagstaff, then Rosemary, who was nine, at a Catholic girls' school in Prescott. I sat in the car watching a nun lead her by the hand into the dormitory. At the doorway, Rosemary turned around to look at me, her cheeks wet with tears. 'Now, you be strong,' I called out to her. I had loved my time at the Sisters of Loretto when I was a girl, and I was sure that as soon as Rosemary got over her homesickness, she'd be fine. 'Some kids would kill for this opportunity!' I yelled. 'Consider yourself lucky!'

When I got to Phoenix, I found a bare-bones boardinghouse and registered for a double load of courses. I figured that if I spent eighteen hours a day going to class and studying, I could get my degree in two years. I loved my time at the university and felt happier than I thought I had a right to be. Some of the other students were astonished at my workload, but I felt like a lady of leisure. Instead of doing ranch chores, tending sick cattle, hauling schoolkids far and wide, mopping the school floor, and coping with belligerent parents, I was learning about the world and improving my mind. I had no obligations to anyone but myself, and everything in my life was under my control.

★ ★ ★

Rosemary and Little Jim didn't share my enthusiasm for academic life. In fact, they hated it. Little Jim kept running away, climbing over fences and through windows, pulling out nails when the windows were nailed shut, and using tied-together bedsheets to shimmy down from upper floors. He was such a resourceful escape artist that the Jesuit brothers started calling him Little Houdini.

But the Jesuits were used to dealing with untamed ranch boys, and they regarded Little Jim as one more rambunctious rapscallion. Rosemary's teachers, however, saw her as a misfit. Most of the girls at the academy were demure, frail things, but Rosemary played with her pocketknife, yodeled in the choir, peed in the yard, and caught scorpions in a jar she kept under her bed. She loved to leap down the school's main staircase and once took it in two bounds only to come crashing into the Mother Superior. She was behaving more or less the way she did on the ranch, but what seemed normal in one situation can seem outright peculiar in another, and the nuns saw Rosemary as a wild child.

Rosemary kept writing me sad little letters about her life. She liked learning to dance and play the piano but found embroidery and etiquette excruciating, and the nuns were always telling her that everything she did was wrong. She sang too loudly, she danced too enthusiastically, she spoke out of turn, she drew whimsical pictures in the margins of her books.

The nuns also complained that she made inappropriate comments, though sometimes she was simply repeating things I'd told her. Once, when she was wondering about the boy who'd died trying to swing to heaven, I'd said maybe it was for the best because he might have grown up to be a mass murderer, but when she said the same thing to a classmate whose brother had died, the nuns sent her to bed without dinner. Other classmates picked on her. They called her 'yokel,' 'bumpkin,' and 'farmer's daughter,' and when Jim donated fifty pounds of beef jerky to the school, they dismissed it as 'cowboy meat' and refused to eat it, so the nuns threw it away.

Rosemary did stand up for herself. One night, she wrote, when she was doing the dishes, a classmate started teasing her about her father, saying, 'Your dad thinks he's John Wayne.'

'My dad makes John Wayne look like a pussy,' Rosemary replied, and dunked the girl's head in the dishwater.

Good for her, I thought when I read the letter. Maybe she's got a bit of her mother in her after all.

In her letters, Rosemary said she missed the ranch. She missed the horses and cattle, missed the ponds and the range, missed her brother and her mom and dad, missed the stars and fresh air and the sound of the coyotes at night. The Japanese had bombed Pearl Harbor in December, and everyone at the school — both the students and the nuns — lived in fear. One girl in Rosemary's class had a brother on the battleship *Arizona*, and when she heard it had been sunk, she fell to the floor sobbing. The nuns kept blankets over the windows at night as part of the blackout — people were fearing that Japanese bombers were going to fill the skies over Arizona — and Rosemary said she felt like she couldn't breathe.

Be strong, was all I could think to say when I wrote her back. Be strong.

I also corrected the grammar in her letters and returned them to her. I wouldn't have been doing that girl any favors to let those sorts of errors go unchecked.

*   *   *

Near the end of Rosemary's first year at the academy, I received a letter from the Mother Superior saying that she thought it would be best if Rosemary didn't return for a second year. Her grades were poor and her behavior was disruptive. I had Rosemary tested that summer, and as I suspected, she was plenty bright. In fact, except for math, she tested in the top five percentile. All she needed to do was knuckle down and get focused. I wrote the Mother Superior, assuring her of Rosemary's intelligence and pleading for another chance. The Mother Superior reluctantly agreed, but Rosemary's grades and rowdiness got even worse her second year, and when it was over, the Mother Superior's decision was final. Rosemary and the school were not a good fit.

Little Jim hadn't done much better. I'd earned my college degree by then, and I took both Rosemary and Little Jim with me back to the ranch. The kids were so happy to be home that they ran around hugging everything — cowboys, horses, trees — and then they saddled up Blaze and Socks and headed out to open country, quirting their horses into a gallop and whooping like bandits.

Now that I had my college degree, I was in demand as a teacher and got a job in Big Sandy, another little town with a one-room school, where I enrolled both Rosemary and Little Jim. Rosemary was delighted not to be returning to the academy. 'When I grow up,' she told me, 'all I want to do is to live on the ranch and be an artist. That's my dream.'

The war was well under way by then, in both the Pacific and Europe, but aside from the shortage of gasoline, it had little impact on our life on the Colorado Plateau. The sun still rose over the Mogollon Rim, the grazing cattle still wandered the range, and while I prayed for the families who put gold stars in their windows because they'd lost sons in the fighting, truth be told, we still worried more about the rains than the Nips and the Nazis.

I did plant a victory garden, mostly to be patriotic, since we had all the beef and eggs we could eat. But a green thumb was not among my talents, and between my teaching and ranch work, I never got around to watering the garden much. By midsummer, those tomatoes and melons had withered on the vine.

'Don't fret about it, honey,' Jim said. 'We're ranchers, not farmers.'

My mother had died back when I was studying in Phoenix. It was blood poisoning that got her, from her bad teeth, and it came on so quick that I didn't have a chance to make it back to the KC before she passed.

During the summer after my first year at Big Sandy, I received a telegram from my dad. After Mom had died, Buster and Dorothy had put Dad in an old folks' home in Tucson, since he needed nursing and I was too busy studying to help out with his care. But now, Dad said, he was fading fast and he wanted to be with his family. 'You've always been my best hand,' he wrote. 'Please come get me.'

It would be a long trip. The government had been rationing gasoline, and we didn't have enough coupons to go the entire distance. But there was no way I was going to let my father die alone in a strange city.

'What are you going to do for fuel?' Jim asked.

'Beg, borrow, or steal,' I said.

★　★　★

I traded slabs of beef for coupons with a few of the people I knew in Kingman and added those to what we'd been issued by the government. We were still short, but I set out in the hearse anyway. I brought along a gas can, a length of hose, and Rosemary, figuring they'd all be useful.

It was the height of summer, a scorching Arizona day that made the roof of the hearse too hot to touch. We headed south, the road wavering in the distance. Rosemary was unusually quiet, staring out the window.

'What's the matter?' I asked.

'I'm sad for Grandpa.'

'If you get down, all you need to do is act like you're feeling good, and next thing you know, you are,' I told her and launched into my favorite song, 'Doodle-dee-doo-rah, doodle-dee-doo-ray.'

Rosemary had her moods, but they never lasted long, and soon enough we were both belting out the tunes — 'Deep in the Heart of Texas,' 'Drifting Texas Sands,' 'San Antonio Rose,' 'Beautiful, Beautiful Texas.'

We always stopped to pick up hitchhiking soldiers — and made them sing along — but none of them ever had gas coupons, and by the time we reached Tempe, the gas gauge was pushing empty. I pulled into a truck stop and parked next to a couple of long-haul rigs. Then, taking Rosemary by one hand and holding the gas can with the other, I went into the diner.

The customers were mostly men wearing sweat-stained cowboy hats, sitting at the counter drinking coffee and smoking cigarettes. A few of them looked up as I walked in.

I took a deep breath. 'Could I have y'all's attention, please?' I said loudly. 'My little girl and I are trying to get down to Tucson to pick up my dying dad. But we're running shy of gas, and if a few of you fellows would be kind enough to pitch in with a gallon — or just a half gallon — we could make it to the next leg of our journey.'

There was a moment of silence as each man

glanced around at the others, waiting to see how the rest of them would respond, and then one nodded, and so did a couple more, and suddenly, it became the right thing for all of them to do.

'Sure enough, ma'am,' one said.

'Happy to oblige a damsel in distress,' another said.

'And if you do run out of gas, old Slim here will push you.'

By then they were all chuckling and getting up from their stools, practically falling over one another for the chance to do a good deed. In the parking lot, the men all siphoned off a gallon or so from their own vehicles, and soon enough we had ourselves almost two-thirds of a tank. I gave each of the men a hug and a kiss, and as we were pulling out, I looked at Rosemary.

'We did it, kid,' I said. I was grinning, feeling like the cat that drank the cream. 'Whoever said I couldn't play the lady?'

We had to stop once more to ask for gas. We had a little problem when a smirker said sure, he'd let me siphon off a gallon if I sucked his hose, but I backhanded him and we went on to the next truck stop, trusting that most of the men we asked for help would turn out to be gentlemen, and they were.

We made it to Tucson the next day. The old folks' home where Dad was staying was really just a ramshackle boardinghouse run by a woman with a few rooms to spare. 'Ain't been able to make out a word of your pa's since he got here,' she said as she led us down the hall to his room.

Dad was lying on his back in the middle of the bed, the sheet up to his chin. We'd visited him and Mom in New Mexico a couple of times, but I hadn't seen him in several years, and he didn't look so good. He was thin, with jaundiced skin, and his eyes had sunk deep into their sockets. He spoke in a croak, but I could understand him as well as I always had.

'I've come to take you home,' I said.

'Won't make it,' he said. 'I'm too sick to move.'

I sat down next to him on the bed. Rosemary sat beside me and took his hand. I was proud to see that she was completely undaunted by the old man's state. She'd been sad about her

269

grandpa on the drive down, but now that she was here, she'd risen to the occasion. Regardless of what those nuns thought, the kid had a brain, a spine, and a heart.

'Looks like I'm going to die here,' Dad said, 'but I don't want to be buried here. Promise me you'll take my body back to the KC.'

'I promise.'

Dad smiled. 'I could always count on you.'

He died that night. It was almost as if he had been holding on until I got there, and when he knew he would be buried back on the ranch, he could stop worrying and just let go.

★ ★ ★

The next morning some of the other men in the boardinghouse helped us carry Dad's body out to the hearse and put it in the back. I rolled down all the windows before we left. We'd need plenty of fresh air. In the middle of Tucson, we stopped at a streetlight, and two kids standing on a street corner started yelling, 'Hey, that lady's got a dead man in the back!'

I couldn't get mad, since what they were saying was true, so I just waved and hit the gas as soon as the light turned. Rosemary, however, sank down below her window. 'Life's too short, honey,' I said, 'to worry what other people think of you.'

In no time we were out of Tucson and flying through the desert, heading east into the morning sun. I was driving faster than I'd ever driven before — cars going the other way flashed past — since I wanted to make sure we got back to the ranch before the body started to turn. I figured if I did get pulled over by any police, they'd cut me some slack once they eyed the cargo.

I had to stop a couple of times to ask for gas. Seeing as how the drivers might notice the body when they came out to siphon me their gas, I varied the pitch. 'Gentlemen,' I said, 'I got my dad's dead body in the back of my car, and I'm trying to get him home to be buried as quick as possible in this heat.'

That sure did startle them — one guy almost choked on his coffee — but they were even more eager to help out than the others had been, and we made it to the ranch before the stench became overpowering.

We buried Dad in the small stone-fenced cemetery where everyone who had ever died on the ranch was buried. At Dad's request, he was laid to rest wearing his hundred-dollar Stetson, the one with the beaded band that had rattlers from two rattlesnakes Dad himself had killed attached to it. Dad had wanted us to use phonetic spelling on his headstone, but we overruled him on that, figuring that folks would think we didn't know how to spell.

Dad's death didn't hollow me out the way Helen's had. After all, everyone had assumed Dad was a goner back when he got kicked in the head as a child. Instead, he had cheated death and, despite his gimp and speech impediment, lived a long life 'doing pretty much what he wanted. He hadn't drawn the best of cards, but he'd played his hand darned well, so what was there to grieve over?

* * *

Dad left the KC Ranch to Buster and the homestead on Salt Draw to me, but going through his papers, which was no small chore, I discovered that he owed thousands of dollars in back taxes on the Texas property. As Rosemary and I set out on the long drive back to Seligman, I considered our choices. Did we sell the land to pay off the taxes? Or did we keep it and pay the taxes by digging into the money we'd saved to buy Hackberry?

We were still stopping to beg for gas, and a couple of times I insisted Rosemary make the pitch. At first she was so embarrassed that she could barely get the words out, but I figured she needed to learn the art of persuasion, and by the end, she was throwing herself into her performances with gusto, relishing the idea that even though she was just twelve years old, she could talk grown-up strangers into doing something for her.

As a reward, I decided to make a detour up to Albuquerque so we could both see the Madonna of the Trail. The statue had been put up several years earlier, and I'd always wanted to have a look at it myself. It stood in a small park, almost twenty feet high, a figure of a pioneer woman in a bonnet and brogans, holding a baby with one hand and a rifle with the other while a small boy clung to her skirts. I thought of myself as the sensible type, not given to a lot of sentimental blubbering — and most statues and paintings struck me as useless clutter — but there was something about the Madonna of the Trail that almost brought tears to my eyes.

'It's kind of ugly,' Rosemary said. 'And the woman's a little scary.'

'Are you kidding?' I said. 'That's art.'

入　入　入

When I returned to the ranch, Jim and I sat down to figure out what we should do about the west Texas land. Jim was of two minds, but for some reason, seeing that statue had made me hell-bent on holding on to the land Dad had homesteaded.

For one thing, land was the best investment. Over the long haul, and provided you treated it with respect, land pretty much always rose in value. And while that west Texas land was definitely parched, they were drilling for oil all over the state — Dad's papers contained some correspondence with Standard Oil — and it might well be sitting on a big field of black gold.

But Dad's west Texas land called to me for a deeper reason. Maybe it was the Irish in me, but everyone in my family, going back to my grandfather — he'd come over from County Cork, where all the land was owned by absentee Poms who took most of what you grew — had always been obsessed with land. Now, for the first time in my life, I had the opportunity to own some outright. There was nothing to compare with standing on a piece of land you owned free and clear. No one could push you off it, no one could take it from you, no one could tell you what to do with it. The soil belonged to you, and so did every rock, every blade of grass, every tree, and all the water and minerals under the land all the way to the center of the earth. And if the world went to hell in a hand-basket — as it seemed to be doing — you could say good-bye to everyone and retreat to your land, hunkering down and living off it. Land belonged to you and yours forever.

'That's one unyielding patch of earth,' Jim

said. He argued that we couldn't raise much of a herd on 160 acres, and paying off those taxes would make a big dent in the fund to buy Hackberry.

'We might not ever be able to buy Hackberry,' I said. 'This is a sure thing. I'm a gambler, but I'm a smart one, and the smart gambler always goes for the sure thing.'

We paid off the taxes and became bona fide Texas land barons. I felt that the Madonna of the Trail would have approved.

We usually took cattle to market in the spring and the fall, but that year the fall roundup was delayed until Christmas because, with the war going on, the military was using the railroad to ship troops and equipment all over the place, and that was the only time the train was available. But that also meant Rosemary, Little Jim, and I could pitch in, which worked out well, because the war had created a shortage of cowboys. We usually had upward of thirty cowboys on a roundup, but that year we had half that many.

Rosemary and Little Jim had both been going on roundups ever since they were old enough to walk, first riding behind me and Jim, then on their own ponies. Even so, Big Jim didn't want them in the thick of the drive, where even the best cowboys could get thrown off their horses and trampled by nervous cattle. So he had Rosemary and Little Jim work as outriders, chasing down strays and stragglers hiding in the draws. I followed the herd in the pickup, carrying the bedrolls and the grub.

It was cold that December, and you could see steam rising off the horses as they cut back and forth, keeping the herd together while it moved across the range. Rosemary was riding old Buck, the buckskin-colored Percheron who was so smart that Rosemary could drop the reins and he'd corner strays on his own, biting them on the butt to drive them back to the herd.

Rosemary loved the roundups except for one thing — she secretly rooted for the cattle. She thought they were kind, wise animals who, in their hearts, knew that you were leading them to their death, which was why their lowing had such a piteous tone. I suspected that from time to time, she'd helped the odd steer escape. One day, well into the drive, Jim noticed a stray sidling up a draw and sent Rosemary after it. We heard old Buck whinnying, but a little later, Rosemary rode back out all innocent-eyed, declaring that she couldn't find the steer.

'Just plain disappeared,' she said, and held up her hands with a shrug. 'It's a mystery.'

Jim shook his head and sent Fidel Hanna, a young Havasupai, into the draw. Soon enough he came trotting out, driving the steer in front of him.

Jim gave Rosemary a hard look. 'What the hell are you doing?' he asked.

'Not her fault, boss,' Fidel Hanna said. 'That steer, he was hiding way up a gulch.'

Jim looked like he didn't completely buy the story, but it got Rosemary off the hook. Fidel glanced at Rosemary, and I saw him give her a sly little wink.

Rosemary had turned thirteen that year, which put her right on the brink of womanhood — girls of my generation sometimes got married at that age — and from that moment on, she was smitten with Fidel Hanna. He was only sixteen or seventeen himself, a tall, good-looking boy with an angular face who was moody and aloof but also sweet. He had a languid way of moving, wore a black hat with a shiny silver concha, and rode like he was part of his horse.

Rosemary by then was quite a looker, with her dark blond hair, wide mouth, and saucy green eyes, but she seemed unaware of it, carrying on instead like a complete tomboy. Her crush on Fidel Hanna left her confused and acting silly. During the day, he'd catch her gazing at him. She'd do things like challenge him to Indian wrestling matches, but she also made drawings of him on his horse and left them under his saddle at night.

The other cowboys noticed and started ribbing Fidel Hanna. I figured I'd have to keep an eye on the situation.

'Watch yourself around these cowboys,' I told Rosemary.

'What do you mean?' Rosemary asked, giving me that same innocent-eyed expression she'd given Jim when she couldn't find the stray.

'You know what I mean.'

★ ★ ★

With demand for beef down because of the war, we rounded up only two thousand head of cattle, not the usual five thousand, and when we put the herd together, we drove it east across the plateau to the loading pens in Williams. Once we got there, I saddled up Diamond, one of our quarter horses, to help with the corralling and the loading. Near the end, two steers ducked out of the chute and headed through an open gate toward the range.

'Go, babies, go!' Rosemary shouted.

I looked sharply at her, and she covered her mouth with her hand, which made me realize she hadn't even known what she was saying. She'd just blurted it out.

Fidel Hanna and I chased down the two runaways and drove them back to the chute, where they were loaded onto the cattle cars with the rest of the herd. I trotted over to where Rosemary was sitting on Buck.

'Didn't you tell me you wanted to live on the ranch when you grew up?' I asked.

Rosemary nodded.

'What in the Sam Hill do you think we do on ranches?'

'Raise cattle.'

'Raise cattle for market, which means sending them off to be slaughtered. If that upsets you — if you're rooting for the cattle to break free — you're not cut out for ranch life.'

* * *

We got back to the ranch and were in the barn unsaddling the horses and cleaning the tack when Rosemary walked up to Jim and me. 'I want to learn to skin a steer,' she said.

'What on earth for?' I asked.

'That's the nastiest job on the ranch,' Jim said. 'Even worse than gelding.'

'Since I'm going to be a rancher, it's something I need to learn,' Rosemary said.

279

'Suppose you're right about that,' Jim said.

At roundup time, when we had a lot of cowboys on hand, we slaughtered a steer at least once a week. A few days later, Jim picked out a healthy-looking three-year-old Hereford. He led it into the meat house, quickly slit its throat, gutted it, sawed the head off, and hooked it, then a couple of the cowboys used the pulley to hoist it up to the cross-pole.

We let the carcass hang for a day, and the following morning we all went back to the meat house for the butchering. Jim used the pedal-driven grinding stone to give the knife a razor-sharp edge, holding it with both hands and moving it back and forth along the spinning stone as sparks shot out.

Rosemary, who was watching silently, looked pale. I knew she thought of cattle as sweet creatures who never harmed anyone, and now she was standing in front of a dead steer her father had killed, steeling herself to cut it apart. When I was growing up, gelding and slaughtering had been part of my life, but since moving to the ranch, we'd had cowboys do the bloody work, and Rosemary had been shielded from it.

But the kid was trying to be brave, and as Jim tied the leather butcher's apron around her waist, she started humming. Jim passed her the knife and guided her hand to the spot on the steer's lower leg where she needed to make the first cut. As she drew the knife down, she started crying silently, but she kept at it, Jim directing her movements, keeping his voice low and steady, cautioning her not to nick the flesh.

Rosemary's hands were soon covered with blood, and she smeared it on her face, trying to wipe away the tears, but she never gave up, and while it took most of the day, they eventually got the hide off and sectioned the meat.

When it was all done, I threw sawdust on the floor while Jim cleaned the tools. Rosemary hung up the leather apron, washed her hands in a bucket, and walked out of the meat house without saying a word. Jim and I looked at each other, but we didn't say anything, either. We both knew that she'd proved she could do it, but she'd also proved that she didn't truly have the heart for it, and none of us ever mentioned it again.

I thought Rosemary might have even lost her appetite for meat, but the girl had a real gift for pushing unpleasantness out of her mind, and that night she tucked into her steak with gusto.

The following summer I received a letter from Clarice Pearl, a senior muckety-muck with the Arizona Department of Education. She wanted to investigate the living conditions of the children of the Havasupai, who lived in a remote stretch of the Grand Canyon. She was bringing a nurse from Indian Affairs to determine if the children met hygiene standards. She asked me to drive the two of them to the canyon and arrange horses and a guide to get us down the long trail to the Havasupai village.

Fidel Hanna, the young Havasupai ranch hand whom Rosemary had a crush on, lived on the reservation when he wasn't staying at the bunkhouse, and I asked him to set things up. He laughed and shook his head when I told him why the superintendent and nurse were making the trip.

'Coming to inspect the savages,' he said. 'My father used to tell the story about how, for centuries, the Havasu men got up in the morning, spent the day hunting and fishing, came home, played with their children, and lay down with their woman at night. They thought life was pretty good, but then the white man came along and said, 'I have a better idea.''

'I get his point,' I said. 'But my father used to sit around pining for the past, too, and I've seen how that kind of thinking just eats away at you.'

282

I drove the hearse into Williams, bringing Rosemary with me, to pick up Miss Pearl and the nurse, Marion Finch, at the depot. Both of them were stout and pucker-mouthed, with short bobby-pinned hair. I recognized the type — disapproving do-gooders. They always had very high standards, and they always let you know that you didn't quite measure up to them.

As we headed north, I tried to entertain my customers with a little Indian lore. 'Pai' meant 'people,' I explained. 'Havasupai' meant 'people of the blue-green water.' There were also the Yavapai, the Sun People, and the Walapai, the Tall Pine People. The Havasupai, who lived in a narrow valley on the banks of the Colorado River, regarded the water as sacred and threw their babies into it when they were a year and a half old.

'Before they've learned fear,' I said.

'That's just the kind of practice we're concerned about,' Miss Finch said.

I glanced over at Rosemary and rolled my eyes. She stifled a smile.

★ ★ ★

After about two hours, we reached Hilltop, a desolate spot out in the sagebrush at the canyon's rim, where the horse trail led down to the village. There was no sign of Fidel Hanna. We all got out of the hearse and stood there listening to the wind, my two customers clearly disgusted with the unreliability of the heathens they'd come to help. All of a sudden a band of young Indians on horseback, half naked and with painted faces, galloped up the trail and circled us, whooping and brandishing spears. Miss Pearl turned white, and Miss Finch gave a shriek and covered her head with her arms.

But by then I'd recognized that the ringleader, under his war paint, was Fidel Hanna.

'Fidel Hanna, what the blazes do you think you're doing?' I hollered.

Fidel pulled up in front of us. 'Don't worry.' He grinned. 'We no scalp'em white ladies. Hair too short!'

He and the other Havasu boys all started laughing, so beside themselves with glee at their success in terrorizing the do-gooders that they almost fell off their horses. Rosemary and I couldn't help chuckling, too, but my customers were outraged.

'You all belong in the reformatory,' Miss Pearl declared.

'No harm done,' I said. 'They're just kids playing cowboys and Indians.'

Fidel pointed at three of his friends, who jumped off their horses and doubled up with others. 'Those are your mounts,' he said to us. Then he held out his hand to Rosemary. 'You can ride with me,' he said. He pulled her up behind him, and before I could say anything, they were galloping down the trail.

★ ★ ★

Miss Pearl, Miss Finch, and I followed at a walk on our horses. The trail to the village was eight miles long, and it took most of the day to travel it. The path wound down the side of the canyon through a series of steep switchbacks, passing walls of limestone and sandstone layered like giant stacks of old papers. Several years earlier, some missionaries had tried to haul an upright piano down to the village so the Havasupai could sing hymns, but it had fallen off the cliff. We passed its smashed remains — black and white keys, twisted rusting wire, and splintered wood — lying among the rocks.

After a few hours, we came to a spot where clear, cold water gushed from an artesian spring, and that was where the stony landscape of the upper canyon gave way to lush greenery. Cottonwood, watercress, and willows lined the trail. The air was cool and moist and still.

Rosemary, Fidel, and his friends were waiting for us by the stream, letting their horses graze, and we all continued on together. The stream, fed by additional springs, gathered in strength and size the farther we went. Eventually, we reached a spot where the stream descended in a series of short falls, then we rode on for a ways before reaching the most breathtaking place I'd seen in my entire life. The creek poured through a gap in a cliff wall and cascaded a hundred feet down to a turquoise pool. The air was filled with mist from the thundering fall. The water's vivid blue-green came from the lime that leached out of the underground springs. The mist in the air had the same lime in it and had covered everything near the fall — trees, bushes, rocks — with a white crystallized crust, creating one big natural sculpture garden.

It was midafternoon by the time we reached the Havasupai village, a collection of wattle huts where the stream flowed into the Colorado River. Around the huts, the stream fed into several pools of the same turquoise water. Naked Havasupai children were splashing in the water. We all dismounted, and Fidel and his friends dove into the biggest pond.

'Mom, can I go swimming, too?' Rosemary asked, so desperate to get in the water that she was hopping from foot to foot.

'You don't have a swimsuit,' I said.

'I could swim in my underwear.'

'Certainly not,' Miss Pearl piped up. 'It was improper enough for you to be riding behind that Indian boy.'

'And it would be unhygienic,' added Miss Finch. 'There's no telling what you'd find in that water.'

* * *

Fidel showed us to the guest hut. It was tight, but there was enough room for the four of us to stretch out on the mat on the dirt floor. Miss Pearl and Miss Finch were tired and wanted to rest, but Rosemary and I still had some gas left, and when Fidel offered to show us the valley, we took him up on it.

He found us all fresh horses, and we set out on a tour. Walls of red Coconino sandstone and

286

pink Kaibab limestone rose steeply on both sides of the river. The narrow strip of bottomland was green and fertile, and we rode past rows of widely planted maize. Once upon a time, Fidel said, the Havasupai had spent the winter hunting game up on the plateau and come down to the valley to farm in the summer. But ever since they lost their traditional hunting grounds to the Anglo settlers, they'd remained holed up down here year-round, in the most remote spot in the entire west, a secret, hidden tribe living life the ancient way while most people on the outside world didn't even know it existed. Fidel pointed out a pair of red rock pillars towering above the cliff wall. Those were the Wigleeva, he told us. They protected the tribe. It was said that any Havasupai who left for good would be turned to stone.

'This place is like heaven,' Rosemary said. 'Even more than the ranch. I could live here forever.'

'Only Havasupai live here,' Fidel said.

'I'd become one,' she said.

'You can't become a Havasupai,' I said. 'You have to be born one.'

'Well,' Fidel said, 'the elders do say Anglos can't marry into the tribe, but as far as I know, none ever really tried to. So maybe you could be the first.'

★ ★ ★

As evening came on, the Havasupai offered us fried cornmeal cakes wrapped in leaves, but Miss

Finch and Miss Pearl would have none of them, so we ate the biscuits and jerky I had packed.

The next day Miss Finch gave medical exams to the Havasupai children while Miss Pearl discussed their education with their parents, sometimes using Fidel as the interpreter. The village had a one-room school, but from time to time over the years, the state had decided that the Havasupai children weren't getting a proper upbringing and had swooped in to round them up and send them to boarding school, whether their parents wanted it or not. There they learned English and were trained for jobs as porters, janitors, and telephone operators.

After a morning of interpreting for Miss Pearl, Fidel sat down next to me and Rosemary. 'You people think you're rescuing these children,' he said. 'But they just end up unfit for both the valley and the world outside. Take it from me. I was sent to that school.'

'Well, at least when you left, you didn't turn to stone,' Rosemary said.

'What turns to stone is inside you.'

★   ★   ★

In the afternoon Rosemary and I walked around the village. She continued to pester me about going swimming. I could tell that she could really see herself living here.

'Mom, it's the Garden of Eden,' she kept saying. 'The Garden of Eden still exists on this planet.'

'Don't idealize this way of life,' I said. 'I was

born in a dirt house, and you get tired of it pretty quickly.'

In the evening, after another meal of biscuits and jerky, we turned in early again, but I was wakened in the middle of the night by a commotion. Rosemary, streaming wet, was standing outside the hut wrapped in a blanket. Miss Pearl had her by one arm and was shaking her, hollering about how she'd gotten up for some fresh air, heard laughter, and found Rosemary, Fidel, and a few other Indian kids swimming buck-naked in the moonlit pool.

'I wasn't naked!' Rosemary shouted. 'I was wearing underwear.'

'As if that makes a difference,' Miss Pearl said. 'Those boys could *see* you.'

What I was hearing made me practically blind with rage. I couldn't believe Rosemary would do this. I knew that Miss Pearl was appalled, not only at Rosemary but at me as well, wondering what kind of mother would raise such a shameless child. Miss Pearl might well decide it made me unfit to be a teacher. But I was also plain furious with Rosemary. I'd slept next to that girl every night to protect her. I thought I had taught her to be smarter than this, taught her that young men were dangerous, that seemingly innocent situations could result in trouble, that one misstep could lead to a disaster she might never recover from. Plus, I'd told her she couldn't go swimming, and she'd outright disobeyed me.

I grabbed Rosemary by the hair, pulled her into the hut, and threw her onto the floor, then whipped off my belt and started hiding her. Something dark came out of me, so dark it scared me, but even so, I kept at that girl, who was scrambling around on the dirt floor whimpering, until I had the sickening feeling that I'd gone too far. Then I threw down the belt and stalked past Miss Pearl and Miss Finch out into the night.

The next day it was a long ride back up to the canyon rim. Fidel Hanna had made himself scarce, but one of the other Havasu boys came along to bring back the horses. Miss Pearl kept going on about how she was going to report Fidel Hanna to the sheriff for committing indecencies with a minor, but Rosemary and I stayed quiet. Whenever I glanced at Rosemary, she had her eyes on the ground.

Back at the ranch that night, I got into bed with Rosemary and tried to put my arm around her, but she pushed me away.

'I know you're mad at me, but you needed that whipping,' I said. 'There was no other way to teach you a lesson. Do you think you learned it?'

Rosemary was lying on her side staring at the wall. For a minute she was silent, then she said, 'All I learned is that when I have children, I'm never going to whip them.'

*   *   *

That trip to the Garden of Eden turned out badly for just about everyone. After I told Jim about it, we agreed that hiring Fidel Hanna again was out of the question. That was a moot point, because when Fidel heard that Miss Pearl was threatening to turn him in to the sheriff, he joined the army.

291

He became a crack sharpshooter and was sent off to fight in the Pacific Islands, but war eventually unhinged Fidel and he was sent home suffering from shell shock. Not long after he returned, he came apart altogether and shot up a Hopi village. No one was killed, and when Fidel was freed from the state pen in Florence, he returned to the valley. But the Havasupai wouldn't allow him into the village because he'd brought shame on the tribe, and he became an outcast, living by himself in a lonely corner of the reservation. He had, in the end, turned to stone.

After that business with Fidel Hanna, I decided the ranch was no place for my teenage daughter. If she'd go skinny-dipping with Fidel, she'd go skinny-dipping with any ranch hand who took her fancy. To instill a proper sense of caution concerning men, I gave Rosemary copies of *True Confessions* magazine with articles like 'We Met in Alleys and He Led Me Down the Path of Sin.' I also wrote to the Mother Superior at the academy in Prescott, telling her that Rosemary had matured and was eager to try boarding school once more.

Rosemary didn't want to go, but we packed her off again. No sooner had she left, it seemed, than we began receiving letters full of homesickness as well as reports of the D's and F's she was earning. All she wanted to do, the Mother Superior wrote, was draw pictures and ride horses. I was getting pretty exasperated with Rosemary, but also with those nuns, who I wished would learn to cut a fourteen-year-old daydreamer a little slack.

But by then we had something a lot bigger to worry about.

★　★　★

The Poms wrote us a letter saying that, with the war on, they were going to sell the ranch to put

293

their money in the munitions industry. If we could pull together a group of investors, they'd entertain our offer, but from that moment forward, the ranch was on the market.

Jim and I had been squirreling away everything we could, and our savings were considerable — particularly because the Poms had given Jim bonuses during good years — but we didn't have nearly enough to buy Hackberry, much less the entire spread. Jim talked with neighboring ranchers about forming various kinds of partnerships. He also met with a few bankers, and I called Buster in New Mexico, but the fact was, because of the war, hardly anyone had two extra nickels to rub together. People were rationing cloth, collecting tin cans, and growing victory gardens.

Most people.

★　★　★

Late on a January morning, a big black car pulled up in front of the ranch house, and three men got out. The first was wearing a dark suit, the second had on a safari jacket and leather gaiters, and the third wore a big Stetson, pressed jeans, and snakeskin boots. Suit introduced himself as the Poms' lawyer. Gaiters turned out to be a movie director famous for his westerns who was interested in buying the ranch. Boots was some rodeo cowboy Gaiters had cast in a few bit parts.

Gaiters, a beefy, red-faced man with a groomed silver beard, was one of those people who acted

294

as if everything that came out of his mouth, even the most obvious remark, was profoundly interesting. Each time he said something, he'd look over at Suit and Boots, who'd either chuckle appreciatively or nod sagely. It took Gaiters about three minutes to mention that he'd worked with John Wayne, or, as he called him, Duke. He said things like 'Duke's the ultimate natural' and 'Duke's first take is always his best take.'

When Old Jake shuffled out from the barn, Gaiters was standing on the porch, surveying the land. He pointed to a willow next to the pond. 'That's picturesque,' he said. 'Good place to plant a willow.'

'Ain't got time around here to go planting no picturesque trees,' Old Jake said. 'I reckon it just growed there.' He limped back to the barn, shaking his head.

Jim and I showed them around, but since we weren't particularly keen on seeing the place sold out from under us, Jim was even more taciturn than usual. Gaiters, for his part, acted almost as if we didn't exist. He never asked questions. He and Boots kept tossing ideas at each other about how to improve the place. They were going to build an air-strip to fly in from Hollywood. They were going to install a gasoline-powered generator and air-condition the ranch house. They might even put in a pool. They were going to double the herd and breed palominos. It was clear that Boots was this rhinestone cowboy who had dazzled Gaiters with horse jargon and rope tricks when, in fact, he didn't know diddly about ranching.

In the middle of our tour, Gaiters stopped and

looked at Jim as if seeing him for the first time. 'So you're the manager?' he asked.

'Yes, sir.'

'Funny, you don't look like a cowboy.'

Jim was wearing what he always wore: a long-sleeve shirt, dirty jeans with the cuffs turned up, and round-toed work boots. He looked at me and shrugged.

Gaiters studied the weathered gray outbuildings with his hands on his hips. 'And this doesn't look like a ranch,' he said.

'Well, that's what it is,' Jim said.

'But it doesn't feel like one,' Gaiters said. 'The magic is missing. We need to goose the magic.' He turned to Boots. 'You know what I see?' he asked. 'I see everything in knotty pine.'

★   ★   ★

And knotty pine it was. After buying the place, Gaiters tore down the ranch house and built a fancy new place with exposed beams and walls of varnished knotty pine. Then he tore down the bunkhouse and built a new one in matching knotty pine. He renamed the spread the Showtime Ranch. True to his word, he put in the airstrip and doubled the size of the herd.

Gaiters also fired Big Jim and Old Jake. They were too old and too old-fashioned — 'old-timers,' he called them — and he said he needed people who would help him goose the magic. Then he fired all the ranch hands, who were mostly Mexicans and Indians, because he said they didn't look like cowboys. He hired Boots to run the place and brought in a bunch of fellows from the rodeo circuit who wore tight new jeans and embroidered shirts with pearl snap buttons.

We had lived on that ranch for eleven years, and we loved the place. We knew each and every one of those 180,000 acres — the gullies and washes and mudflats, the sagebrush plateau, the boulder-strewn mountains and juniper-covered foothills — like we knew our own hearts. We'd respected the land. We knew what it could and couldn't do, and we'd never pushed it beyond its limits. We'd never squandered the water, and we'd never overgrazed the grass, unlike our neighbors. Anyone riding the fence line would see grass four inches high on our side and one inch on theirs. We had been good stewards. The buildings may have been a little rough on the eyes, but they were in good repair, still solid and true. There wasn't a more honestly run ranch in all of Arizona. We'd known all along, of course, that we didn't own the place, but at the same time, we couldn't help considering it ours, and we felt dispossessed, like my dad and his pa did when the settlers started fencing in the Hondo Valley.

'Guess I've been put out to pasture,' Jim said after Gaiters delivered the news.

'You know you're the best at what you do,' I told him.

'Just seems like what I do don't need to be done anymore.'

'We've never felt sorry for ourselves before,' I said, 'and we're not going to start now. Let's get packing.'

We had our savings, so we weren't in a bind financially. I decided we should move to Phoenix and make a fresh start. Arizona was changing, money was pouring in. Because it had perfect weather for flying, the air force had discovered the state, building bases and landing strips all over the place. At the same time, lungers — folks with breathing problems — were arriving in droves, and what was more, air-conditioning had become affordable, making places like Phoenix appealing to all those eastern lace-panties who couldn't tolerate its true temperatures. The city looked like it was going to take off.

When I called Rosemary to tell her we were leaving the ranch, she became almost hysterical. 'We can't, Mom,' she said. 'It's all I've known. It's inside me.'

'It's behind you now, honey,' I said.

Little Jim was beside himself as well and said he outright refused to go.

'It's not up to us, and it's not up to you, either,' I told him. 'We're gone.'

Since ranching was going to be in our past, I wanted to get rid of most everything that had to do with it. We sold all the horses to Gaiters except Patches, who was pushing thirty. I gave her to the Havasupai. Rosemary might never see the Garden of Eden again, but at least she'd know that a horse she loved was there.

I did keep the English riding pants and the pair of field boots I'd been wearing the day I'd fallen off Red Devil and met Jim, but that was about it. Everything we owned fit into the back of the hearse, and on a beautiful spring day when the lilac was blooming and warblers were singing in the hoptrees, we packed it all up and headed down the drive. Rosemary was still at boarding school. She'd never returned to the ranch. Little Jim, who was sitting between me and Jim, twisted around for one last glance.

'No looking back,' I said. 'You can't. You just can't.'

VIII

GUMSHOES

Rosemary, age sixteen, Horse Mesa

Jim decided that we should start our new life in Phoenix by splurging.

'Name something you've always wanted,' he said.

'New choppers,' I said immediately. My teeth had been giving me trouble for years, but folks on the Colorado Plateau weren't big on dentists. If a tooth wouldn't stop aching, you found yourself a pair of pliers and pulled the bugger. I also had a gap between my two front teeth where they had rotted in from the sides. I tried to keep the gap plugged with a piece of white candle wax, but when the wax fell out from time to time, I had to admit it looked a little scary. Jim's teeth were every bit as bad.

'You get yourself a pair, too,' I said.

Jim grinned. 'Two new sets of choppers. That should get us going just fine in this here town.'

We found a nice young dentist who shot us full of Novocain, pulled out our worn-down brown teeth, and fitted sets of new dentures to our gums. The first time he put them in place and held up the mirror, I was thrilled by those two flawless rows of big gleaming white porcelain, as shiny and square as kitchen tiles. Overnight I'd gotten myself the smile of a movie star, while Jim looked about thirty years younger. The two of us walked around the city beaming radiantly at our new neighbors.

We also bought a house on North Third Street. It was a big old place with high windows, sturdy wooden doors, and adobe walls about two feet thick. Finally, we junked that beater of a hearse and bought a maroon Kaiser, a new kind of sedan made in California, with wide bumpers and running boards. I was proud of that house and proud of that car, too, but nothing made me prouder than my new set of choppers. They beat the pants off real teeth, and from time to time when I was in a restaurant or someplace telling someone about them, I couldn't help it, I had to pull them out and show them off to prove that they were the genuine article.

'Look!' I'd say as I held them up. 'They're not teeth. They're real dentures!'

At first I thought Phoenix was terrific. Our house was near the center of town, and we could walk to stores and movie theaters. I made a point of going to every single restaurant on Van Buren Street. I especially loved cafeterias, because you could actually see the food before you ordered it instead of flying blind with a menu. After all those years of sitting on orange crates and drinking from coffee cans, I went out and bought a carved mahogany dining set and Bavarian china. For the first time in our lives, we got a telephone, which meant people who wanted to get in touch with me didn't have to leave a message with the sheriff.

Little Jim, however, hated Phoenix from the get-go. 'You feel penned in,' he said. 'You feel puny.'

And when Rosemary's boarding school let out and she joined us in the city, she hated it, too. They hated the black asphalt and the gray concrete. They thought air-conditioning was weird and noisy, and the telephone just allowed busybodies to pester you day and night. Phoenix was square and straight, boxy and boxed in, and above all, fake.

'You can't even see the ground,' Rosemary complained. 'It's all covered up with pavement and sidewalks.'

'But think of the advantages,' I said. 'We eat at

cafeterias. We have indoor plumbing.'

'Who cares?' Rosemary said. 'Back at the ranch, you could hunker down and take a pee whenever you had the urge.' She added that living in Phoenix was even making her question her faith. 'I've been praying daily to go back to the ranch,' she said. 'Either God doesn't exist or he doesn't hear me.'

'Of course he exists and of course he hears you,' I said. 'He has the right to say no, you know.'

But I did begin to worry about the effect Phoenix was having on that girl. She had no use for indoor plumbing, questioned the existence of God, and even acted all embarrassed when, the next day at a luncheonette, I took out my dentures to show them off to the waitress.

★ ★ ★

I didn't care to admit it to the kids, but after a few months, I started feeling a little penned in myself. The traffic drove me crazy. Back in Yavapai County, you drove wherever you wanted at whatever speed you wanted, and left the road whenever you were so inclined. Here there were stop-lights, cops with whistles, yellow lines, white lines, and all manner of signs ordering you to do this and forbidding you from doing that. Cars were supposed to mean freedom, but all these people stuck in traffic on one-way streets — where you weren't even allowed to make a U-turn to get the hell out of the jam — might as well have been sitting in cages. I found myself

306

constantly arguing with other drivers, sticking my head out the window of the Kaiser, which was always overheating, and hollering at those dimwits that they should go back east, where they belonged.

Nothing had ever made me feel as free as flying, and I was only a few hours away from getting my pilot's license, so I decided to take up lessons again. The airport had a flying school, but when I showed up one day, the clerk passed me an entire sheaf of forms and started yammering about eye exams, physicals, takeoff slots, elevation restrictions, and no-fly zones. I realized that these city folks had boxed off and chopped up the sky the same way they had the ground.

$$\star \quad \star \quad \star$$

One thing about Phoenix, though: There were a lot more jobs available than in Yavapai County. Jim was hired as the manager of a warehouse stocking airplane parts, and I landed a teaching position in a high school in South Phoenix.

There were also investment opportunities in the city. After paying for our house on Third Street, we still had money left over, and we used it to buy a few other small houses that we rented out. Distressed properties were always coming onto the market at bargain prices. Jim and I attended courthouse auctions and bid on foreclosures, and I started carrying a ten-thousand-dollar cashier's check in my purse, just in case I happened across anyone needing to sell quickly at a discounted price. For the first time in our lives, we were living on the backs of others, but that was how you got ahead in the city. When Jim said it made him feel like a vulture, I told him that scavengers got a bum rap. 'Vultures don't kill animals, they live off the dead,' I said. 'And that's what we're doing. We're not bringing misfortune on these people, we're just taking advantage of it.'

I worried constantly that someone might snatch my purse and make off with the check, so I kept the bag clutched to my chest when I walked through town. That was only one of a number of things I found myself worrying about in Phoenix. We had bought ourselves a radio that we could listen to all day long now that we were living in a house wired for electricity. At first I thought that was just grand, but it meant that for the first time I was also listening to the news every day, and about every day, it seemed, there was a report about some crime or another in town. People were always getting robbed or having their cars stolen or their houses burgled if they weren't getting raped, shot, or stabbed. A Phoenix woman named Winnie Ruth Judd — known as the 'Blonde Butcher' and the 'Trunk Murderess' because she'd killed two people and put their bodies in her luggage — kept escaping from the insane asylum she'd been sent to, and the news was always filled with accounts of possible Trunk Murderess sightings, along with warnings to the citizenry to lock all doors and windows.

So I kept my pearl-handled revolver under my

bed. I also bought a little twenty-two pistol to carry in my purse along with the check. Every night I made a point of bolting the doors, which we had never done at the ranch, and I slept on the outside of the bed I still shared with Rosemary, keeping her next to the wall so if anyone got through the locked doors and attacked us, I could fight them off while Rosemary escaped.

'Mom, you've become such a worrywart,' she said.

Rosemary was right. On the ranch, we worried about the weather and the cattle and horses, but we never worried about ourselves. In Phoenix people worried about themselves all the time.

People also worried about bombs. Every Saturday at noon, the air-raid siren was tested, and an earsplitting whoop-whoop-whoop blared throughout the city. If the siren sounded at any other time, that meant an attack was under way and you were supposed to run to the bomb shelters. Rosemary couldn't abide the siren, and when it went off, she buried her head under a pillow. 'I can't stand that noise,' she said.

'It's for your own good,' I said.

'Well, all it's doing is scaring me, and I don't see the good in that.'

The girl was developing a pronounced contrarian streak. One morning that August, when Rosemary and I were walking down Van Buren Street, we passed a storefront where a bunch of people were gathered, gawking at an automatic donut-making machine. Next to it was a newsstand, and it was when I glanced down at the headlines that I first learned about the atom bomb falling on Hiroshima. I bought the paper, and as I read, I tried to explain to Rosemary what had happened. Rosemary couldn't believe that a single bomb had obliterated an entire city — hundreds of thousands of people, not only soldiers but also grandparents, mothers, children, as well as dogs, cats, birds, chickens, mice, every living thing. 'Those poor, poor creatures,' she kept sobbing.

I tried to argue that it was the Japs who'd started the war, and because of Hiroshima, thousands more American boys would not have to die fighting them, but Rosemary decided there was something sick about the atom bomb. The deaths of all those mice and birds was just as upsetting to her as the deaths of the people. After all, she said, the animals hadn't started the war.

She also decided there was something sick about Americans who would stand there gawking at a donut maker while there was so much agony on the other side of the world.

'Focus on the positive,' I said. 'You live in a country where no one has to make donuts by hand.'

★   ★   ★

Rosemary's feelings got even darker that fall. We'd enrolled her at St. Mary's, a Catholic school a few blocks from the house, and the nuns, who kept reminding their students that all life was sacred, showed some Japanese news reels of the devastation at Hiroshima and Nagasaki. The scenes of flattened city blocks, incinerated corpses, and babies deformed by radiation gave Rosemary nightmares. The nuns told her that we needed to pray for the Japanese because they were God's children, too, and they had lost their sons and daughters and fathers and mothers. I was less sympathetic. 'That's what happens when you go around starting wars,' I said. But Rosemary was distraught. No one but God, she thought, should be able to kill so many people so easily and so quickly as we had done with the atomic bomb. That her own government had that kind of power made her very afraid of it. Now that it had the bomb, who was it going to bomb next? What if it decided she was the enemy?

When I got tired of explaining that the end justified the means, I told Rosemary to stop talking about Hiroshima, because if she stopped talking about it, she'd stop thinking about it. She did stop talking about it, but one day I looked under the bed we still shared and found a folder full of drawing after drawing of animals and children, all with Japanese eyes and angels' wings.

Rosemary started drawing and painting more obsessively than ever. As far as I could tell, it was her one talent. Her grades were still terrible. I signed her up for violin and piano lessons, but her instructor said she lacked the discipline to practice. I tried to defend her, arguing that improvisation, not recitation, was her musical forte, but one day the instructor said if he had to listen to her torturing that poor violin one more minute, he'd puncture his own eardrums.

'What are we going to do with you?' I asked her.

'I'm not worried about me,' she said. 'And no one else should be, either.'

A lot of pretty girls lost their looks when they reached adolescence, but Rosemary was still a stunner, though I'd kept my promise to myself never to tell her this. However, I was getting a little desperate, and one day when I read a newspaper article about a beauty contest, I figured maybe Rosemary should go ahead and play that card. 'I have an idea,' I said. 'You can be a beauty queen or a model.'

'What are you talking about?' Rosemary asked.

I told her to put on a bathing suit and walk back and forth in front of me. It wasn't promising. She had the looks and the figure, but she moved like a cowgirl, not a beauty queen, swinging her arms vigorously with each big stride. So I enrolled her in modeling school, where she learned how to walk with a book on her head and get out of a car without showing her underpants. But at her first photo session, when the photographer told her to flirt with the camera, she couldn't stop giggling self-consciously, and the man shook his head.

What Rosemary really wanted to do was be an artist.

'Artists never make any money,' I said, 'and they usually go crazy.'

Rosemary pointed out that Charlie Russell and Frederic Remington had both gotten rich painting western scenes. 'Art's a great way to make money,' Rosemary said. For the cost of a piece of canvas and some paint, she went on, you could create a picture worth thousands of dollars. In what other line of work could you do that? A blank canvas, she kept arguing, was a treasure waiting to happen.

I finally took some of her drawings to a few frame shops and asked the clerks if they thought my daughter had any talent. They said she showed promise, so I arranged for her to take lessons with Ernestine, an art teacher who wore a beret just in case you couldn't tell from her accent that she was a Frog.

Ernestine taught Rosemary that white wasn't really white, that black wasn't really black, that every color had other colors in it, that every line was made up of more than one line, that you should love the weeds as much as the flowers because everything on the planet had its own beauty and it was up to the artist to discover it, and that for the artist, there was no such thing as reality because the world was as you chose to see it.

This all struck me as a lot of hogwash, but Rosemary really lapped it up.

'You know what's the greatest thing about painting?' she said one day.

'What?'

'If there's something about the world that you don't like, you can paint a painting that makes it the way you want it to be.'

With Ernestine's lessons, Rosemary's paintings became less and less about the thing she was painting and more about what she was feeling at the moment. Around this time, she started spelling her name Rose Mary because she thought it made for a prettier signature. I continued to pay the Frog for the lessons, but I kept reminding Rosemary that art was an iffy proposition, that most women still had to choose between being a nurse, a secretary, and a teacher, and for my money, teaching beat the others hands down.

*　*　*

The funny thing was, even while telling Rosemary this, I was not, for the first time in my life, enjoying my job. I was teaching math and English at a large high school. A lot of the kids came from highfalutin families, wore fancy clothes — a few actually drove their own cars — and refused to obey me if they didn't feel like it. It was also the first time I had not been on my own, teaching in a one-room school. I had principals and other teachers second-guessing me, forms to fill out, and committees to sit on. Half my day was spent doing paperwork for the bureaucracy.

There were more rules for teachers than for students, and those bureaucrats were awfully persnickety about you following those rules. Once when I opened my purse in the teachers' lounge, one of the other teachers saw my little pistol and just about had a fit.

'That's a gun!' she gasped.

'Barely,' I said. 'It's only a twenty-two.'

Still, she reported me to the principal, who warned me that if I ever brought a gun to the school again, I'd be fired.

'How am I going to protect myself and my students?' I asked.

'That's what the police are for,' he said.

'Who's going to protect us from the police?'

'Just leave the gun at home.'

Jim never complained, but I could tell his job chafed him as much as mine did me. He was bored — a big, broad-shouldered guy sitting awkwardly behind a little metal desk, checking his inventory list and watching the Mexican workers boxing up airplane parts. Jim wasn't a desk man. He also had a lot of downtime, which he wasn't used to, and he spent a fair amount of it shooting the breeze with the warehouse bookkeeper, a tarted-up divorcée I did not take to named Glenda. She called Jim 'Smithy' and was always asking him to light her cigarettes.

My husband just didn't see the point of city life, didn't understand why anyone would want to live like this. So many things about it struck him as contrary to the proper and natural way of the world. Shortly after we moved to the city, they cut down all the orange and cottonwood trees that shaded the streets to make room for more parking. 'Seems to me you lose more than you gain,' Jim said.

The simple truth was, he missed the outdoors. He missed the sweat and dust and heat of ranching, the smells and hard labor. He missed the way that ranch life forced you to study the sky and the land every day, trying to anticipate nature's intentions. On Sundays we took walks in Encanto Park in the middle of the city, and out of habit, Jim continued to be mindful of what the

317

plants and animals were telling him. As fall came on that year, he noticed that the birds were migrating south earlier than usual, squirrels were storing extra nuts and their tails were unusually full, acorns were especially large, the bark on the cottonwoods was thicker, and so were the hulls on the pecan nuts.

'Going to be a hard winter,' he said. The signs were all there. He hoped other people were reading them, too.

★ ★ ★

And that winter was hard. It came on early, and in January it snowed in Phoenix for the first time in most folks' memory. Back on the ranch, a blizzard like that would have been a call to action, forcing us to run around collecting firewood, bringing in the horses, and carting hay to the range. Jim would build a windbreak to protect the cattle. He'd empty all the wagons out of the garage and make a wall of them between the house and the barn, covering it with tarps, coats, and blankets, then buttressing it with old trunks and anvils and dirt and rocks and whatever he could find. He'd round up as many cattle as could fit into the barn, and when the storm reached us, he was outside on horseback, keeping the cattle moving, keeping their blood circulating. Every couple of hours, he'd rotate a new group into the barn and behind the wall of wagons so they could get a break from the wind and snow.

Living in the city, all we did was turn up the radiator and listen to the hiss and clank of the pipes.

*   *   *

The snow kept falling, and the next day the governor went on the radio, declaring a state of emergency. School was canceled and most businesses were closed. The National Guard was called out to rescue people stranded in remote parts of the state. Jim said he hoped that Boots and Gaiters knew what they were doing. He hoped all the cattle had been moved off the plateau down to the winter range and the hands had broken the ice on the ponds. 'The first thing you got to do is break the ice,' he said. 'The cattle'll die of thirst before they starve.'

*   *   *

On the third day of the storm, we got a knock on the door. It was a man from the Arizona Department of Agriculture. Cattle were dying across the state, he said. Ranchers needed help, and the name that kept coming up was Jim Smith. It had taken them a while to track him down, the man said, but he was needed.

Jim threw some heavy clothes into his old army duffel bag, grabbed his hat, and was out the door in less than five minutes.

*   *   *

The first thing Jim did was organize drops of hay. He had a big cargo plane filled with round bales, and they took off into the storm. When they reached the range, the crew rolled the bales

319

out the back of the cargo bay and watched as the hay tumbled through the snow and bounced on the ground.

Since the roads were impassable, Jim asked the government for a small plane and a pilot, and they flew across the state, touching down at isolated ranch houses. Jim explained to the ranchers, most of whom had never seen a blizzard the likes of this one, what to do. You got to break the ice on the ponds, he told them, and cut down the fence wire. Let the cattle roam. They need to move to keep their blood circulating, and they'll instinctively move south, but if they hit a wire fence, they'll all press up against it and die. Let them get into big herds and huddle for warmth. You can sort them all out by the brands later.

At one ranch up in the hills, there was no place to land. Jim had never put on a parachute before, much less jumped, but he strapped one on. 'Count ten, pull the cord, and roll into the fall,' the pilot said, and Jim heaved himself out of the plane.

★ ★ ★

The storm had stopped, but the temperatures were still frigid when Jim reached the Showtime Ranch. Even before he landed, he could see from the air that no one had broken the ice on Big Jim. Carcasses of frozen cattle lay clustered along the pond's edge. When he got to the ranch house, he found Boots and the new hands sitting around Gaiter's fancy propane stove, their feet up, drinking coffee.

Any muttonhead can run a ranch during good times. You only find out who the real ranchers are when calamity strikes. Those dunces sitting around that stove may not have been able to read tree bark, but at the very least, they should have been listening to the weather reports, and when they heard that a devil of a storm was coming down from Canada, they would have had twenty-four hours to prepare. I would have lit into that fool Boots and those other chumps, but that was not Jim's way. He did, however, get their sorry butts out and mounted up to cut wire, break ice, and start the cattle moving.

There were thousands of dead cattle lying rock-hard in the snow, piled along the southern fences. Some of the cattle that had survived were so weak they couldn't walk, so Jim had the men bring hay and water and hand-feed them. He massaged their legs, which were cut from where they'd tried to break the ice themselves, and helped them stand again. If he could get them moving, he knew, they'd live.

★ ★ ★

Jim was gone two weeks. That whole time I didn't know where he was or how he was doing, and it was the longest two weeks of my life. When he finally came back, he'd lost twenty pounds. His face and hands were raw. He hadn't slept for days, and there were dark circles under his eyes. But he was happy. He hadn't felt this useful since leaving the ranch. He'd been out

321

doing what he was meant to do. He was Big Jim again.

★   ★   ★

A few days after Jim returned, he got a call from Gaiters. When Jim had been back in Yavapai County during the blizzard, people had told him that Gaiters had been going around referring to him as a 'relic' and a 'washed-up old geezer.' But that was before the storm. Now Gaiters was so impressed with the way Jim had salvaged what remained of the Showtime's herd that he offered Jim his old job as ranch manager. He'd even build us our own knotty pine caretaker's cabin. 'You're the real thing,' Gaiters said.

Jim and I discussed it, but we agreed right away that it was not for us. Before, we had been the ones running the ranch, making all the decisions. The storm had humbled Gaiters somewhat, but he still had his cockamamie notions for goosing up the Showtime. Jim didn't want to do Gaiters's bidding or have to spend his time arguing the man out of foolish ideas. What was more, there was no possibility of us someday buying the place. I told Jim I didn't want to live in a caretaker's cabin, even a knotty pine one, waiting for the owner to fly in with his Hollywood friends for weekend parties and leading dudes on trail rides. I'd been a servant before, and once was enough.

322

The following month I had a school holiday and was in town running errands when I decided to swing by the warehouse. An article about the work Jim had done saving herds during the blizzard had appeared in the newspaper, along with a photograph of him standing by the plane he'd jumped out of. The headline read COWBOY PARACHUTES THROUGH BLIZZARD TO RESCUE CATTLE. My husband had become a bit of a local hero. People recognized him on the street and stopped to shake his hand. One guy even hollered: 'It's the Parachutin' Cowboy!'

Jim thought it was all a little ridiculous, but I couldn't help noticing the way women smiled and flirted with the Parachutin' Cowboy when he doffed his hat or opened the door for them.

Jim didn't expect me that day, and when I walked into the warehouse, Glenda the floozy bookkeeper was standing in his doorway, talking to him. She had jet-black hair and blood-red lipstick, wore a tight purple dress, and was leaning with her back against the door frame to show off her figure. She had on one of those wire bra contraptions, and it pushed her bosoms forward like a couple of airplane nose cones.

When she saw me, instead of seeming contrite, she gave her bosoms a little jiggle and looked at my husband. 'Uh-oh, Smithy,' she said. 'Are we in trouble?'

My blood boiled up, and I was sorely tempted to backhand that hussy, but instead I looked at Jim to get his reaction. If he was all hot to trot, there was going to be hell to pay, but Jim just seemed embarrassed, more for the tart than for anything he'd done. 'Knock it off, Glenda,' he said.

The two of us went out to a cafeteria for lunch, and I didn't say anything about Glenda's little display, but I made a mental note to keep an eye on the two of them.

★　★　★

Truth be told, as the days went by, I couldn't help wondering if there was actually something going on between Jim and the floozy. At times the two of them were all alone in that big warehouse, and there were plenty of hidden nooks and crannies to provide sites for hanky-panky. And then they both had lunch hour, again giving them ample time to duck into some hot-sheets hotel. In other words, they both had opportunity, and she clearly had motive. The question was, did my husband?

There was no point in confronting Jim, because if he was turning out to be another crumb bum like my first husband, he'd simply lie. I thought I knew Jim, but I also knew you couldn't — or shouldn't — trust men. An otherwise sensible man might be driven wild if an irresistible temptation presented itself. And there was a heck of a lot more temptation wagging its tail in Phoenix than there ever had been in Yavapai County. Also, men can change. Maybe this Parachutin' Cowboy business had gone to Jim's head, all the adoring ladies with their battering eyelashes and nose-cone bosoms making him think he was the prize stallion at the stud farm. Maybe it had brought out the latent polygamist in him.

Whatever the case, as the days went by, I realized I was not going to get any peace from these thoughts unless I got to the bottom of the matter. I needed to investigate.

I didn't want to hire a private detective, the way they did in all those movies. The gumshoes were always men, and I couldn't trust them, either. I also didn't want to follow Jim around myself, the way I did my first husband in Chicago. I'd known that crumb bum was a louse, I'd just needed to prove it. With Jim, I was trying to make a determination of the facts, the more quietly the better. Besides, Phoenix was a lot smaller than Chicago, and people knew me. I was a schoolteacher with a reputation to maintain. I didn't want to be caught lurking in alleys.

So I enlisted Rosemary's help.

★　★　★

'But, Mom, I don't want to spy on Dad,' she said when I explained the enterprise.

'It's not spying, it's investigating,' I said. 'He might be cheating on me, but we don't know. He might be innocent. That's what we hope, and that's what we're trying to prove — that he's innocent.'

How could the girl say no to that?

325

I figured that if something was going on between Jim and the floozy, the odds favored lunchtime assignations. The consequences of being caught in the warehouse with your pants around your ankles were a little too serious.

Rosemary had spring break coming up. My plan was for her to spend her week off school following Jim during his lunch hour. If Jim and the floozy were going at it, they were probably doing so at least on a weekly basis. If, during that week, there was no suspicious activity, I decided I could let him off the hook.

The first day of our investigation, it was hot for spring, and the cloudless sky was a deep, almost dark blue. I parked the Kaiser a couple of blocks from the warehouse. I told Rosemary to hide in the alley across the street and follow Jim when he came out at lunchtime, making sure to keep several other people between them in case he happened to turn around. I gave her a pencil and pad. 'Take notes,' I said.

She had a look of resignation about her, but she took the pad and got out of the car.

'It'll be fun,' I said. 'We're gumshoes.'

I sat there for half an hour, trying to read the paper, but mostly checking my watch and studying passersby. Then Rosemary came up the street and got back in the Kaiser.

'So what happened?' I asked.

'Nothing.'

'Something must have happened.'

Rosemary sat there staring at her shoes. 'Dad

ate lunch. In the park. By himself.'

She'd followed him, she said, and he'd gone into a grocery store, come out with a paper bag, and walked to the park, where he'd sat on a bench and taken out a packet of saltines, a chunk of bologna, a chunk of cheese, and a carton of milk. He'd used his pocketknife to cut a slice of bologna and a slice of cheese for each cracker, and he'd drunk the milk in little swallows, nursing it so it would last.

Rosemary smiled as she said that, as if the sight of her father sitting in the sun eating his bologna and crackers and rationing his milk had made her feel good about the world.

'That was it?' I asked.

'When he was done, he brushed the crumbs off his fingers and rolled himself a cigarette.'

'Good,' I said. 'We'll do it again tomorrow.'

★　★　★

On the second day, Rosemary got out of the car with her pencil and pad, and I sat there for a while drumming my fingers on the steering wheel, then around the corner came Jim with Rosemary. He was holding her hand, and she looked a lot happier than she had when she'd left.

Jim knelt down by my window. 'Lily, what the hell is going on?'

I thought of coming up with some complicated lie, but Jim was smarter than that, and I knew the game was up. 'I was trying to prove to myself and Rosemary what I hoped would be the case — that you are a faithful husband.'

'I see,' he said. 'Let's all go have lunch.'

He took us back to the grocery store, where we bought bologna and crackers and cheese and milk and had us a right fine picnic in that same park.

But that night, when he got home, Jim said to me, 'What say the two of us have a little sit-down.'

I fixed myself a whiskey and water and we sat out in the yard behind the adobe house, where little fruits were starting to come in on the orange trees.

'I wasn't spying,' I said. 'I was just confirming that everything between us was copacetic. I don't want you cheating on me with that floozy.'

'Lily, I'm not cheating on you. But it's a part of city life that men are going to find themselves, from time to time, in the company of women who are not their wives. You got to trust me.'

'It's not that I don't trust you,' I said. 'But I'm not going to stand idly by while some floozy tries to steal my man.'

'Maybe we're all feeling a little penned up in this city. Maybe it's making us all a little crazy.'

'Then maybe we should leave,' I said.

'Maybe we should.'

'So that's settled.'

'Now we just got to find us a place to go.'

IX

THE FLYBOY

Rex and Rosemary after their wedding

Horse Mesa was a flyspeck of a place, a glorified camp, really, built for the men who worked at Horse Mesa Dam, which held back the waters of the Salt River, formed Lake Apache, and generated electrical power for Phoenix. Only thirteen families lived in Horse Mesa, but those families had kids, and the kids needed a teacher, and that summer I got the job.

We traded in the fancy but unreliable California Kaiser for a good old made-in-Detroit Ford and, one day in July, packed our suitcases in the trunk and headed east, first to Apache Junction, then up to Tortilla Flats, where the asphalt ended. From there, we followed the Apache Trail, a winding dirt road, up into the Superstition Mountains, which for my money were even sweeter on the eyes than the Grand Canyon. We drove by massive cliffs of red and gold sandstone, their layers of collapsed sediment pushed up at an angle like a bunch of books leaning against one another on a shelf. The mountains were studded with saguaros, stag horns, and prickly pears, which were ugly as hell, but you had to admire their ability to thrive in even the driest, stoniest, most inhospitable cliffside cranny — and darned if they didn't manage to produce some tasty fruit.

After several miles on the Apache Trail, we came to an even narrower dirt road leading off to the north. We followed it over a ridge and down through a series of sharp, steep switchbacks, passing beneath overhangs and around other-worldly rock formations. Jim was at the wheel, and he made the Ford crawl along, hugging the mountainside, as there was no guardrail and the ground fell away so abruptly on the other side that with one miscalculation, we would plunge into the abyss. The road was called Agnes Weeps, after the town's first schoolteacher, who had burst into tears when she saw how plunging and twisting the road was and realized how remote the town must be. But from the first moment I laid eyes on it, I loved that road. I thought of it as a winding staircase taking me out of the traffic jams, news bulletins, bureaucrats, air-raid sirens, and locked doors of city life. Jim said we should rename the road Lily Sings.

We followed Agnes Weeps all the way to the bottom of the canyon, then came around a bend and saw a deep blue lake with red sandstone cliff walls rising on all sides around it. Across a short bridge, perched up on one of the cliffs and looking down on that lake, was Horse Mesa. It was just a cluster of stucco houses, and it was remote — Agnes had been right about that. A truck brought in groceries twice a week from the commissary at Roosevelt Dam. There was only one telephone, in the community center. If you wanted to make a phone call, you had to put in a request through the operator at the Tempe substation, who gave you an appointment and, at the designated time, routed the call through Mormon Flats, and everyone at the community center got to hear your conversation.

But from the get-go, we were all darned happy to be at Horse Mesa. Since it was summer, the kids spent the entire day at the lake, diving off the cliffs into the cool water. The river and the lake attracted all sorts of animals, and we saw bighorn sheep, coatimundi cats, Gila monsters, Green Mountain rattlesnakes, and chuckwallas.

Jim got a job with the Bureau of Land Reclamation driving a gravel truck — he filled potholes and rebuilt eroded washes along the entire length of the Apache Trail — and the work made him content. He was riding something powerful, on his own, out in the open.

And I was back where I belonged, in a one-room schoolhouse, with no fish-faced bureaucrats second-guessing me, teaching my students what I thought they needed to know.

The school at Horse Mesa went only through the eighth grade, so that fall, for the third time, we had to send the kids off to boarding school. We enrolled Rosemary at St. Joseph's, a small, fancy school in Tucson. I knew that a lot of the other girls came from rich families, so before Rosemary left, I gave her a present.

'Pearls!' she exclaimed when she opened the box. 'They must have cost a fortune.'

'I got them with S&H green stamps,' I said. 'And they're not real, they're fake.' I told her for the first time about my crumb-bum first husband and his other family. 'The louse gave me a fake ring,' I said. 'But for years I thought it was real and acted like it was, and so did everyone else.' I fastened the pearls around her neck. 'The point being,' I said, 'if you hold your head up high, no one will ever know.'

★ ★ ★

With the kids away at school, our life in Horse Mesa settled into a tranquil routine. Part of it was the setting itself. Living there was like living in a natural cathedral. Waking up every morning, you walked outside and looked down at the blue lake, then up at the sandstone cliffs — those awe-inspiring layers of red and yellow rock shaped over the millennia, with dozens of black-streaked crevices that temporarily became waterfalls after rainstorms. During one downpour I counted twenty-seven waterfalls.

Just as important, everyone in Horse Mesa got along. We had to. Since we all worked together and depended on one another, arguments were a luxury none of us could afford. No one complained or gossiped. We only got intermittent radio signals, so in the evening, while the children played, the grown-ups strolled about visiting one another. None of us had much money, so we didn't talk about the things people with money talked about. Instead, we talked about what mattered to us — the weather, the level of the lake, the big-mouth bass someone had caught under the bridge, the mountain-lion scat someone else had seen along Fish Creek. It may have seemed to city folk that we had precious little to do, but none of us felt that way, and the quiet routine contributed to the tranquility of our little cliffside camp.

★   ★   ★

Peaceful as our life had become, I still had my moments of high dudgeon. I'd always been interested in politics, but I discovered I actually had a talent for it after the Department of Education tried to close down a couple of schools in our area and I hooked up with the United Federation of Teachers to stop it. I saw how easy it was to get things done if you were willing to use your elbows and your lungs, and how easily cowed some politicians got if you grabbed them by the tie or jabbed them in the chest with your finger.

I started visiting Phoenix regularly, making sure those double-talking politicians followed through on their campaign promises, and on one occasion I burst into the governor's office, Rosemary in tow, to berate him for not funding the education bill. When he threatened to have me arrested, I said if he did, I — a taxpayer, teacher, and loving mother of two — would hold a press conference and remind everyone what a lying son of a bitch he was.

I became the Democratic precinct captain for Horse Mesa. I always carried around voter registration cards, and in grocery stores I'd ask the people in line if they were registered to vote. If they weren't, I'd hand them a card. 'Anyone who thinks he's too small to make a difference has never been bit by a mosquito,' I'd tell people.

I had all thirteen families in Horse Mesa register to vote, and on election day, Jim drove me into Tortilla Flats. I kept the ballots in one hand and my pearl-handled revolver in the other, daring anyone to try to hijack democracy by stealing the twenty-six votes I had been entrusted with. 'Hold on, everyone!' I declared when I arrived. 'The votes from Horse Mesa are here, and I'm proud to announce we had one hundred percent turnout.'

★ ★ ★

Jim and I also all took up a new hobby — hunting for uranium. The government needed

336

the stuff for its nuclear weapons and offered a reward of one hundred thousand dollars to anyone who discovered a uranium mine. A penniless couple up in Colorado had actually stumbled across one and were now rich. Jim bought a used Geiger counter, and on the weekends we drove out into the desert, hunting for rocks that ticked.

I was surprised to find a lot of them out there, mainly near a place called Frenchman's Flat, and it didn't take us long to fill several crates. We took them into an assayer in Mormon Flats, but he told us they weren't in fact uranium — all the radioactivity was on the surface. The rocks, he said, had been in an area where the government had been doing nuclear testing.

I figured ticking rocks would have to be worth something someday, so we stored them under the house and from time to time collected more.

★   ★   ★

After they finished high school, both Rosemary and Little Jim went off to Arizona State. At six foot four and two hundred pounds, Little Jim was now bigger than Big Jim. He played college football and ate half a box of cereal every morning, but he'd never been much of a student. During his first year in college, he met Diane, a full-lipped beauty whose father was a big cheese at the Phoenix postal system. They got married, and Jim dropped out of college and became a police officer.

One down, I thought, and one to go.

I felt I had come to an understanding with Rosemary. Or at least I considered it an understanding — Rosemary still thought I was imposing my will on her. But we agreed that she could study art in college as long as she majored in teaching and got her certificate. After the war, young men had poured into Arizona, and Rosemary was always being pestered for dates. In fact, several men had already proposed to her. I told her to hold out, she wasn't ready yet. But I did have a good notion of the type of man she needed — an anchor. That girl still had a tendency to be flighty, but with a solid man beside her, I could see her settling down, teaching elementary school, raising a couple of kids, and dabbling in painting on the side.

There were plenty of solid men out there — men like her father — and I knew I could find her the right one.

The summer after Rosemary's third year in college, she and her friends started driving over to Fish Creek Canyon to swim. One day she came home with what she thought was a funny story. A group of young air force pilots had been at the canyon. When she'd dived off the cliffs into the water, one of them had been so impressed that he'd jumped in after her and told her he was going to marry her.

'I said that twenty-one men had already proposed to me, and I turned them all down, so what made him think I'd say yes to him. He said he wasn't proposing, he was telling me we were going to get married.'

Someone with that sort of moxie, I thought, was either a born leader or a con artist. 'What was he like?' I asked.

Rosemary considered the question for a moment, as if trying to figure it out herself. 'Interesting,' she said. 'Different. One thing about him — he wasn't a very good swimmer, but he jumped right in.'

★ ★ ★

The jumper's name was Rex Walls. He had grown up in West Virginia and was stationed at Luke Air Force Base. Rosemary came back from her first date with him practically giggling

339

with glee. They'd met at a Mexican restaurant in Tempe, and when some guy had flirted with her, Rex had started a fight that became a general brawl, but she and Rex had ducked out and run off hand in hand before the cops arrived.

'He called it 'doing the skedaddle,'' she said.

Just what she needs, I thought. A hellion. 'That sounds very promising,' I said.

Rosemary ignored the sarcasm. 'He talked all night,' she said. 'He has all sorts of plans. And he's very interested in my art. Mom, he's the first man I've ever dated who's taken me seriously as an artist. He actually asked to see some paintings.'

★ ★ ★

The following weekend Rex showed up at Horse Mesa to look at Rosemary's art. He was a rangy fellow with narrow dark eyes, a devilish grin, and slicked-back black hair. He had courtly manners, sweeping off his air force cap, shaking Jim's hand vigorously, and giving mine a gentle squeeze. 'Now I see where Rosemary gets her looks,' he told me.

'You do know how to spread it,' I said.

Rex threw back his head and laughed. 'And now I also see where Rosemary gets her sass.'

'I'm just an old schoolmarm,' I went on. 'But I do have a nice set of choppers.' I slipped out my dentures and held them up.

Rosemary was mortified. 'Mom!' she said.

But Rex laughed again. 'Those are fine indeed,

but I can match you there,' he said, and slipped out his own set of dentures. He explained that when he was seventeen, his car had hit a tree. 'The car stopped,' he said, 'but I kept going.'

This fellow did have a way about him, I thought. And at the very least, you knew anyone who could laugh off a car accident that took out all his teeth had to have a little gumption.

Rosemary had brought in some of her paintings — desert landscapes, flowers, cats, portraits of Jim — and Rex held each one up, praising it to the skies for originality of composition, brilliance of color, sophistication of technique, and on and on. More horseshit, as far as I was concerned, but Rosemary lapped it up, just the way she did that existential hogwash from the Frog art teacher Ernestine.

'Why aren't any of these paintings hanging on the walls?' Rex asked.

In the living room, we had two woodland prints that I had bought because the blue of the sky perfectly matched the blue of the rug on the floor. Without so much as a by-your-leave, Rex took them down and replaced them with two of Rosemary's paintings that didn't have any blue at all in them.

'There,' he said. 'On display, where they belong.'

'Well, they're nice, but they don't match the rug,' I said. 'It took me a long time to find prints with exactly the right shade of blue.'

'To hell with matching,' Rex said. 'You got to mix things up every now and then.' He pointed at my prints. 'Those are just reproductions,' he said, and then gestured toward Rosemary's paintings. 'These are originals, and not just that, they're goddamned masterpieces.'

I looked at Rosemary. She was glowing.

By the end of the summer, Rex and Rosemary were dating regularly. I couldn't tell how serious she was, but that polecat Rex was sure persistent. I felt I could read the man like a book. He was charming, but most con men were, since before they fleeced you, they needed to gain your trust. My crumb-bum first husband had taught me that. This Rex fellow always had a joke on hand, could talk about any subject, passed out compliments like candy, and made you feel you were the center of the world, but you couldn't trust him farther than you could throw him.

He also had all sorts of grand plans and was always talking about new energy sources — solar energy, thermal energy, wind energy. Jim thought Rex was all talk. 'If we could harness the hot air coming out of that gasbag,' he said, 'we could power the whole of Phoenix.'

I didn't actively discourage Rosemary from getting serious, since there was no more surefire way to make that willful young woman want to do something, but I did try to point out that he might not make the ideal mate for the long haul.

'He's not exactly a rock,' I said.

'I don't want to marry a rock,' she said.

* * *

What she liked about Rex, Rosemary told me, was that when he was around, things always happened. He loved to start conversations with absolute strangers. He loved to act on whims. He loved pranks and surprises. Once he sneaked one of Rosemary's smaller paintings into an art museum in Phoenix, hung it in an empty spot, then invited Rosemary to come to the museum with him. She'd never been so startled — or tickled — than when Rex led her over to it and, feigning surprise, said, 'Well, lookie here. Best painting in the whole damned building.'

Some of the things that happened around Rex were strange, Rosemary explained, some were exciting, some were funny, some were scary, but he made everything into an adventure. Because of his own wild streak, he had a way of recognizing it in others, as if they were Masons communicating by secret hand signals. You'd go to a circus and meet the clowns, the bareback rider, and the sword swallower, wind up after the show tossing back shots in a bar with all of them, the sword swallower showing you how to stick a knife down your throat, the bareback rider describing how the Nazis had sent her to a concentration camp because she was a gypsy, then one of the clowns — the sad-eyed one — would confess that his old sweetheart was living nearby and he'd never loved anyone since, so you'd all pile into the car and drive over to the sweetheart's house and you'd find yourself at four in the morning standing under this strange woman's window serenading her with 'Red River Valley' in the hope of rekindling her love for the sad-eyed clown.

★ ★ ★

Early one Saturday morning that fall, when Rosemary was home from college, Rex showed up at Horse Mesa. He was wearing cowboy boots and a ten-gallon hat. Rosemary, Jim, and I were finishing our Cream of Wheat at the kitchen table. I asked Rex if he wanted me to fix him a bowl.

'No, thank you, ma'am. I got a big day planned and I don't want to weigh myself down.'

'And what are your plans?' I asked.

'Well, you're all true horse people,' he said. 'And I figure that since I'm going to marry this here daughter of yours, I gotta show you all that even though I've never been astride a horse, I got what it takes to ride one. So I'm off to find myself a horse today, and if you all want to come along and give this hillbilly a few pointers, I'd be most obliged.'

Jim and I looked at each other. This fellow just was not going to go away. Meanwhile, Rosemary was saying that the Crebbses, who lived on a ranch at the foot of the mountains and sent their two kids to my school, had some quarter horses that they'd be happy to let us ride. So when we finished our Cream of Wheat, we all dug out our boots and set off in the Ford for the Crebbs place.

Ray Crebbs told us the horses were in the corral and the tack was in the barn and we were free to saddle up, but the horses hadn't been ridden for a couple of months and might be a bit fresh. We picked out four, but all of them were herd-bound and didn't want to come to us, so Jim had to lasso those buggers before we could get them into the barn.

Rosemary always had to have the most spirited horse in the herd, and she chose a hot little bay. I had my eye on a quiet gelding for Rex, but he said there was no way in hell he was riding a horse whose balls had been cut off, so I gave him the mare I'd picked out for myself, even though she was acting a tad scutchy and head-shy.

After we saddled up, we headed out to the corral. Rosemary and Jim started trotting around to limber up their horses, and I sat on mine in the middle to give Rex some tips. The poor fellow was being pretty game about it, but you could tell right off he was not a natural horseman. He was trying too hard. He was tensed up and leaning forward, which put all his weight in his shoulders. I told him to relax, sink down into the saddle, and take his hands off the horn, since it wasn't going to save him.

Instead of relaxing, Rex kept up a steady patter about what a cinch this riding business was, what a blast he was having, and how he wanted to put this old nag through her paces. 'How do I get her out of second gear?' he asked.

'First you got to learn to keep your fanny in the saddle,' I said.

After a while I let Rex trot, but he kept popping out of his seat and jerking leather. Still, he insisted that he wasn't getting off until he'd

346

galloped because, he said, until you'd galloped on a horse, you couldn't say you'd really ridden one.

'You want to make her gallop, just kick her,' Rosemary called.

And that was what Rex did, whacking the mare in the ribs. The horse started but didn't break into a gallop, probably figuring that it wasn't a good idea with this unbalanced rider. Rex was nonetheless surprised, and he started shouting, 'Whoa! Whoa!' and sawing at the reins. All that noise and commotion spooked the poor mare, and that was when she took off.

As the horse tore around the corral in a big circle, I yelled at Rex to sit back and grab mane, but he was so deep in the hole of his panic that he didn't hear a thing. He kept shouting at the horse and jerking the reins, but the horse just leaned against the bit and galloped on.

Jim and Rosemary scooted into the center of the corral to get out of her way. The mare had made a few circuits without slowing down, and I could tell that Rex was starting to come unglued. I could also tell by looking at the mare's eyes that she was frightened, not angry, and that meant she wanted to stop but needed permission.

I jumped off my horse and walked into the path of the galloping mare. I was prepared to dive to the side if she didn't stop, but as she got close, I slowly raised my arms, looked her in the eye, and in a quiet voice said, 'Whoa.' And right in front of me, she stopped.

In fact, she stopped so suddenly that Rex

pitched forward, clung to her neck for a moment, then fell to the ground.

Rosemary slid off her horse and ran over. 'Are you okay?' she asked him.

'He's fine,' I said. 'He just had the lace knocked off his panties.'

Rex got to his feet and dusted off his jeans. I could tell he was shaken up, but he took a deep breath and ran his fingers through his hair. Then a big grin spread across his face. 'I found the gas,' he said. 'Now all's I need to do is find the brake.'

★ ★ ★

Rex insisted on getting back on, which I was glad he did, and we had ourselves a nice little ride around the Crebbs' spread. It was late afternoon by the time we got back to Horse Mesa. I heated up some beans and, after we'd eaten, suggested we play a few hands of poker.

'You won't ever hear me say no to that,' Rex said. 'I got a bottle of hooch in the car. How's about I get it and we can have ourselves a pop or two.'

Rex got the bottle, Jim set out glasses — including one for himself, just to be polite — and we all took a seat at the kitchen table. Rex poured everyone two fingers of whiskey. I dealt. There was no better way to read a man's character than to watch him play poker. Some played with the aim of holding on to what they had, others played to make a killing. For some it was gambling pure and simple, for others it was a game of skill involving small calculated risks. For some it was about numbers, for others it was about psychology.

Rosemary, for example, was a terrible poker player. It didn't matter how many times I explained the rules, she was always asking questions that revealed her hand. No sooner had I dealt the cards than she looked at hers and asked, 'Does a straight beat a flush?'

'You'll never win if you give yourself away like that,' I said.

'Winning's not all it's cracked up to be,' Rosemary said. 'If you win all the time, no one wants to play with you.'

I let that one pass.

As we got deeper into the game, I could tell Rex was a good player. To him, the game was not about reading your cards, it was about reading your opponents, and at first he seemed to know exactly when to fold and when to raise the stakes.

But he'd kept the bottle of hooch at his elbow. Jim and Rosemary hadn't touched their whiskeys, and I'd taken only a few sips of mine. Rex kept refilling his glass, and as the evening wore on, he started playing too grandly, overbluffing, overbetting, losing pots he never should have tried to win, and getting mad at his cards when they let him down.

After a while he stopped pouring himself shots and started swigging straight from the bottle. That was when I knew I could take him to the cleaners. I waited until I had a solid hand — a full house, eights over fours — and then I let him think he was bidding me up, but I never called him, and soon he was in deeper than he realized.

I laid my cards on the table. Rex studied them, his expression turning sour, then threw his own cards facedown at the pot. After a few seconds, he chuckled. 'Well, Lily,' he said, 'that gelding didn't have any balls, but you sure got yourself a pair.'

Rosemary giggled. I had the feeling she liked the way her boyfriend had just gotten cheeky with her mother. Truth be told, he was the first fellow she'd brought home who hadn't been even a little bit scared of me.

Jim looked at Rex with raised eyebrows. 'Watch yourself, flyboy,' he said.

'No offense, pardner,' Rex said. 'I was paying the lady a compliment.'

Jim shrugged. 'She's taken many a ranch hand's paycheck that very same way,' he added.

Rex reached for his bottle to take another swig, but it was empty. 'Guess we polished that off,' he said.

'You polished it off,' I said.

'Maybe we've played enough,' Rosemary said.

Rex nodded. He set the bottle on the table, stood up, then lurched to one side.

'You're drunk,' I said.

'Just got a little buzz,' Rex said. 'But I do believe I'll be taking my leave.'

'You can't drive that road in the condition you're in.'

'I'm fine,' Rex said. 'I drive like this all the time.'

'Maybe Mom's right,' Rosemary said.

'You can sleep in the garage,' Jim said.

'I said I'm fine,' Rex told him, and started fishing in his pocket for his keys.

'Listen, you boneheaded boozer,' I said, 'you're too drunk to drive, and I'm not allowing it.'

Rex leaned both his fists on the table. 'Listen, lady, Rex Walls don't take orders from anyone, certainly not some old leather-faced, hard-assed biddy. And with that, I will bid you good night.'

We all sat there in silence as Rex staggered out, slamming the screen door. We heard him turn the engine on, gun it, and then, with a screech of tires, he drove off into the darkness, down the mountainside on Agnes Weeps.

The next day I felt I needed to have a serious talk with my daughter about her boyfriend.

'That scalawag might be fun,' I said, 'but he's also a danger to himself and others.'

'Nobody's perfect,' she said. 'We're all just one step up from the beasts and one step down from the angels.'

'True enough,' I said, 'but not everyone lines up exactly in the middle. Rex is unstable. You'll never have any security with him.'

'I don't really care about security,' she said. 'And anyway, I don't believe I'll ever really have it with anyone. We could all be killed by an atom bomb tomorrow.'

'So you're telling me the future's not important? That you're going to live your life like there's no tomorrow?'

'Most people spend so much time worrying about the future that they don't enjoy the present.'

'And people who don't plan for the future get ambushed by it. Hope for the best but plan for the worst, my dad always used to say.'

'You can't prepare for everything that life's going to throw at you,' she said. 'And you can't avoid danger. It's there. The world is a dangerous place, and if you sit around wringing your hands about it, you'll miss out on all the adventure.'

I felt there was a lot more I could say about

the subject of danger. I could have given her an entire lecture on it, talking about my dad getting his head staved in by a horse when he was three, about my Chicago friend Minnie getting killed when her hair got caught in machinery, about my sister, Helen, taking her own life after accidentally getting pregnant. Life came with as much adventure and danger as any one body needed. You didn't have to go chasing after them. But the fact of the matter was, Rosemary hadn't really listened to what I had to say ever since that time we visited the Havasupai and I gave her the whipping for swimming with Fidel Hanna.

'I don't know what I did wrong raising you,' I said. 'Maybe I tried too hard. But I still say you need an anchor.'

★ ★ ★

Later that day there was a knock on the door. When I answered it, Rex Walls was standing outside. He had a big bouquet of white lilies in one hand, and he held it out to me.

'Lilies for Lily, by way of apology,' he said. 'Though they're not as lovely as their namesake.'

'That's not exactly the tune you were whistling last night.'

'What I said was inexcusable, and I'm the first to admit it,' he said. 'But I was hoping you'd cut a fellow some slack.' He'd had a tough day, he went on, falling off a runaway horse in front of the woman he loved, then getting beat by her mother in poker, all of which led him to take a few nips too many. 'But you started it, you know, calling me a bone-head.' He paused. 'And I do know how to drive drunk.'

I shook my head and looked at the lilies. 'I could cut you all the slack in the world, but I still think my daughter needs an anchor.'

'The problem with being attached to an anchor,' he said, 'is it's damned hard to fly.'

What a scoundrel, I thought. Always having to have the last word. But the lilies were pretty. 'I'll go put these in water.'

'You like to fly,' Rex added. 'If it would get me back into your good graces, I'd be honored to take you up for a spin.'

I hadn't been up in a plane for years, and though I was still steamed at that hooligan, the idea thrilled me, so of course I agreed. When Rex arrived to pick me up the following Sunday, I was standing outside in my aviator's jumpsuit, carrying my leather helmet.

Rex leaned out the window of the two-toned Ford sedan he was always borrowing from a friend. 'Amelia Earhart!' he called. 'You're alive after all!'

Rosemary wanted to come along, but Rex told her the plane was only a two-seater. 'This trip's just me and Amelia,' he said.

Rex drove like a demon, the way I liked to, and in no time at all, we had hurtled down Agnes Weeps, climbed out of the canyon, and were heading along the Apache Trail.

I asked Rex a little bit about his background.

'Ma'am,' he said, 'if you're looking for pedigree, you're going to find more in the local dog pound.' He'd grown up in a coal town, he said. His mother had been an orphan, his father had worked as a clerk for the railroad. His uncle made moonshine, and as a teenager, Rex sometimes ran the hooch into town.

'Is that where you learned to drive like this?' I asked. 'Trying to get away from the revenuers?'

'Hell, no,' he said. 'The law was our best customers. And Uncle wouldn't allow no speeding. It was fine moonshine, and he bade me drive slow so as to let it age.'

I told him about my days selling hooch stored under the baby's bassinet and how Rosemary had saved me by bawling at the sight of the cops who'd come to investigate. We got along just fine, chatting away until we reached the flats and came to a beat-up trailer surrounded by junk: car axles, metal sinks, old fuel drums, stacks of folded canvas tarps, and a rusting truck up on cinder blocks.

Rex slammed on his brakes and swerved into the yard in front of the trailer. 'Look at all that crap!' he exclaimed. 'Being from West Virginia, I'm a mite touchy about white-trash eyesores, and I'm going to give that fellow a piece of my mind.'

He got out and started pounding on the door. 'Will the sorry-ass lowlife who lives in this heap of rubble have the balls to show his butt-ugly face?'

A scrawny fellow with a crew cut opened the door.

'My future mother-in-law's in that car,' Rex hollered. 'And she's sick of driving past this pigsty. So the next time I come down this road, I want to see it cleaned up, understand?'

The two men stared at each other for a moment, and I was certain one was going to deck the other, but then they both started laughing and slapped each other on the back.

'Rex, you ornery son of a bitch, how you been?' the fellow said.

Rex brought him over to the car and

introduced him as Gus, an old air force buddy. 'You may think I've got the long-lost Amelia Earhart here, but she's Lily Casey Smith. She could teach Amelia Earhart a thing or two about flying, and she really is the mother of my future bride.'

'You're going to let this AWOL jackass marry your daughter?' Gus cried. 'Keep the bullwhip handy!'

They both thought that was just hilarious.

★ ★ ★

Rex explained that, strictly speaking, it was against regulations for air force pilots to take civilians up in military planes, though everyone did it all the time on the QT. Since they couldn't take off from the airbase, in front of the controllers, the pilots picked up the civilians at the different grass fields outside the base where they practiced landings. One of those fields was right behind Gus's trailer, so Rex was going to leave me with Gus, take off from the base, and fly the plane back to the trailer. I didn't mind a man who ignored stupid regulations, so Rex got another check in the plus column — though the minus column was still well in the lead.

I sat in back of the trailer, shooting the breeze with Gus. There was an orange wind sock on a pole by the landing field, but since there was no wind, it just hung there. Finally, the plane appeared. It was yellow, a single-engine two-seater with a glass canopy that Rex had shoved back. He landed and taxied toward us. After Rex stopped, Gus pointed out the footstep below the flap, and I scrambled onto the wing. Rex had me sit in the front while he got in the back. I plugged in my headphones and watched the needles on the instrument panel jiggle from the engine's vibration. Rex throttled up, and we bumped across the field into the air.

As we gained altitude, I again had the sensation that I was an angel, watching tiny cars creep along ribbons of road far beneath me, and gazing toward the earth's distant curve, with that infinity of blue space behind it.

We flew toward Horse Mesa, and Rex dropped down to buzz the house a couple of times. Rosemary and Jim came running out waving like maniacs, and Rex dipped the wings.

Rex climbed, and we followed the spine of the mountains to Fish Creek Canyon. Then we dropped down into the canyon itself, flying above the winding river with the red stone cliff walls sweeping in and out on either side of us.

When we came up out of the canyon, we circled back over the flats, and Rex, who could talk to me over the intercom, let me take the controls. I banked left, brought her level again, banked right in one big circle, climbed, and dropped. Nothing in life was finer than flying.

Rex took the controls again. He sent the plane on a big rolling loop, and I couldn't help grabbing on for dear life when we went upside down. Coming out of the loop, we dove steeply and then went skimming along barely fifty feet above the ground. Trees, hills, rock formations zoomed up at us and flashed by.

'We call this flat-hatting,' Rex said. 'A friend of mine was doing it over the beach, and when he leaned out to wave at the girls, his plane went right into the drink.'

Then we were flying toward a road with a string of telephone poles running alongside it. 'Watch this!' Rex shouted over the intercom. He dropped the plane down even lower until we were practically touching the ground.

I realized he was going to try to fly under the telephone wire. 'Rex, you fool! You'll kill us!' I yelled.

Rex just cackled, and before I knew it, we were lining up to shoot between two poles, then they zipped past, along with the blur of the wire overhead.

'You're a goddamned crazy man!' I said.

'That's what your daughter loves about me!' he hollered back.

He climbed again and headed north until he found what he wanted, grazing cattle. He dropped down behind the herd and approached it, once again almost skimming the earth. The cattle started stampeding away from us at their lumbering gallop, streaming out to the sides as we came onto them, but Rex banked right and then left, driving the cattle toward the center. Only when he had them back together did he pull up and away.

'Can't do that on a horse, can you?' he asked.

That spring Rex and Rosemary decided to get married. She gave me the news one evening after dinner while we were doing the dishes.

'You need someone solid,' I told her. 'Haven't I taught you anything?'

'You sure have,' she said. 'That's all you've been doing my whole life. 'Let this be a lesson.' 'Let that be a lesson.' But all these years, what you thought you were teaching me was one thing, and what I was learning was something else.'

We stood there, staring at each other. Rosemary was leaning against the kitchen sink, her arms crossed.

'So you're going to marry him even if I don't approve?' I asked.

'That's the plan.'

'I always liked to think I'd never met a kid I couldn't teach,' I said. 'Turns out I was wrong. That kid is you.'

★   ★   ★

At the same time, Rex announced that his tour of duty was coming to an end and he'd decided not to re-enlist. The air force wanted him to fly bombers, and he wanted to fly fighters. Also, he didn't want Rosemary to waste her life raising a brood of kids in a broiling trailer on a desert air base. Besides, he had other plans. Big plans.

The whole idea was half-baked.

'Where are you going to live?' I asked Rosemary.

'I don't know,' she said. 'It doesn't matter.'

'What do you mean, it doesn't matter? The place where you live — your home — is one of the most important things in a body's life.'

'I feel like I haven't really had a home since I left the ranch. I don't think I'll ever have a home again. Maybe we'll never settle down.'

★ ★ ★

Jim was philosophical about Rosemary's decision, figuring that since her mind was made up, we'd only turn her against us by arguing with her.

'I feel like I failed,' I said.

'Don't beat yourself up,' Jim said. 'She might not have turned out like you planned, but that don't mean she turned out wrong.'

We were sitting on the front step of our house. It had rained earlier. The red rock cliffs around Horse Mesa were wet, and runoff was pouring over crevices, creating dozens of those temporary waterfalls.

'People are like animals,' Jim went on. 'Some are happiest penned in, some need to roam free. You got to recognize what's in her nature and accept it.'

'So this is a lesson for me, then?'

Jim shrugged. 'Our daughter's found something she likes, this painting, and someone she wants to be with, this Rex fellow, so she's way ahead of a lot of folks.'

'I guess I should try to let it go.'

'You'll be happier if you do,' Jim said.

★ ★ ★

I told Rex and Rosemary I'd pay for everything if they'd get married in a Catholic church, and we'd do it in style. I was hoping that a big traditional wedding would get them off on the right foot and might even lead to a traditional marriage.

We rented a banquet hall at the Sands Hotel, which had just been built in downtown Phoenix. I got a good deal, since the hotel was new and trying to drum up business. I helped Rosemary pick out a wedding dress, and I got a good deal on that, too, because another bride-to-be had returned it when her wedding had fallen through. But it fit Rosemary perfectly.

I invited practically everyone I knew: ranchers and ranch hands, teachers and former students, administrators, members of the Arizona Democratic Party, people from my past like Grady Gammage, who got me that first teaching job in Red Lake, and Rooster, who wrote back to his old writing teacher that he'd be bringing the Apache girl he'd married. I was going to wear my *Gone with the Wind* gown, but Jim put the kibosh on that idea. He said he didn't want me upstaging the bride.

'What are you going to do for a honeymoon?' I asked Rosemary as the day approached.

'We're not going to plan one,' she said. 'It's Rex's idea. We're just going to get into the car after the wedding and go where the road takes us.'

'Well, honey, you're in for a ride.'

★　★　★

Rosemary did look beautiful at her wedding. Her dress reached to the floor, with layers of lace over white silk, a long lace veil, and matching lace gloves that came up to her elbows. In her white high heels, she was almost as tall as Rex, who looked rakish as hell in his white dinner jacket and black bow tie.

Rex and his buddies were nipping from their pints all day, and things got a little wild at the reception. Rex gave a big speech, calling me 'Amelia Earhart' and Jim 'The Parachutin' Cowboy' and Rosemary 'My Wild Rose.' When the music started, he twirled Rosemary around the room, dipping and spinning her. She was having the time of her life, flouncing her lace dress and kicking up her white high heels like she was a cancan girl. Then Rex led everyone in a conga line and we all snaked around the room, swaying our hips and kicking out.

At the end, when the newlywed couple came out of the hotel, Rex's borrowed Ford was waiting for them at the curb. It was a late afternoon in May, and that golden Arizona light filled the street. We all crowded onto the steps to wave good-bye. When they reached the sidewalk, Rex grabbed Rosemary by the waist, leaned her backward, and planted a long, deep smooch on her mouth. They almost fell over, and that set them laughing so much it brought tears to their eyes. As Rosemary climbed into the car, Rex patted her behind like he owned it, then got in beside her. They were both still laughing as Rex gunned the motor the way he always did.

Jim put his arm around me and we watched them take off up the street, heading out into open country like a couple of half-broke horses.

EPILOGUE

THE LITTLE CRITTER

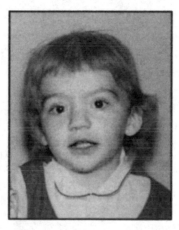

Jeannette Walls, age two

Jim and I lived on in Horse Mesa. Jim was getting along in years, and he soon retired, though he stayed busy as our little camp's unofficial mayor — giving one neighbor's wayward child the stern talking-to he needed, helping another neighbor patch a roof or unclog his gummed-up carburetor. I kept teaching. Like Jim, I was never one to lounge around with my feet propped on the porch rail, and knowing my students would be waiting for me made me wake up every morning raring to go.

Little Jim and Diane settled into a tidy ranch house in the Phoenix suburbs, and they had a couple of kids. Their life seemed pretty stable. Rex and Rosemary, meanwhile, drifted around the desert, Rex taking odd jobs while working on his various harebrained schemes, sipping beer and smoking cigarettes as he drafted blueprints for machines to mine gold and giant panels to harness the sun's energy. Rosemary was painting like a fiend, but she also started dropping babies right and left, and every time they visited us — which they did a couple of times a year, staying until Rex and I started hollering at each other to the point that we darned near came to blows — she was either expecting another one or nursing the one that had just popped out.

Rosemary's first two babies were girls, though crib death got the second before she was one year old. The third was also a girl. Rex and Rosemary were living in Phoenix at the time she was born, in our house on North Third Street, but they didn't have the money to pay the hospital bill, so I had to drive down with a check — and some choice words for that reprobate Rex. Rosemary named the baby Jeannette and, probably still under the influence of her old art teacher, spelled it with two Ns the way the Frogs do.

Jeannette was not a raving beauty — and for that I was thankful — with carroty hair coming in and such a long, scrawny body that when people saw her lying in the stroller, they told Rosemary to feed her baby more. But she had smiling green eyes and the beginnings of a strong, square jaw just like mine, and from the outset, I felt a powerful connection to the kid. I could tell she was a tenacious thing. When I took her in my arms and stuck out a finger, that little critter grabbed it and held on like she'd never let go.

With the way Rex and Rosemary's life together was shaping up, those kids were in for some wild times. But they came from hardy stock, and I figured they'd be able to play the cards they'd been dealt. Plus, I'd be hovering around. No way in hell were Rex and Rosemary cutting me out of the action when it came to my own grandchildren. I had a few things to teach those kids, and there wasn't a soul alive who could stop me.

AUTHOR'S NOTE

This book was originally meant to be about my mother's childhood growing up on a cattle ranch in Arizona. But as I talked to Mom about those years, she kept insisting that her mother was the one who had led the truly interesting life and that the book should be about Lily.

My grandmother was — and I say this with all due respect — quite a character. However, at first I resisted writing about her. While I had been close to her as a child, she died when I was eight, and most of what I knew about her came secondhand.

Still, I'd been hearing the stories about Lily Casey Smith all my life, stories she told over and over to my mother, who told them to me. Lily was a spirited woman, a passionate teacher and talker who explained in great detail what had happened to her, why it had happened, what she'd done about it, and what she'd learned from it, all with the idea of imparting life lessons to my mother. My mother — who struggles to remember my phone number — has an astonishing recall for details about her mother and father and about their parents as well as an amazing knowledge of the history and geology of Arizona. She never once told me something, whether about the Havasupai tribe or the Mogollon Rim, slaughtering cattle or breaking horses, that I could not confirm.

369

While interviewing my mother and other family members, I came across a couple of books about her paternal grandfather and maternal great-grandfather that confirmed some of the family stories: *Major Lot Smith, Mormon Raider*, by Ivan Barrett, and *Robert Casey and the Ranch on the Rio Hondo*, by James Shinkle.

Although those books substantiated certain events, such as the murder of Robert Casey and his children's feud over the herd, they contradicted others. Shinkle noted that while researching his book, he came across conflicting versions of events and was frequently unable to get to the ultimate truth. In telling my grandmother's story, I never aspired to that sort of historical accuracy. I saw the book more in the vein of an oral history, a retelling of stories handed down by my family through the years, and undertaken with the story-teller's traditional liberties.

I wrote the story in the first person because I wanted to capture Lily's distinctive voice, which I clearly recall. At the time I didn't think of the book as fiction. Lily Casey Smith was a very real woman, and to say that I created her or the events of her life is giving me more credit than I'm due. However, since I don't have the words from Lily herself, and since I have also drawn on my imagination to fill in details that are hazy or missing — and I've changed a few names to protect people's privacy — the only honest thing to do is call the book a novel.